DEAD MEAT

William G. Tapply has lived in New England all his life. He has taught history in both private and public schools and has written articles for *Field & Stream* and *Sports Illustrated*. He lives in Concord, Massachusetts, with his wife, Cindy, and his three children, Michael, Melissa and Sarah. *Dead Meat* is his fifth novel starring Attorney Brady Coyne. The first, *Death at Charity's Point* won the Scribner Crime Novel Award for 1984.

WILLIAM G. TAPPLY

Dead Meat

Attorney Brady Coyne's fifth case

FONTANA/Collins

First published in Great Britain by
William Collins Sons & Co. Ltd, 1988

First published in Fontana Paperbacks 1989

Printed and bound in Great Britain by
William Collins Sons & Co. Ltd, Glasgow

For Michael Fosburg

My thanks to Rick Boyer, my wife, Cindy, and
Betsy Rapoport – once again – for their immeas-
urable contributions to this manuscript, and to
my father, H. G. Tapply, for introducing me to
loons and moose and landlocked salmon and the
wilderness of Maine.

We saw a pair of moose horns on the shore, and I asked Joe if a moose had shed them; but he said there was a head attached to them, and I knew that they did not shed their heads more than once in their lives.

HENRY DAVID THOREAU: *The Maine Woods*

Prologue

'Even a broken clock is right twice a day,' said Charlie. 'Even a monkey chained to a typewriter –'

'Yeah, yeah. I know,' I said. 'So I made a couple good guesses.'

'Sheer luck. Random chance. Anyhow,' he said, tapping the flat plastic box on the top of his desk, 'through the wonders of modern technology, the unlimited resources of the United States government, and the expertise of the Federal Bureau of Investigation, I have here the piece of the puzzle that you're missing. The piece that makes sense of it.'

'Well, hell, Charlie. You gonna make me grovel, or what?'

He leaned back and grinned at me. 'Naw. Makes me sick to see a grown man grovel.'

'Then play the damn tape, will you?'

'Lunch. On you, right?'

'Sure, sure.'

'Jimmy's?'

'Agreed.'

'Lobster.'

'Sure. Lobster. Whatever the hell you want.'

'Good. It's done, then.' Charlie went to the cabinet and took out a tape recorder. He brought it back and placed it on the center of his desk.

'The one who sounds like he's got throat cancer is Uncle Fish,' he said, threading the tape through the old-fashioned reel-to-reel recorder.

'Vincent Collucci,' I said.

'Himself. And the other guy is Joseph Malagudi.'

'The one they call Ceci?'

'Yep.'

'And he's the button from Atlanta.'

Charlie smirked at me. 'You've got the terms down pretty good, Counselor. Watching reruns of the *Godfather* flicks, huh? Yeah. Ceci Malagudi is the button from Atlanta. One of the best – or worst, depending on your point of view – on the East coast. High up on everybody's most-wanted list, especially after taking out a promising witness in Baltimore last spring. The law, as you know, is a bit intolerant of guys who shoot other guys in the back of the head with twenty-two-caliber pistols. Anyhow, this recording came from a tap the boys downstairs had on Collucci's phone, all legal and everything. The call was made last April.'

'Before I went to Maine.'

'Right. Before you went salmon fishing and started to run into dead bodies.'

Charlie McDevitt's office is high in the J. F. K. Federal Building in Boston's Government Center. The single window looks out over a broad brick-paved plaza toward what used to be, in my youth, Scollay Square, where my buddies and I would catch the Saturday morning strip shows at the Old Howard before the ball game started over at Fenway Park. On this particular summer morning a hot breeze was coming in off the ocean, and through Charlie's window I could see sharp-dressed ladies hurrying across the plaza, leaning into the wind, their flimsy skirts plastered against the fronts of their thighs, and I thought how it was a long way from Raven Lake, way up there in northwestern Maine, a few miles from the Canadian border.

'There,' said Charlie. 'All set. Remember, now. That's Collucci, at his modest mansion up there in Hamilton, hard by the Myopia Hunt Club. Fox hunting. Polo ponies. Tallyho. Just imagine Uncle Fish in jodhpurs. Anyway, the other one's Malagudi. They failed to trace where he was calling from. Not that it especially matters.'

'Play the damn tape, Charlie.'

'Okay. Here goes.' He depressed a button. I heard static, then a click. Then a voice like sandpaper.

'Yeah?'

A hesitation. 'This my uncle?'

'Yeah. Whosis?'

'Ceci.'

'Mr M. Long time.' Collucci sounded as if he had his mouth full.

'I need someone to say a prayer for me.'

'Want some salvation, huh?'

'Salvation. Right.'

'Only Jesus saves, Mr M.'

'Ain't how I hear it.'

Collucci made a noncommittal grunt.

'How many angels it take for salvation, Uncle?'

'Fifty angels, Mr M.'

'You still talkin' to our lord, Uncle?'

Collucci burped. 'I can arrange your salvation, Mr M. Call back Friday.'

'With fifty angels, huh?'

'You need them fifty angels on your side, Mr M.'

There was a click and then static. Charlie reached over and turned off the machine.

I sat back and lit a cigarette. Charlie smiled at me. 'See what I mean?'

I nodded. 'Yeah. That explains it, all right. Okay. Let's go to lunch.'

'Jimmy's, right? Lobster?'
'As promised.'

Charlie McDevitt's tape recording gave me the final link in a chain of events that had begun on a warm noontime the previous June, when I walked from my office in Copley Square to meet a man near the duck pond in the Boston Public Garden.

Chapter One

The voice boomed over the phone, all the way from the pay phone in Greenville, Maine. 'Brady, it's Anthony Wheeler. How the hell are you?'

He was the only one who called himself Anthony. He was a boulder of a man, with a cavern for a chest and a great hard stomach and a bush of a black beard, only lately gone over to gray. So naturally everyone else called him Tiny.

Tiny Wheeler was an old-time Maine guide, half owner and manager of the Raven Lake Lodge up there in the wilds of the Pine Tree State, not far from the Canadian border.

Tiny liked to tell how he had once punched a black bear on the nose. 'Sonofabuck was gnawing at my best paddle,' he said. 'Gave him my best shot, and by God he went cross-eyed before he turned tail and ran.' No one really doubted the story.

'You didn't dial me person-to-person collect to ask how I am,' I said. 'I happen to be fine. So's my ex-wife and two boys. What's up, Tiny?'

'Salmon are bitin' like snakes up here. Naturally made me think of you.'

'Naturally,' I said.

'Wonderin' if you might enjoy a week or two up here on Raven Lake. Have Gib meet you at the seaplane dock in Greenville, fly you in. Old Woody's available for guidin'. Bud Turner's still the best cook north of Boston. Whaddya say?'

'I say what do you really want?'

'Aw, hey,' said Tiny. Then he chuckled. 'Wouldn't do no harm if you were to stop in on a fella named Seelye Smith in Portland on your way up.'

'Who's this Smith?'

'Lawyer fella, like yourself. I just hired him to help out with a little problem. Would have asked you to take care of it, 'cept this Smith's a Maine boy, specialist in Indian problems, and he was recommended.'

'So what do you want me to do, Tiny?'

I imagined his broad grin as he spoke into the phone, his gold incisor glittering from inside his gray beard. 'Check out this fella. Make sure I didn't hire me a wimp. While you're at it, get a handle on my situation if you can. Then hike your tail up here and explain it to me.'

'What situation?' I swiveled around in my office chair to stare out at the Boston skyline. A helluva long way from Raven Lake, up there northwest of Moosehead Lake.

'Aw, it's the damn Indians. They wanna buy me out.'

'So tell them to stuff it.'

'These are the Indians, Brady.' I heard Tiny sigh. 'Smith'll explain it to you. Okay? Check him out, get the dope for me, then get your ass up here and catch some salmon.'

'What's Vern say about this?'

Vern Wheeler was Tiny's older brother, half owner of the Raven Lake Lodge, one of Boston's most prominent businessmen, and my client. Vern was the main brains of the Wheeler family. Tiny was the charm and the brawn. Tiny rarely did anything without Vern's approval.

'I don't want to bother Vern about this,' said Tiny after an instant's hesitation. 'I can handle it.'

'You ought to apprise Vern,' I said.

'You can do that for me.'

'You've got to tell me more, then.'

He sighed. 'Okay, Counselor. It's your dime. It goes like this. The Indians have offered to buy Raven Lake, lock, stock, and barrel. I have turned down their offer. Told them the place wasn't for sale. They came back, threatened a suit. Claim the old burial ground entitles them to the place.'

'Burial ground?'

'Yeah. Up there where Harley's Creek divides there's a place we always called the burial ground. Local folks think it's haunted. These Indians are saying that if we won't deal with them, they'll claim the place.'

'Can they do that?'

'Well, dammit, Coyne, that's what I want to know, okay?'

'Have they actually filed suit?'

'Nope. Just threatened. What they really seem to want to do is dicker with me. I've told 'em nothin' to dicker about.'

I hesitated. 'They really biting like snakes, Tiny?'

'Swear to Christ. Best salmon fishin' in years.'

'I'll have to check it out with my boss.'

'Boss? You don't have a boss, Brady. You're your own boss.'

'You forget Julie.'

'She's your secretary, ain't she? The one who answered the phone?'

'Same difference,' I said.

The old man had chosen a bench with a view of both a formal garden of yellow roses and the duck pond. Behind him, George Washington, dressed in full Revolutionary War regalia and about twice life-size, sat astride his horse, which was frozen in mid-canter atop a big granite pedestal. A starling perched on the general's left shoulder.

The Public Garden was at its lushest on this sunny afternoon in June. It looked as I imagined Frederick Law Olmsted must have visualized it when he designed it a hundred-odd years ago. The flower beds glowed in pastels and neons, weeded clean and freshly mulched. The lawns shimmered emerald green. The grand old willows and beeches and maples had leafed out thickly, grateful, it seemed, that this was a down year in the gypsy-moth cycle.

I stood beside General Washington, sniffing the mingled aromas of the flowers, the ocean, and the fresh-cut grass – that rare clean-air miracle created by the driving rain of the previous day and the purging easterly breeze that followed in its wake.

It was the kind of day I'd prefer to spend casting dry flies for brown trout on the Deerfield River rather than walking the streets of Boston. On the other hand, if I had to be in the city, there were worse places than the Boston Public Garden.

The old man on the bench wore a rumpled seersucker jacket and baggy chino pants. Thin strings of white hair hung over his ears and forehead. He hunched forward arthritically as he scattered popcorn to the flock of city pigeons that had gathered at his feet. They fluttered and flapped and scrambled over each other in their greed. The old man seemed to be studying their behavior.

I strolled over and slid onto the bench beside him. He glanced up at me, grinned briefly, and held out the half-filled bag of popcorn to me. I grabbed a handful and popped one into my mouth. 'Hell, it's stale,' I said.

'The birds seem to like it better stale,' he answered.

I threw the rest of my popcorn as far from the bench as

I could. I was gratified to see the pigeons scramble stupidly away in pursuit.

'They're filthy creatures, Vern,' I said to the old man. 'They'll shit all over your shoes.'

'It's all relative, my friend,' he said mildly. 'Pigeons are much like people, don't you think? They'll go wherever we toss the popcorn, and they'll shit on anybody's shoes to get there. Including the shoes of the man who's handing out the popcorn.'

'Especially the shoes of the popcorn man,' I amended.

He smiled. 'Well, anyhow, it's about all we've got for wildlife around here.'

Anyone who didn't know him would have mistaken Vernon Wheeler for another derelict enjoying the delicious comfort of a warm June afternoon with the pigeons. He was, in fact, the founder and owner of one of the world's most successful industries and a man who could, if he chose, conduct his business from the office building he owned on Tremont Street or from one of his offices in Los Angeles, Denver, Antwerp, or Tokyo.

Those were the places he met with his bevies of corporate lawyers.

He preferred to meet with me, his personal legal adviser, on a bench in the Boston Public Garden.

Vern Wheeler was typical of my clientele. He was old, smart, eccentric, and rich. I've found that most rich people tend to be old, smart, and eccentric. I like them best when they're all those things. In fact, I specialize in solving the legal problems of old, smart, eccentric, rich people. They rarely come to me for specialized expertise or courtroom savoir faire. When they do, I help them find it elsewhere than the office of Brady L. Coyne, Attorney-at-Law. Mostly they come to me because I offer a surprisingly rare commodity: discretion.

I am discreet as hell. I can't help it. I can't take credit for it. It's my nature. It's how I was raised. Or perhaps it's in my cautious WASP genes. I am always surprised how old, smart, eccentric, rich people want to pay me lots of money for this accident of my personality.

'You didn't call me because you wanted to help me feed the pigeons,' said Vern. 'What's on your mind?'

I told him what Tiny had told me over the phone. 'So I'm going up there, check up on Seelye Smith, see if I can give Tiny a hand. Tiny wanted me to fill you in.'

'Tiny's afraid of talking to his own brother?'

'I don't think he wanted to bother you.'

'I'm half owner of the place. I've got a right to know what's going on.'

I put my hand on his bony knee. 'That's why we're here.'

He held the paper bag upside down and dumped what was left of the popcorn onto the pavement. Then he wadded up the bag and stuffed it into his jacket pocket. He sighed, then turned to face me. 'Goddamn Indians, anyways.'

Vern had a way of saying 'goddamn' that betrayed his Skowhegan, Maine origins. It sounded like 'gawd day-em' when he said it. I always suspected that he consciously cultivated the down-easterliness of his speech. In fact, it seemed to me that over the years I had known him he actually injected 'ay-yuh' more and more often into his conversation – on the assumption, I figured, that the simple country-bumpkin façade gave him an edge over yuppies and other city types. He saw through people with the same clarity as an old Maine lobsterman, and he outsmarted them routinely.

During the Depression, Vern had paid for an engineering degree from MIT by guiding city sports on summer

16

fishing expeditions up the Kennebec River and into the Allagash wilderness. He taught demolition during the war, on the government's theory that a man who knew how to construct things would be the best man to tell others how to destroy them. Vern liked to say that the science of destruction was not much different from the art of creation, anyway.

After the war, he went back to Maine and bought into a small printing firm. By 1949 he owned it outright, and by 1957 he had amassed a tidy little fortune. He wet his forefinger, stuck it into the breeze, and Vern Wheeler saw the future – not plastics, as Dustin Hoffman was informed in the movie, but computers. And those computers would need programs to tell them what to do.

So Vern came to Boston and started up a firm that created and marketed educational software long before the machines to use it properly had been sufficiently refined. He understood what 'programmed learning' promised, and he was able to envision the day when technology would catch up. When it did, Vern Wheeler was ready. By 1970 he had expanded, diversified, and opened corporate offices in strategic locations throughout the world.

He had also acquired ownership of at least one United States congressman – which, as he liked to say, 'didn't do a damn bit of harm'.

He also liked to say, 'You can take the man out of Maine, but you can't take Maine out of the man.' So as soon as he could afford it, Vern bought a run-down sporting camp and most of the acreage on the shores of Raven Lake, a crescent-shaped body of water tucked up in the northwest corner of the state. He gave his younger brother, Tiny, half interest in the place and hired him to run it.

17

Raven Lake Lodge was more than a business diversion and tax write-off for Vern. It was a place he loved. He refused to let Tiny open the place for business until two weeks after ice-out, normally in early May. Those first two weeks belonged to Vern and his friends, because that's when the landlocked salmon fishing was best.

With Vern's money and Tiny's hard work, Raven Lake Lodge became one of the classiest – and most expensive – sporting camps in Maine. In the spring and summer, city sports could count on superior fishing for landlocked salmon, brook trout (which the natives called 'square tails'), lake trout ('togue'), and smallmouth bass. In September, hunters flocked to the place, hoping to kill a black bear. Come October, they could shoot partridge and woodcock over the points of Tiny's kennel of English setters, and in November Raven Lake was a hot spot for whitetail deer.

It was, in fact, at Raven Lake in 1976 where I first met Vernon Wheeler. The ice had been out for three weeks, so the place had opened for official business. My friend Doc Adams, the master oral surgeon, had gotten wind of the fabulous salmon fishing there, and he had no trouble persuading me to take a week off to share it with him.

On the third day of our stay Doc claimed his arms were tired from hauling in so many large salmon, a complaint that I didn't share, and he decided to test the trout fishing at Harley's Creek for the day. I hadn't had my fill of hauling in large salmon, so I found myself in a canoe with Woody, our Penobscot Indian guide, and a taciturn old guy who was known around the lodge only as 'Vern'. I didn't realize until later that he owned the place. It turned out to be one of those rare days when the salmon refused to bite, and although Vern and I flailed away with our fly rods until our arms ached, we returned to the

18

lodge in the afternoon empty-handed. Doc resumed salmon fishing the next day, promising to show me how it was done, and I saw little of Vern during the rest of our stay.

But a couple of weeks later he called me at my office back in Boston. 'This is Vernon Wheeler,' he said.

'Yes?' I answered, drawing a blank.

'You and I got skunked up on Raven Lake.'

'Oh sure,' I said. 'How are you?'

'Been checking up on you. I like to check up on people. Especially on men who stick to the fly rod when the salmon aren't biting. There's usually something to be said for men like that.'

'You stuck to the fly rod, too.'

'That's what I mean,' he said. 'I spoke to an old friend of mine this morning. Florence Gresham.'

Florence Gresham had been my very first client. She was a flinty old Yankee lady who owned a mansion on the water in Beverly Farms, on Boston's North Shore, and spent her summers in what she called her 'cottage' in Bar Harbor, the swankiest part of Maine. 'Florence is one of my favorite people,' I said.

I heard Wheeler chuckle. 'That's exactly what she said you'd say. Anyhow, you come well recommended. I need a man I can trust. I figured I could trust a man who'd stick to the fly rod. Florence assures me that while my body is decaying, my instincts remain acute.'

'What do you need me for?'

'Right now, nothing special. But things come up. I like to be prepared.'

'Well, I'm like you, Mr Wheeler,' I said. 'I like a man who sticks to the fly rod. I can also afford to be particular, and, like you, I always check out what my instincts

19

suggest. So why don't you leave me your number and I'll get back to you.'

He chuckled again. 'Florence said you'd say that, too. She's waiting for your call.'

Florence Gresham's recommendation was, for her, effusive. 'Vernon Wheeler's not half bad,' she told me. 'Of course, I wouldn't want to be married to the man.'

So Vern Wheeler joined my small but select group of clients. I fiddled with his will every year or so, advised him on matters that were usually more personal than legal, served as a sounding board for his opinions, checked on the reliability of some of the advice he received from his corporate attorneys, and let him buy me lunch at expensive Boston restaurants.

For this he paid me an outrageous retainer.

It seemed to be an arrangement that, all in all, we both found eminently satisfactory.

And several times after that he invited me and my friends up to Raven Lake right after ice-out, before the paying sports arrived. Doc Adams and Charlie McDevitt and I usually made a threesome of it. We caught lots of salmon on flies, which was worth more to me than the retainer.

Vern's curse about the 'goddamn Indians' reminded me of the Passamaquoddy and Penobscot guides who worked at Raven Lake. 'Tiny mentioned old Woody,' I said. 'He's the last of the Indian guides, isn't he?'

'Yep. The rest've died or gone back to the city.' He looked down at the pigeons, which were still scratching around for bits of popcorn. 'Hell, maybe it's time to sell the place, anyways.'

'I don't think Tiny wants to sell.'

Vern shrugged. 'Tiny usually goes along with what I say. Raven Lake ain't a big money-maker.'

'It's Tiny's life, Vern.'

He nodded. 'Yes. That it is.' He sighed. 'You'd think, in this land of the free, that a man wouldn't have to sell anything he didn't want to sell. But we're talking about Maine, now, and Maine, as you know . . .'

'Is the home of the braves,' I finished for him. 'An old line, Vern.'

He chuckled. 'This any kind of a case, Brady?'

'I'll know better when I talk to this Smith in Portland. On the one hand, the land settlement made by the feds some years ago says no, the Indians can make no more claims in Maine. On the other hand, the fact that this is sacred land we're talking about may make Raven Lake an exception. Complicated.'

'Umm,' he grunted. 'Indians got more lawyers working for them than squaws these days, and since that settlement, they've got more money to throw around than they know what to do with. They have discovered the joys of litigation.'

'It can be profitable,' I agreed. A pigeon pecked at my shoe. I shoved it away with a sideways swipe of my foot.

'Makes you wonder,' said Vern.

'What?'

'What the Indians really want with Raven Lake.'

I shrugged.

He put his hand on my shoulder and pushed himself into a standing position. He was a tall man, still straight and broad-shouldered in spite of his years. He peered down at me. 'Hope you have good fishin', Brady.'

I stood beside him. 'There's one thing I especially like about Raven Lake, even when the fish don't bite.'

'What's that?'

'No pigeons.'

I shook hands with Vern, and he wandered off through

the gardens toward his office on Tremont Street, while I strolled back to my office in Copley Square via Boylston Street, plotting my trip to Raven Lake. I decided to bring my new Orvis four-weight boron rod as well as my old faithful Leonard split bamboo. I'd have to pick through my boxes of bucktails and streamers. Maybe tie up a few Grey Ghosts and Dark Edson Tigers and Warden's Worries for the trip.

Of course, I still had to clear it with Julie. There was only one way to do it. I'd give her the same couple of weeks off, in addition to her regular vacation. A little bonus for her. A nonrefusable offer. Julie would call all our clients to tell them we'd be gone. That was the sort of small courtesy that set my practice apart. Then we'd put the 'Gone Fishin'' sign on the door, call the answering service, and depart.

Julie was my secretary, my sole employee. In the actual practice of things, she was more like a partner. Hell, she really was more like my boss than the other way around. I once tried to bestow upon her the title of 'Administrative Assistant'. I had been struggling to elevate my consciousness to the ever-increasing heights expected of an enlightened man in these days of sexual equality and liberated womanhood, and it never occurred to me that I might have committed another faux pas. Julie instantly set me straight.

'There's nothing wrong with being a secretary,' she told me hotly. 'You just have to keep in mind that secretaries do not brew and fetch coffee, buy birthday presents for ex-wives, sign and mail their employer's Christmas cards, or stand in line for Celtics tickets. So don't you try to buy my goodwill with any phony new title. I am your secretary. It's an important job. And don't forget it.'

Indeed. Julie knows the business. She's smart,

efficient, imaginative, self-starting, self-reliant. She utterly charms all my clients. She is, in a word, all the things that I would like to be.

She also happens to be young and beautiful, which has not proved to be a serious hindrance to our working relationship.

As I sauntered along Boylston Street, sniffing the air and peering into the store windows, I tried to anticipate Julie's reaction to my announcement that we would be closing the office for a week or two. She would tell me I was being irresponsible again. I would deftly parry her thrust by reminding her that I had to see Seelye Smith in Portland and that Tiny and Vern Wheeler, who were, after all, important clients, wanted me to hang around Raven Lake for a little while.

She'd remind me that she wasn't stupid.

I'd tell her to remember that she would have the time off, too.

She'd tell me that was even more irresponsible.

I'd ask her just who the hell she thought was the boss around here.

She'd give me one of her sardonic grins.

No sweat.

When I walked into the office, Julie had the telephone tucked against her ear. With one hand she was flipping through her Rolodex file. With the other hand she was tapping on our new office computer. I decided to wait a while to tell her about the Raven Lake trip.

I kissed the top of her head, and she rewarded me by rolling her eyes and crinkling her nose at me.

I went into my inner office and called Charlie McDevitt. In addition to being golf and fishing partners, Charlie and I liked to exchange favors with each other.

23

This was a businesslike arrangement. We paid each other off with lunches in Boston restaurants.

I swapped flirtations with Shirley, Charlie's grandmotherly dumpling of a secretary. When Charlie came on the line, I said, 'Need a favor.'

'Will this be a Burger King favor or a Locke-Ober favor?'

'Probably somewhere in between,' I said. 'More like a Jake Wirth or maybe a Durgin Park favor. Depends on what you can do for me.'

'Who gets to decide?'

Charlie always did drive a hard bargain. 'You decide the category, I'll pick the place,' I told him. 'Fair enough?'

'I think you better tell me what you want, first.'

'Okay. I want a rundown on an attorney by the name of Smith. First name of Seelye. He's got an office in Portland. You guys should have something on him, because he represented some landowners in the Maine Indian cases. I seem to recall that Justice was involved in that one.'

'We were,' said Charlie. 'Interior and Justice both helped to negotiate the settlement.' He paused. 'This sounds to me at least like a Jimmy's Harborside favor.'

'You must know somebody who could help.'

'I can talk with the folks in the Augusta office. Tell me what you're after.'

'You remember Vern Wheeler? Runs Raven Lake?'

'Ah, those salmon. Of course I remember.'

'Vern's brother, Tiny, has hired Smith. Seems that the Indians want to buy Raven Lake.'

'And Smith is doing the dickering?'

'Not exactly. Smith is advising. Tiny doesn't want to sell. Question is, if he refuses, can the Indians win in court? They're hinting at a suit, claiming that since the

24

place sits on one of their sacred burial grounds, the old settlement doesn't hold. So Tiny is depending on this Smith to handle the litigation, if necessary, or to advise him with regard to the transaction. He wants to know if Smith's any good.'

'And,' added Charlie, 'if he's in somebody's pocket. Sure. It'll take me a few days, probably. I'll get back to you.' He paused. 'Did I tell you the one about the pope dying and going to heaven? See St Peter's there at the pearly gates talking with a guy –'

'I'm kinda busy now, Charlie,' I said.

'No, listen. St Peter's talking to this guy, who's wearing a pinstripe suit, expensive worsted charcoal, pale blue button-down shirt, nice silk tie, black wing tips. St Peter says, "So we've been saving a super place for you. Think you'll like it. Three bedrooms, two full baths, nice balcony to catch the morning sun, view of the golf course, trout stream out back. Agreeable girls to bring your coffee in the morning, make your bed, whatever. Tennis courts, Jacuzzi, Olympic pool, exercise room. Couple nice restaurants within walking distance. How's that sound to you?" And Pinstripe says it sounds great. Sounds like heaven, he says. And all this time the pope is standing there next in line, listening, thinking, *Man, this sounds great. They must have something terrific for the pope.*'

'Charlie, really,' I said. 'I'm on a tight schedule. Gotta run.'

Charlie pressed on. 'So the gates swing open, and two gorgeous angels, look like Loni Anderson and Joan Collins, they come down and take Pinstripe by the hand and lead him inside, and the gates close again. Then St Peter turns around and sees the pope standing there, and he drops to his knees and kisses the pope's ring and murmurs, "Welcome to Heaven, Your Holiness. We are honored to have you here." And the pope is thinking, hot diggity, this is gonna be great. So he says, "Rise, my son." So St Peter stands up and he says, "We want you to be happy, Holy Father. We have a lovely efficiency apartment for you. Nice Army cot, bedside table, windup alarm clock, communal bathroom just down the hall. The hot water works most of the time, and you get an extra blanket for when the heat goes off. I think you're going to love it." Now, the pope, he doesn't want to admit it, of course, but he's pretty disappointed. So he says to St Peter, "It sounds very nice, of course. But I was wondering. That man who was in front of me, the man in the pinstripe suit. You seem to have really rolled out the red carpet for him. His accommodations sounded, er, even more luxurious than those you have set aside for me. And I was the pope. Who was that man, anyway?" And St Peter, says, "Oh, that man was a lawyer." And the pope frowns and says, "A lawyer, huh? Well, how come he got such a nice place?" And St Peter says, "Well, see, Your Eminence, we never had a lawyer up here before."'

I snorted through my nose. 'You trying to tell me something?' I said.

'Hell,' he said. 'I'm a lawyer, too, you know.'

Charlie called me back the following Tuesday. 'Good news,' he said. 'This Seelye Smith is a straight arrow. And a very sharp one. Back in the seventies, while everyone else in the state of Maine ignored the Indians, Smith was warning them that the tribes had a helluva case. He predicted exactly what was going to happen. That they'd win *Passamaquoddy* v. *Morton*, that they'd follow up with that big lawsuit, and that Congress would settle. Nobody listened to Smith. Now everybody does. The boys in Augusta respect the hell out of him. And they like him, too. The Wheeler brothers've got themselves a good attorney.'

'Your sources, Charlie. You trust them?'

'Oh, yes. Absolutely.'

'Well, good, then. That's a big help.'

'So when you taking me to Jimmy's?'

'When I get back.'

'Back?'

'From Raven Lake. Didn't tell you? I gotta go up there.' I sighed elaborately. 'Leaving Friday. Probably have to do a lot of fishing.'

'Jesus, Brady. That's rough.'

'Well, you know, this isn't an easy racket I'm in.'

Chapter Two

When I grasped Seelye Smith's hand to shake it, I thought for a panicky moment that I had somehow managed to grab on to his bare foot. I looked down at the thing I held in my hand before I could stop myself. Then, with what I imagined was a sickly grin, I quickly lifted my gaze to his eyes.

He had a plump woodchuck face. Two large front teeth with a space between big enough to wedge a matchstick into. Fiftyish, fat cheeks, thinning reddish-gray hair. Small, closely spaced pale blue eyes. He wore a hearing aid in his left ear, the old-fashioned kind with a wire running from a white button down into a battery pack in his shirt pocket. He was smiling broadly.

'It's okay, Mr Coyne. Everybody sneaks a look the first time.'

He held his right hand up for me to see. Where the thumb and forefinger should have been was a red mound of scar tissue. He had half a middle finger. His ring finger and pinkie remained intact.

He jerked his head toward his office. 'Come on. Let's go in. Hey, Kirk,' he said to his receptionist. 'Bring Mr Coyne and me some coffee, will you?'

I followed Smith into an unprepossessing office. One wall was dominated by a window giving a view down the hill to the Portland harbor. There were the standard wall-to-wall bookshelves lined with legal tomes, a few framed diplomas, plain gray metal desk, and a small conference table. We sat opposite each other at the table.

Smith put his mangled hand on the table. Again, I had trouble not staring at it.

'Mill accident,' he said, flip-flopping his hand around on the table so that I could see all sides of it. 'Happened when I was fifteen. My old man owned a sawmill in Lewiston. Did finish work – moldings, valances, door-frames, mostly fancy stuff like that. I worked there after school, summers, weekends. Learning the trade, the old man called it. Started by sweeping up the offices, and when I got bigger, I helped with the heavy outside work. Learned to drive the machinery – forklifts, what have you. Summer I was fifteen, Pop figured I was big enough to do some cutting. Thing was, there was this old French-man who worked with me, supposed to be breaking me in. Told the damnedest stories. Dirty stories. Raunchy. Very flattering for a kid, the boss's son, to have this old Canuck tell him dirty stories. One day he really broke me up, and when I started laughing, I ran my hand right through the saw. Didn't even feel it. The old Frenchie stopped in the middle of his sentence and started bellow-ing. I looked down, saw the blood gushing out of my hand, and passed out.'

Smith rubbed his scarred right hand with the palm of his left. 'I spent five days in the hospital. For a long time those fingers that weren't there anymore hurt like hell. After that, they started itching. Still do. Damnedest thing. The itch is up where the thumb and finger ought to be. Can't scratch it. Drives me nuts sometimes. Anyways, when I came home, the old man sat me down. "Boy," he said, "you sure'n hell ain't gonna be no use now. Anyone dumb enough to saw his hand off belongs in college." So he shipped me off to a private school down in Berwick, then got me into Bowdoin. After that I went off to Stanford for the law degree, then came back and set up shop right here in Portland.'

He smiled at me. 'Imagine that was some of the stuff you came to find out. Checking up on me. Tiny Wheeler wants you to corroborate his judgement, way I figure it.'

'Something like that,' I admitted.

Kirk, a dark young man in an expensive-looking suit, brought in a tray with two cups of coffee on it. He set it before us and stood back expectantly.

'That's just fine, Kirk. Thank you,' dismissed Smith. When Kirk had left the room, Smith said, 'You want someone to fetch the coffee, you sure as hell can't hire a woman. Know what I mean?'

I grinned and nodded. 'I certainly do.'

He stirred some cream and sugar into his coffee. I sipped mine black.

Smith settled back in his chair. 'Portland's a good city for lawyering lately. Getting all citified, in its own small way. Yuppieized. We got the most architects and ortho-dontists per capita in the state. That kind of city.'

I lit a cigarette. Behind Seelye Smith's gap-toothed grin and country-boy chatter, I detected a shrewdness that made me cautious. Charlie McDevitt had reported that Smith was honest and able. I felt confident about the able part.

He had the habit of touching his hearing aid with his left forefinger and cocking his head sideways at me when he expected me to speak. I found myself raising my voice a notch when I talked to him.

'So what can you tell me about the offer for Raven Lake?' I said.

He scratched his scarred hand absentmindedly. 'Right now, probably not any more than you already know. The offer came from an Indian law firm, acting for a partner-ship in Bangor. What they're saying is they want to make some kind of retreat out of Raven Lake, a kind of memorial. Place where Indians can go to find their roots. Some damn thing like that.'

'They're claiming it's sacred old Indian ground, I understand.'

He nodded. 'Well, there *is* a certifiable burial ground on the property. They're right about that. But it's way the hell across the lake and into the woods from where the lodge sits.'

'So the question is, how can they claim the whole place?' I asked.

Smith touched his hearing aid and nodded. 'What they're saying is that to the Indians the whole place was sacred. It was like a great big Mecca. They made pilgrim-ages there. To the lake. One of their gods resided there. They never hunted or fished there. The burial ground is all that's physically left of it. If we go to discovery, we'll see what sort of evidence they've got. In the meantime, they're only hinting at a lawsuit. No lawsuit, of course, no discovery – and no access to their evidence. They'd rather make a straight purchase, avoid litigation.'

'Meaning they haven't got the evidence to back up their claim,' I said.

'Maybe. Or maybe it just means they'd rather avoid the hassle.' Smith shrugged. 'We call them on it, we gamble they haven't got it. Meantime, they've tendered an offer. One million, seven hundred thousand for the whole operation. Shorefront, buildings, docks, the works.'

'Is that a good offer?'

He shrugged. 'It's on the low side of fair. As you'd expect. They'd assume we'd dicker around some. One point seven million is in the ballpark. It's a serious offer.'

'My clients, the Wheeler brothers, don't want to sell, as you know. At any price. They're worried what happens next.'

'And they're wondering how Seelye Smith is going to handle it,' Smith added. 'Fair enough. If the Wheeler boys don't want to sell, the Indians are saying they'll take it to court. My job is to figure out if they can win. I understand that.'

'And that means deciding if they've got a case.'

'Tell you one thing,' he said, downing the last of his coffee. 'Potentially, at least, they've got a case. The government has been very receptive to claims based on religious factors. It's case by case, of course, but there is this burial ground up there on Raven Lake. Whether that entitles them to a claim of the entire lake is another question.'

'I thought,' I said slowly, 'that they forfeited all future claims in 1980.'

Smith cocked his head at me. 'What do you know about the Maine Indian land grab, Mr Coyne?' He fingered his hearing aid.

I lifted my hands, palms up, and let them fall back onto the table. 'Just the outline of it, I guess. The Indians claimed the entire state of Maine originally belonged to them and that the white man took it illegally. They filed suit, and their claim was upheld in federal court. Congress settled by buying big chunks and turning it over to the Indians, along with lots of cash. The Indians agreed to abandon future claims.'

He nodded. 'All true. It was the biggest settlement the Indians ever got. The United States Congress gave them three hundred thousand acres, which we taxpayers bought from governments and corporations. Lumber companies, mainly. Uncle Sammy paid fifty-four point five million for that land. Plus, just to make sure they were happy, Congress set aside another twenty-seven million in a trust fund for them.'

'I've never entirely understood the legal aspects of the case,' I said. 'The whole deal. Will those principles be applied to Raven Lake, or what?'

He touched the button in his ear. 'I can summarize it for you. The thing is, nobody took it serious at the beginning. Except me. I visualized the whole thing. It all started when this illiterate old Passamaquoddy lady by the name of Lena Brooks came across an old treaty in a cardboard box up in the attic of an old house at the Pleasant Point Reservation. This was the 1794 treaty between the Passamaquoddies and the state of Massachusetts. Massachusetts, as you remember, included Maine back then. This treaty ceded all Indian lands to the state except for a few thousand acres and a couple islands. Some smart Indian got ahold of it and said, "Aha! Those acres and islands belong to us, and we ain't got them anymore." An even smarter Indian remembered the Indian Non-Intercourse Act, which was about the first thing the United States Congress ever did back in 1790. This Non-Intercourse Act set up a trust relationship between the federal government and all the Indian tribes. Specifically, it said that Congress had to supervise and ratify all land transactions between the Indians and the non-Indians. The idea was to protect the ignorant heathens, you understand. White man's burden, all that shit.'

I nodded. 'Obviously,' I said, 'the 1790 act of Congress superseded the 1794 treaty with the state of Massachusetts.'

Smith grinned. 'Why, sure. Simple law. And on that basis, the Indians filed a relatively small claim in the Federal District Court of Maine. Claimed the 1794 treaty

33

was null and void. Laid claim on a relatively small hunk of land.'

'That was *Passamaquoddy* v. *Morton*, right?'

'Good for you, Mr Coyne. June 22, 1972. Very important date for the good folks in Maine. *Morton* settled for the Indians. Gave them one hundred and fifty million bucks.' Smith rubbed his scarred hand. 'I worked for Morton on that one.'

'For the state,' I said.

'Right. The state's attorney general. I told them we were going to lose. I recommended we settle. The law was against us. So was the temper of the times, if you understand me.'

'Those were good days for minorities,' I said.

'They sure as hell were. Flushed with victory, as the fella says, the Penobscots and Passamaquoddies filed another suit in 1976. This was the blockbuster. They figured, what the hell, if that 1794 treaty ain't any good and if that was the one that cost us the state of Maine, let's get that sucker back. Their claim was for a mere twelve point five million acres. That's nearly sixty percent of the state, Mr Coyne.'

He paused, and I nodded appreciatively. 'As an afterthought,' continued Smith, 'they claimed an additional twenty-five billion in what they called back rents and damages. And they had the backing of the United States Departments of Interior and Justice. Now, the thing was, the tribes were perfectly willing to negotiate. They expected to bargain. No dummies, those Indian lawyers. They knew how it worked. Give a little, take a little. Right, Mr Coyne? Ain't that the way they do law in Boston?'

I smiled. 'Exactly.'

'It was my position right along,' said Smith, 'that we

should bargain with them. Play the damn game. Give them some respect. After all, they clearly had legal precedent in *Morton*.' He paused and cocked his head at me. 'You familiar with the concept of laches, Mr Coyne?'

I hastily flipped through the musty, dog-eared law book I kept in my head. 'Long-neglected rights lose their standing, I think. Something like that.'

Smith nodded. 'Close enough. Rights that have been consistently and uniformly neglected cease to be rights and cannot later be invoked. That was the position of the state. If you rest on that principle, you can't turn around and negotiate. Fact is, even after *Morton*, folks figured the claim was just too outrageous to take seriously. So they refused to bargain. The state litigated. Congress finally settled it.'

'I see,' I said. 'But the Indians did give up their prerogative for further suits.'

'Well, yes and no. They can't litigate on the basis of the 1790 treaty, or *Morton*, anymore. But there's nothing to stop them from finding new approaches.'

'Like the special status of sacred land.'

'Exactly.' Smith stared out the window at the deep-water harbor in the distance. There was very little maritime activity on the water that I could see except for the brightly colored sails of pleasure craft. 'There are some precedents for this. Other tribes in other states have made some headway based on similar claims. That's why it's my job to try to find out just what kind of evidence there is that this claim falls outside the *Morton* settlement.'

'You think there's some other agenda?' I said. 'Some other reason they want Raven Lake?'

'Well, the obvious thing is they just want it and they're

gambling that the Wheeler brothers won't risk going to court.'

'Is that likely?'

Smith shrugged. 'Probably that's the most likely. Straightforward real estate deal, with just the hint of a threat tossed in for bargaining purposes. Also likely is just what they're saying. They want to set up some kind of shrine or park or reservation. A memorial to their heritage. The Indians aren't all cynics, Mr Coyne.'

'And third?'

He flapped his one-and-a-half hands in the air. 'Third is one of those things I've got to check out. Third is they want the place for something else. I don't know what.'

I glanced at my watch. It was eleven-thirty, and I faced close to a five-hour drive to Greenville at the foot of Moosehead Lake. I pushed myself back from the table. Seelye Smith stood up.

'I've got a plane that'll be taking off at five this afternoon in Greenville,' I told him. The extra loudness in my voice by now had become habit. 'I appreciate the information, Mr Smith. We'll keep in touch. I hope you can find out just what's behind this thing.'

He came around the table and began to walk me toward the door. 'Sorry I can't buy you some lunch, Mr Coyne.'

'Next time.'

We paused at the door. He looked up at me, his eyes twinkling. 'Well, tell me.'

'What?' I said, frowning.

'Did I pass?'

I laughed. 'If you don't know what you're talking about, Mr Smith, you sure as hell have fooled me. Takes a good lawyer to fool me. So I guess either way, you pass.'

He chuckled. 'I fooled you on one thing, I reckon. You noticed my hearing aid.'

I nodded.

'Best damn hearing aid there is. This wire here – you probably think I got it hooked into a battery, right?'

I shrugged.

'Look.' He pulled the end of the wire out of his pocket. It wasn't hooked into anything.

I frowned. 'What good does that do?'

'Well, I had no trouble hearing what you had to say to me, Mr Coyne.' He grinned. 'People see this thing in my ear, they just naturally talk louder. So I hear them fine. Helluva hearing aid.'

Seelye Smith accompanied me through the reception area. I nodded to Kirk, the receptionist, and turned to Smith. I held out my hand, and he stuck his own mangled appendage into it.

'Good fishing, Mr Coyne,' he said.

'And good hunting to you. I'll be in touch soon. I hope you can scare up some answers.'

'I expect I will,' he drawled.

I walked out into the crisp June sunshine, climbed into my BMW, and pointed it at Greenville, nearly two hundred miles to the north and west. I was heading into the vast, still largely untracked Maine wilderness. I couldn't wait to get there.

Chapter Three

'Pretty, ain't it?'

Bailey Gibbons grinned sideways at me and then banked the Cessna so that I could peer down at Moosehead Lake two thousand feet below us. I swallowed back the bile that suddenly tried to squeeze up into my throat and nodded. 'Pretty. Yes,' I said through clenched teeth.

He frowned at me. 'You okay there, man?'

I nodded vigorously. 'Oh, sure. Fine.'

'You feel like blowin' lunch, I got a bag somewhere.'

'I'm fine.'

'That's Lily Bay down there. Elephant Mountain off to your right. You can see Mount Kineo up ahead.' He leveled the floatplane off. We were following the ragged eastern shoreline of Moosehead, heading north. Raven Lake was a half hour's flight away. Barring air pockets or unnecessary acrobatics by my pilot, I thought I might make it without embarrassing myself.

Evergreen and water. That's the northwest quarter of Maine. Red, white, and black spruce. Balsam and hemlock, white pine and cedar and tamarack (which the natives call 'hackmatack'). From the air it looks like a lumpy green velvet cloth onto which someone has spilled handfuls of glittering gems – big odd-shaped diamonds, tiny round emeralds – all linked up with serpentine silver chains. Maine's waterways make a complex circulatory system. Moosehead is the big heart at the center of it. The Kennebec and the Penobscot rivers, the St John and the Allagash, are the main arteries. The thousands of feeder streams are the veins and minor arteries and capillaries, which bulge into hundreds of ponds and lakes, many of them still nameless and uncharted.

I was not deceived by the tranquillity of the scene from two thousand feet. I had spent time in the Maine woods, and I knew just how treacherous they were. Those gentle lumps on the velvety surface were, from ground level, sheer mountainsides interlaced with blowdown and brier and surrounded by blackfly-infested bogs where a man could wander for weeks and never find a sign of human existence.

Wolves used to prowl those woods. They're virtually extinct here, now. Mountain lions, too. Natives called them 'catamounts'. The Indians thought they were devils and called them 'Lunk Soos'. The last catamount was killed in 1891, although from time to time a possibly sober woodsman or trapper claims to have seen one. The last caribou in Maine was killed in 1908.

There are black bear, still, and whitetail deer. Sportsmen and other sorts of men armed with guns trek from all over the northeast to the Maine woods hoping to slay a deer or bear. There are moose and beaver, porcupines and musk-rats ('musquash' to the Indians). These creatures, sublime and lowly alike, get shot by gunners now and then, sometimes perfectly legally.

Winter fur trappers, those hardiest of all souls, prize the sable and the weasel in its winter white, which is called an ermine.

In the Maine woods, too, lurk lynx and bobcat, red and gray fox. There are skunks, squirrels, hares, rabbits, and chipmunks. Mice, moles, shrews, and voles. Mosquitoes, deerflies, blackflies, and no-seeums.

A man might be lost in those vast woods. But he'd never be alone.

'Don't really look that much like the head of a moose, does it?' remarked the pilot. 'I reckon that's how she got her name, though.'

Neither, I thought, did Raven Lake look like a raven's beak, which is how, according to Tiny Wheeler, that little body of water acquired its name. From the air, Raven Lake looked like a banana. 'Lake Banana,' I once told Tiny. 'That's what you should call it.'

'I was thinkin' more along the lines of Penis Pond,' he had said, his gold incisor flashing with his grin.

'Spencer Bay down there,' announced Gib, as the pilot told me he preferred to be called. 'We'll be passing over the North East Carry in a minute. Follow the West Branch up to Chesuncook. Then we come to Umbazookeus, Mud Pond, Chamberlain, Eagle, Allagash, and Chemquasabamticook. We'll cut west over the St John, and then it's a short way to Raven.' The names rolled easily off his tongue. I was impressed.

'You must know these parts like the back of your hand,' I said.

'Nobody knows these parts, man,' Gib answered quickly. 'Except maybe some old Indians. I know it from the air. I recognize the lakes, the landmarks. It's like a map to me. I can read it pretty good from up here. But, hell, no, I don't know it. Not like the old boys used to, when you had to paddle the length of the lake from Greenville to the Carry and portage over to the West Branch. Hell, Thoreau made the trip three times. Took him twenty-four hours just to get to Greenville. All-night steamer from Boston to Bangor, then all day by stage overland, before he even stepped into a bark canoe. He spent weeks out in those woods, just him and his friends and their Indian guides. And Thoreau didn't even pretend to know this land.'

I had initially pegged Gib as a Maine woodsman, wise, perhaps, in the ways of whitetail deer and landlocked salmon. No inconsequential wisdom, that, but I figured him for crude and unschooled and not the sort of man who had read Thoreau. I knew better than to share my misperception with him.

'You watch close, now, man,' he said as we climbed a little and sailed smoothly through the clear afternoon sky. 'This little doodad here, you move it this way and she banks left.' He demonstrated, a little too abruptly for the serenity of my gastric system. 'This way here and she banks right.' We banked. 'When you pull on her, she goes up. Push forward, she goes down.' Gib put the machine through some paces. It responded instantly.

'Why' – I gulped – 'are you telling me this?'

'This thing here's a throttle,' he continued, ignoring my question. 'Do this and she slows down. Do it too much and she stops, of course. Then we crash onto the ground. Do this here to it and she goes faster. Course, you don't want her to go too fast. Okay, you got all that, man?'

'Up, down, left, right. Sure, I guess so. I really don't want to fly this thing, though.'

'If'n I have another one of them heart-attack things, you're the one who's going to have to get us down,' said Gib. I studied his face for the glint of a grin. I saw none.

'You're joking, of course,' I said hopefully.

Gib was a compact guy with a prematurely weathered face. He wore a Grateful Dead T-shirt and Boston Red Sox cap twisted around backward on his head. A little pigtail hung down the back of his neck. I had initially taken him for about my age, but as I saw him more closely, I revised my estimate. He was younger than I. Perhaps in his early thirties. A lifetime in the out-of-doors had eroded premature gullies in his cheeks and forehead.

41

'Way off to your right there,' he said, 'you can see Mount Katahdin. The Indians think it's haunted. Biggest mountain in the state. That hunk of land beyond the mountain is Baxter State Park.' He chuckled, his eyes sweeping the landscape in front of us. 'Sound like a goddamn tourist guide, don't I? Keep forgetting you've been up here before.'

'Several times,' I said. 'But it's new to me each time.'

'It's pretty awesome the first time you fly your own plane over it. I've talked to boys who do this kind of flying in Alaska. They say the same thing. Thank God for skis and floats. Bring a plane down just about anywheres. You can land a floatplane on grass if you've got to. Course, you have a helluva time getting her up again.'

'You've been doing this a long time,' I said.

'Learned to fly after ROTC. Then the first chance I had I went into hock to buy this machine. Been flying out of Greenville several years now. Best kind of flyin' there is. Take off and land where you want, when you want. No flight plans to file. No traffic. Just me and the sky and the lakes.' He paused and crinkled his eyes as he studied the landscape below. 'Fact is, business ain't what I thought it would be. Folks come to Maine lookin' for what they call a wilderness experience. Shit, man, this hasn't been wilderness for a long time. Here. Take a look over there.'

He banked the plane a few degrees so that I could peer out over the right wing. I saw an area several acres square that looked as if it had been shaved clean. The earth lay raw and exposed. It was studded with stumps. 'Fresh clear cut,' said Gib, leveling off the Cessna again. 'That's how the loggers do it nowadays. Ever since they outlawed the river drives. They cut roads into the woods, strip the land clean, load the logs onto trucks, and lug them out

that way. They've cleaned up the Kennebec and Penobscot rivers that way. They claimed that all the bark and
sunken logs and shit was poisoning the water. What they
got instead was this clear-cutting and a wilderness full of
passable roads. Shit, man, there's hardly a pond or stream
up here now that ain't fished – and fished hard. You could
drive your Caddy right up to most of 'em. Places that
twenty years ago you had to fly into, and you could cast a
fly to trout that had never seen a lure before, now you go
there and you find beer cans and Big Mac wrappers the
assholes dump along the shore. There's a stream up there
– I ain't sure it's even got a name – where there's a
boulder in it. You fish there, you'd swear you were the
first white man ever been there. Then you look at this
boulder, and there's a bronze plaque on it. Says, "Presi-
dent Eisenhower fished here." Wilderness! Shit, man.
You really want wilderness, you've got to go to Alaska.'

I studied the landscape beneath us more carefully, and
I could detect the web of narrow, twisting roadways that
meandered through the forest and the areas that had
been cut clean over the years. There were whole mountainsides that were beginning to grow back, where the
foliage was a light green, and other areas already thick
with new second-growth forest. To the untutored eye, it
still looked primeval. There were no paved highways, no
housing developments. But a careful look revealed a
scarred and wounded landscape.

'Is business that bad?' I asked Gib.

He shrugged. 'It's a struggle. There are fewer of us
now than there used to be, so I guess it evens out. Before,
a plane was the only way to get into the woods, and there
were plenty of folks who wanted to do that. Nowadays I'd
guess there are more folks than ever who want wilderness
and come to Maine for it. But they find out they can drive

right in. I still get a lot of first-timers. And, of course, flyin' in gives you the illusion of wilderness, if you can fool yourself into thinkin' it's the only way and if you don't look too close while you're up in the sky.'

'It's also a hell of a lot quicker,' I observed.

'True enough,' he said. 'And that's typical, too. I mean, folks want the wilderness, and they want it instant. I can get them a long way up in a short amount of time, that's true.'

'What is the range of this plane?' I asked.

'Comfortable seven hundred miles. She'll do about one-twenty at a sixty-five percent cruise. Gets about twelve gallons per hour. She'll carry four adult men, fuel, floats, a hundred pounds of gear, easy. Nice little plane. There, up ahead. That's Chamberlain Lake. Headwaters of the Allagash. Still damn fine trout fishing in the Allagash. Big water.'

The lakes, ponds, rivers, and mountains had begun to take on a sameness to my eye. I'd had a glut of the beauty of it. I was ready to set my feet onto solid ground. I relaxed back into my seat and closed my eyes. It had been a long day – long in time, a sense that was further heightened by the distance I had travelled. I had awakened in my apartment overlooking Boston Harbor, driven to Portland, Maine, spent an hour with Seelye Smith, and then ground over two-lane roads for the afternoon to Greenville, stopping only at a two-pump gas station for a fill-up, a can of Pepsi from the machine, and a Hershey bar. I was tired, and I was hungry. I looked forward to a healthy slug of Old Hipboot at Tiny Wheeler's rustic but well-stocked bar and then something fancy from Bud Turner's kitchen. A good night's sleep and I'd be ready to spend a day in a canoe hauling in big salmon.

'How soon?' I mumbled to Gib without opening my eyes.

'Running into a little headwind,' he said. 'Going to take her up a ways, see if we can get on top of it. We should be there fifteen, twenty minutes.'

I glanced out my window. The tiny ponds below glittered as the slanting afternoon sun caught their riffled surfaces. 'Looks like it's getting rough down there,' I said.

'The four o'clock chop. Wind always picks up in the afternoon. So does the salmon fishing. Cause and effect.'

'I remember,' I said. 'That chop must make it tough to land this thing.'

Gib turned to peer at me. He seemed mildly amused. 'If I don't have one of them heart attacks, no problem. Damn sight better than glassy smooth. It's a pure bitch putting one of these ladies down on a mirror. Can't see where the hell the top of the water is. Hit it wrong, just like hitting concrete. Nice little chop, you can see it. Makes it easy.'

I shrugged and nodded. Flying floatplanes was another one of those things I knew nothing about.

I settled back again and allowed my eyelids to droop. The hum of the engine drugged me, and the faint vibration in the fuselage was a gentle body massage.

Abruptly we tipped onto our side and dropped. The plane's engine whined at a higher pitch. I swallowed hard, both against the sudden tightening in my inner ears and against the flip-flopping of my stomach.

I sat forward. 'What the hell?'

Gib was peering out his side window. 'Down there. See it?'

I leaned over to look out his window. 'What? What is it?'

'Moose with her calf. There, in the cove.'

He had circled around as we descended, so that we

45

came across the pond toward the cove, where I could now see the two moose. The cow was enormous – bigger and bulkier and longer legged than a full-grown steer. As the plane approached her, she lifted her head and then began to trot with surprising quickness and grace through the weedy shallow water toward the woods that bordered the shoreline. Her calf, a miniature version of herself, followed. As they slid into the underbrush, Gib veered away, and we skidded over the tops of the trees.

'They move like ghosts through the woods,' he said softly as we slanted upward to regain altitude. 'You'd think they'd crash around, but they can slip away from you so you'd never know they'd been there. Amazing animals.'

'How in the world did you ever spot them?'

He shrugged. 'You develop an eye for something that doesn't quite belong, I guess. The wrong shape, the wrong color. I've hunted a lot of deer. Usually I spot a deer by detecting a horizontal line. Think about it. The woods are all vertical lines – trees, saplings, brush, weeds. A horizontal line'll be the belly or the back of a deer. That or the white tail flipping, though usually if you see the tail it's too late. By then the deer's hightailing it.' He paused. 'I reckon that's where the word came from, isn't it? Hightailing, I mean. That's what deer do when they're running away. They stick that tail up there high so's the white shows.' He rubbed his face with his hand. 'Anyway, I saw those dark shapes down there in the water, and there wasn't anything else they could be except a couple of moose. When there's nothing else they can be, man, then they've got to be moose.'

'Unassailable logic,' I said, smiling. 'They say the moose are coming back in Maine.'

'Well, yes, they are. Not so much that you don't want to circle back to take a closer look, of course. The plane scares them. Which, to my way of thinking, ain't such a bad thing. They may not be as stupid as they look, but they sure'n hell ain't hard to kill if you've got a mind to. They don't have any enemies except man, so they don't scare easily. I figure I can save a few moose if I buzz them when I can. Put a little fear into them. Anyways, I do like to look at them.' He glanced out the window. 'St John River below. Just a few minutes to Raven Lake.'

'Moose are legal now, I understand,' I persisted.

'Oh, yes. Big controversy up here. The Audubon-type assholes think it's horrible that people want to shoot moose. It's very closely regulated. There's a lottery for permits. The Fish and Game fellas study the herd, figure out how much of it needs to be harvested each year to keep it healthy. Not much sport to it, moose hunting. But a rack of moose antlers looks nice in the pine-paneled dens down there in Wellesley and Greenwich and Scarsdale. Sorry, man.'

I laughed. 'Don't mention it. I don't hunt animals.'

'Best damn eatin' critter on the face of the earth,' said Gib. 'Bar nothin'. Ever eaten moose, man?'

'Not that anybody told me.'

'Even Thoreau said so. Like sweet, supertender beef. Look at what they eat. Lily shoots, watercress. Stands to reason. A Maine family can get through a whole winter eating off the carcass of one adult moose. Makes perfect sense to let folks shoot them rather than have them starve to death in the winter. Even if there ain't any sport to it. The guides love it. Naturally. They can absolutely guarantee their sport gets a point-blank shot at a moose. Sometimes they'll dick around for a few days before they show them the moose, just so the sports'll think they've done some hunting. But if they wanted to, any asshole who can point a gun could fill his permit in half a day with a decent guide. I guess the bleedin' hearts think it's okay to kill a deer because it's harder to find. I imagine the deer don't like gettin' shot any better than a moose does, though.' He craned his neck and squinted out over his wingtip. 'There's your lake.'

I peered down. Raven Lake looked like a dozen others we had flown over – crescent shaped, perhaps two miles long, with the silver threads of an inlet at the north end and an outlet at the south. Except this one, unlike most of the others, had a dock stretched over the water halfway down the eastern shore and a clearing where several buildings huddled, backed up to the dense woods. 'Lake Banana,' I muttered.

'Huh?'

'Nothing,' I said.

We approached the lake from the north end. Gib brought the plane down to about five hundred feet and flew the length of the lake. He studied the surface of the water as it slipped past under us. At the southern end we tilted up, banked in a tight circle, and returned. He came back at it low. We seemed to be barely skimming the treetops. When we had water under us, we sank down so that our eyes were at treetop level. Gib paralleled the shoreline. The engine roared as he throttled back. We touched, bounced, touched, skipped, and touched again. This time we stayed down, and I could feel the water brake us. Then we taxied toward the dock in front of Raven Lake Lodge, rocking on the rippled surface of the water.

'Nice job,' I said.

Gib shrugged. 'Made it that time. Always a relief.'

'I didn't realize you were concerned.'

'I'm always concerned, man. That's what keeps me alive.'

I studied his face for a hint of irony. I saw none.

48

Chapter Four

Marge Wheeler was standing on the dock, and as soon as Gib had maneuvered the Cessna up onto the sand beach, she came bounding down. 'Damn,' she said, smiling broadly, 'it's good to see you, Brady Coyne. It's been too long.'

She laid a wet kiss on my cheek and gave me an awkward one-armed hug around the waist. Marge had flashing eyes. She wore her hair in a short ponytail, which I noticed had begun to streak with silver since I had last seen her. She was about forty now, a full twenty-five years younger than Tiny, who loved to boast about how he had snatched her away from the preppies of Princeton.

I held her at arm's length. 'You're looking fine, Marge.'

'Damn straight. Wood choppin' and canoe paddlin'.' Her plaid flannel shirt was open at the throat that one extra button, which, on slick lady attorneys in their off-white silk blouses, always looks calculated. On Marge it just looked careless. And sexy. She patted her hip. 'I can still squeeze into these old jeans.' She jabbed my stomach with her forefinger. 'You could use a little wood chopping yourself, Counselor.'

'The only exercise I want is hauling in big salmon,' I said.

'That can be arranged. Come on up. You'll be staying at the lodge, if that's okay. The cabins are full.'

Gib had unloaded my gear from the plane and was busy making it fast. 'Be staying for supper, Gib?' Marge said to him.

'Yup. Need a sack, too.'

'There's room with the guides, if that'll be all right.'

She picked up my aluminum rod cases, and I shouldered my big duffel bag. We walked up the slight incline to the main lodge.

'Too bad you weren't here on Monday,' she said. 'We could've used a level head around here.'

'What happened?'

'We lost a sport.'

'What do you mean?'

'Fella disappeared. Ken Rolando, from Albany. He was up here by himself. Came in Sunday night. Monday it was raining. All the others went out, anyway. They usually figure, you pay two hundred and fifty bucks a day, you don't want to sit around the lodge playing solitaire on a rainy day. But Mr Rolando, he said he was going to hang around for the morning, wait and see if the weather was going to break. Around noon we noticed he wasn't around. Figured he went out for a walk, maybe casting from the shore. Or he could've just gone back to his cabin for a nap. But when he didn't show up for dinner, Tiny went to his cabin. He wasn't there. We asked all the guides and guests. Nobody'd seen him all day.' She shrugged. 'Still haven't. We never had that happen before. Oh, once or twice every fall a deer hunter'll get twisted around in the woods. But the guides always manage to find him. Generally they have enough sense to build a smoky fire, shoot off their rifles. But Mr Rolando just disappeared. Five days now. It doesn't look that good.'

We climbed the broad steps onto the front porch of the lodge. 'Want to sit and rock for a bit?' Marge said. 'Tiny's inside changing. He should be out in a minute. This thing's really thrown him for a loop.'

On the porch a receiving line of rocking chairs waited with open arms for the weary fisherman. 'Brumbys,' Vern had once told me with pride. 'Best damn rockers on earth. Made from good Georgia oak.'

The porch extended the full width of the spruce log lodge. A railing ran along the front at just the right height for propping up a man's feet while rocking. The only thing missing was a penknife and a stick to whittle on. Marge and I hitched up Brumbys and sat down beside each other. Before us lay Raven Lake, the ripples catching and reflecting the slanting rays of the late-afternoon sun. Beyond it the endless spruce and balsam forest rolled north and westward toward the Canadian border.

I sighed deeply. 'I think I love the smell best of all.'

'Pitch pine and woodsmoke,' Marge said. 'Tiny's smells. I think it was the smell of that man that seduced me.'

I lit a cigarette. 'So what have you done about Mr Rolando?'

'By the time we figured out that he was gone, it was nearly dark. We sent the guides out. Couple of them took out the square enders with motors to look around the shoreline of the lake. Couple others went through the woods as best as they could with flashlights. Shot off their guns, hollered a little, looked for tracks or something. Bud got into the truck and went down the road a ways. They didn't find him. No trace. It had rained hard all day, of course. Next morning Tiny got ahold of Thurl Harris – he's the sheriff down in Greenville. Called him on the shortwave. Thurl flew in that afternoon after the weather finally broke. Asked a bunch of damn-fool questions. Wanted to get the state police up here with dogs. Tiny reminded him ever so gently that we'd just had about three inches of rain and it was unlikely the dogs'd be able to smell anything. So Thurl, he huffed and puffed a bit, pretending he knew what he was doing, and then kinda shrugged and got back into his airplane and flew away. I checked Mr Rolando's registration form, got his phone number. Next day Tiny took the truck down to Greenville and called it. Got a man name of Philip Rolando. Kenneth Rolando's brother.'

'Not his wife?' I said.

Marge shrugged. 'Evidently he lived with his brother. Guess he wasn't married. Look. Why don't I go and get us a beer?'

'Sounds good.'

She was back in a minute with two cans of Budweiser. She handed one to me. 'Gimme one of those cigarettes, will you?'

I lit one of my Winstons and handed it to her. She took a big drag. 'I keep quitting. But I do love them. Anyway, Mr Rolando's brother's coming up. Tiny doesn't know what to expect. He'll want to talk to you about liability, I suspect.'

'Have you given up on Rolando?'

'Well, no, I haven't. Of course, he wasn't here long enough for anyone to figure out how resourceful he was. This was his first time. But this time of year, hell, the woods are full of nice fresh water. The nights aren't all that cold. Take a man a long time to starve to death. If he's got sense enough to find running water and follow it downstream, he's pretty likely to come to something.' She tipped up her beer can and drank deeply. 'Tiny, of course, he's imagining the worst.'

'The worst?'

'Mr Rolando's down at the bottom of the lake somewhere. Or he's lying in a gully with a broken leg. You know Tiny.'

'Isn't there anything somebody can do?'

She shrugged. 'It's up to the sheriff, I guess.'

A woman's voice from behind us said, 'Hey, Ma? Can you – '

Marge answered sharply without turning around. 'Excuse me?'

The last time I had seen Polly Wheeler was three years earlier, when she was a coltish girl-child of fourteen, all jutting hipbones, knee knobs, and flipping ponytail. Now she was a woman. She was seventeen or eighteen, I knew, but she could have passed for twenty-two or even older. Her honey-colored hair was cut into a short wedge, giving flattering emphasis to the angles and shadows formed by the delicate bones of her face – high, sharp cheekbones, long, straight nose, pointed chin. Her snug white jeans revealed that her hipbones no longer jutted. Polly wore a yellow T-shirt with 'Maine Black Bears' printed on it. She wore no bra underneath.

She moved beside Marge's chair. She moved, I noticed, very gracefully. 'Excuse me, mother,' she said, a sarcastic edge to her voice. 'Bud needs an idea how many for dinner.'

'Aren't you going to say hello to Brady?'

The girl frowned at me. 'I don't . . .'

I held out my hand to her. 'Brady Coyne. You don't remember me. That's all right. It's been three years, at least.'

She took my hand. 'I'm Polly.'

'I know,' I said.

'Well, at least you didn't say how much I've grown since the last time you saw me.' She turned to Marge. 'Anyway, Bud wants to know.'

'Tell him the usual plus Gib and Brady.'

'You guys want another beer?'

'We'll be in in a minute. Tell your father Brady's here if you see him.'

When Polly left, I said to Marge, 'She *has* grown since the last time I saw her.'

Marge laughed quickly. 'Little Polly is a pregnancy waiting to happen. As maybe you noticed. Can't wear clothes tight enough to satisfy her. I think she practices walking in front of a mirror, make sure her butt wiggles just right. She drives the guides nuts, I can tell. Some of the guests, too. I'm not sure that fancy private school was such a good idea. Oh, well. She's off to college in September. She's her own woman, I guess. Hope to hell she's on the Pill.'

'I would have to say that she's probably the second sexiest lady at Raven Lake,' I said.

'I know a compliment when I hear one,' she said. 'And I also know when it's time to change the subject. Come on. Let's go in and get a real drink.'

The downstairs of the lodge was one enormous room, half lounge and half dining room. The lounge half was dominated by a big fieldstone fireplace where a fire was blazing away. A well-stocked L-shaped bar stood in one corner. A variety of easy chairs, sofas, and Brumby rockers were scattered among the several large braided rugs. A wide central stairway leading to the bedrooms upstairs separated the lounge from the dining room. The walls were hung with mounted heads and fish – moose and deer with big racks, a bear, lake trout and squaretails and salmon of trophy size.

Tiny had once told me that he didn't find the taxidermist's work especially attractive, but he felt that he had to decorate the lodge to fulfill the guests' expectations. 'They want rustic, see?' he said. 'Wide plank pine floors. Log walls. Fieldstone fireplaces. Stuffed heads. That's why we don't run electric lights to the cabins and why we keep the outhouses. The sports want it that way. Give them television and running hot water, they'd think they were getting gypped. They pay seventeen fifty a week, they want wilderness. Go home to the city and talk about how they roughed it. Wild animals, all that shit. Of course, they want their booze, they want Bud's fancy cooking, they want the guides to pamper them. So we give them what they want. We got electricity here in the lodge. Plumbing, too. This is where we live.'

Marge took my hand and led me toward the bar. 'I've got to play hostess, here,' she said. 'Want me to introduce you around?'

'I'll manage. Introduce me to a glass of bourbon.'

Polly was behind the bar, pouring drinks. Three middle-aged men wearing L. L. Bean chamois shirts and chino pants that looked brand-new had hitched up stools and sat there with their elbows on the bar, keeping her company. I stood behind them, waiting to catch Polly's attention. She had a way of tossing her hair and bending for things under the bar that was not going unnoticed.

'You boys have any luck today?' she said to them as she plunked three bottles of beer onto the bar.

'Not yet, honey,' said one. 'But the night is young.'

'Party in Cabin three tonight,' said another one to her. 'You like to party?'

Polly leveled an unsmiling gaze on them. 'I love to party,' she said.

'Hey, come on, you guys,' said the third man. 'This is Tiny's kid.'

'No kid,' said Polly.

'For sure,' said the first sport.

'Hey, hi,' she said, seeing me for the first time. 'Drink?'

'Bourbon. Ice.'

The three men at the bar turned their heads to look at me. I nodded at them. 'Brady Coyne,' I said.

They mumbled greetings. 'Where you from, friend?' said the guy who was planning the party.

'Boston.'

'Hey! So are we. Small world.'

'Boston's a big city,' I observed.

'What the hell's that supposed to mean?'

'Nothing. Actually, I came here to get away from the city.'

'Yeah, well we did, too.'

'So,' I said, 'if you'll excuse me,' and I walked away from them, bearing my glass of bourbon. I looked around the room for Tiny. There were about twenty people in there by now. Some of them were guides I recognized from previous trips. There were two middle-aged women dressed in spanking new blue jeans that they appeared unaccustomed to wearing and one woman, not much older than Polly, who was clutching the arm of a tall guy with a prominent Adam's apple. The rest were men. Marge was chatting with the young couple. I didn't see Tiny.

I wandered back out to the porch. Two men had taken the rocking chairs that Marge and I had used. I dragged a third chair over beside them, propped my feet up onto the rail, and lit a cigarette. I decided that I could happily spend a good part of my two weeks right there.

'Right purty evenin', ain't she?' I said, using a poor imitation of a down-east twang.

The man beside me turned to look at me. 'By God, it's you, Mr Coyne! Tiny said you'd be comin' up.' He turned to the other man. 'This here's Mr Coyne from Boston. He lost the biggest damn salmon I ever seen few years ago.'

'Poor guiding,' I said.

'When they jump, you gotta go slack on 'em, else they come down on the leader and tear the fly out. Good guide puts you into the fish. Good fisherman don't mess up once he's hooked into 'em.' He held out his hand. 'Real good to see you again.'

The old Penobscot hadn't aged since I first met him a dozen or more years earlier. He always looked ageless. His skin was the color of rich red clay. Two deep gullies arced down from each side of his great beak of a nose to bracket his mouth. His coal-black eyes glittered behind narrowed, slightly down-tilted lids. His thick, straight hair, which he pulled back into a short ponytail, was the color of storm clouds. He had broad shoulders, powerful forearms, and an otherwise skinny frame. He could paddle upstream all day without breaking a sweat. Woody might have been fifty. He might have been seventy-five.

I shook his horny mitt. 'Good to see you, Woody. Glad to know you haven't gone to live in the city.'

'All us Indians didn't get rich,' he said. ''Sides, I'd go crazy anywheres else but here.'

'You don't have any room in your canoe, do you?'

The old guide rubbed his seamed face with the palm of his hand. 'I reckon. Mr Schatz here is by himself. You come on out with us tomorrow, Mr Coyne. They're bitin' faster'n blackflies, and that's a fact.' He paused and grinned. 'I must be keepin' my manners up my asshole. Mr Coyne, this here is Mr Schatz. He's from New Jersey.'

I reached across Woody and shook the other man's hand. 'You're keeping bad company, Mr Schatz.'

He grinned. 'Don't I know it. And it's Frank, please.'

I nodded. 'Brady. You don't mind if I join you?'

'Fine with me. This old Indian doesn't talk much. I could use the company.'

'He hasn't told you how he beats up bears?'

'He did tell me that one,' said Schatz.

'What about the time he lined up the partridge, the rabbit, and the whitetail and got all three with one shot?'

'Well, hell, Mr Coyne,' said Woody. 'Now you went and told it. I was savin' that one.'

'Tell him the moose story, then,' I said.

Woody turned to look at Frank Schatz. 'This here is absolutely true, Mr Schatz. See, I made camp up on the north shore of the lake. About this time of year, it was. Well, I woke up – pitch-black out, it was – and I heard the goddamnest thumpin' goin' on – '

'I didn't mean now,' I said, grinning at Woody. 'I've heard it already. Have you seen Tiny around?'

'Tiny had a couple of fellas out this afternoon. Got in after we did, all covered with fish slime and gurry. I'm telling you, the lake's paved with salmon, Mr Coyne. Anyways, I haven't seen Tiny since then.'

Schatz stood up. 'I'm going to get another drink. Tell me about the moose later, Woody. I promise to believe you.'

He left, and Woody and I rocked in silence for a few minutes. The sun was setting behind the hills beyond the distant shore. The surface of the lake had smoothed over. It looked like a pale pink pane of glass.

'That fella can't fish,' declared Woody quietly. 'He don't even appear to like it much. I asked him, does he want to try one of the streams for trout, he says no, he'd just as soon lay around in the canoe. So we've been trollin' for four days, now. Draggin' streamer flies up and down the shore. Catch a salmon now and then. Don't seem to matter to him whether he catches one or not. Almost like somebody told him he had to come up here for a while, so he's puttin' in his time.'

'Pretty expensive way to put in time,' I said.

'We get them now and then,' said Woody. 'Fellas come in here, usually alone, all they want to do is sit around the lodge, play poker, drink whiskey. Take 'em out on the lake, they fall asleep in the canoe. They get sick of it soon enough. Fly out after a few days of it. This Mr Schatz is like that. Friendly enough. But still, a strange bird.'

'Who's a strange bird?'

The voice came from the doorway behind us. 'Hey, Tiny!' I said.

'By Jesus, Brady. It's good to see you.' He came over and whacked my shoulder with his fist.

Tiny perched on the railing facing me. He looked like an aging black bear balancing on a clothesline. His gold tooth glinted in a smile from the undergrowth of his gray beard.

'How's Doc and Charlie, anyways?' he said.

'They're good,' I answered. 'Jealous as hell that I'm here and they're not. Wanted to be remembered to you, both of 'em.'

'You still gettin' rich swindling folks like my brother?'

'Still swindling them,' I said. 'Still not rich enough, though.'

'A man's never rich enough. Look at Woody, here. Government give him half the state of Maine, he's still trying to squeeze big tips from the city sports.' A beer can materialized in his big paw, and he drank from it and then wiped his mouth on the back of his hand. 'Damn,' he said, 'I am glad to see you. Lots of things going on.'

'So I understand. Marge filled me in a little.'

He frowned. 'That, and the Indians. Excuse me, Woody, but you know what I mean. You talk to Seelye Smith? Hell, we gonna lose this place, Brady?'

'You want to talk about it now?' I said. 'That's why I'm here.'

'You're here for the fishin', and don't try to kid me. We can talk about it later. Let you get a couple drinks, dinner, into you first.'

'What about your Mr Rolando?' I said.

He shook his head slowly. 'I just don't know. Nothing like this has ever happened up here before. Don't make any sense at all. But he's gone. Five days now. His brother's coming up in a couple of days. I dunno, Brady. If we don't have something by then . . .'

'You're worried about liability.'

'Hell, yes, I'm worried about liability. We get sued, Vern'll have my ass on a platter.'

'From what Marge told me, I don't see how you're liable, Tiny. But we can talk about that, too. When do we eat around here, anyway?'

'That's what I came out here for. Marge said to drag you in. Bud's got baked lake trout and a roast. Nice smells in that kitchen.'

Woody and I stood up. 'We'll talk some more later,' said Tiny as we followed him inside. 'We got troubles here.'

Tiny set a democratic table. Guides, guests, host, and hostess all ate together without regard for rank or status. I sat between Frank Schatz and the young man with the Adam's apple, who told me he was an accountant named Fisher, up from Hartford on his honeymoon. His bride sat across from him and didn't say a word during the entire meal. She kept her eyes on her plate except when Fisher spoke, at which time she lifted her gaze to him hopefully. He was, I gathered, an avid angler. He discoursed at length about the relative merits of boron and graphite in the manufacture of fly rods. He told me his strategies for fishing the spinner falls at the Henry's Fork. I told him I had never been there, but it only spurred him on to more elaborately detailed treatises. I turned off my mental hearing aid when he switched topics to the advantages of custom-designed shooting heads for winter steelhead fishing in Oregon. His wife continued to listen raptly.

At the other end of the table the guides were speculating on the fate of the missing Mr Rolando. 'Bears got 'im, sure'n hell,' one said.

'I thought bears were timid,' said one of the party boys from Boston.

'This time of year, a big ol' mother bear with her cubs'll take a man's head clean off with one swipe of that big paw of hers. Nothing meaner'n a mamma bear in June.'

'Catamount got 'im you ask me,' chimed in another guide. 'Folks say them big cats're extinct, but I seen their tracks. They'll jump outa trees, sink them old teeth into the back of a man's neck. Your poor Mr Rolando's a goner, 'fraid.'

The sports from Boston chuckled at this, but I sensed a nervous edge to their laughter. A glance at Tiny told me that he wasn't enjoying the conversation a single bit.

Lew Pike, who had guided me on one of my earlier trips to Raven Lake, said, 'It ain't the animals that got 'im. It's the Injuns. Hell, everybody knows there's only one thing Indians like better'n findin' a white man alone in the woods, and that's findin' a white woman. Peel their skin clean off, they will, in neat little strips, one at a time. Them squaws is worst of all. When the Indians want to do some serious torturin', they leave it to their squaws. Ain't that right, Woody?'

Woody looked up from his plate. 'That is so, Lew,' he said mildly. 'Learned all about it from the white man.'

Between the bantering from that end of the table and the pontificating of young Mr Fisher, there was no call for me to fabricate small talk. Which suited me fine. Bud Turner had performed his customary miracle – baked lake trout steaks with a sharp white sauce, roast beef with popovers and smooth brown gravy, baby baked potatoes, red kidney beans, fresh bread, and pitchers of cold milk and ice water.

I ate it all with great appetite and kept my silence. Diagonally across from me, Polly sat beside Gib. They seemed to have their own conversation going. At the head of the long rectangular table Tiny reigned, trying, it seemed to me, to keep tabs on all the conversations at once. At the other end sat Marge, a bemused smile on her face. Once when I glanced her way, she caught my eye and winked wickedly.

After dinner I went into the kitchen. Polly and Bud Turner were working side by side at the big double sink, scraping off plates and loading up the dishwasher.

'Hey, Bud,' I called.

Turner turned around. 'Hey, there, Mr Coyne. How you doin'?'

The Raven Lake cook was a gaunt man a few years younger than me. He was losing his sandy hair rapidly. His beaky nose and hollowed cheeks looked more fitting on a prisoner of war than on a talented chef.

He dried his hands on a towel and stalked across the kitchen. He thrust his bony hand at me, and I shook it. 'Good to see you,' I said. 'Another culinary masterpiece tonight.'

'Aw, just a little somethin' I threw together,' he said with a grin.

'You haven't lost your touch. The lake trout was special.'

He chuckled. 'They came out good, didn't they?'

'What was the flavor of the sauce? I couldn't identify it.'

'Herbs. Professional secret.'

'I'd love to have your recipe.'

'Sorry, Mr Coyne. Maybe I'll write a cookbook someday.'

'You gotta learn to write first,' said Polly over her shoulder. 'Come on. Cut the yakking and get back to work. I'm not going to do this all by myself.'

Turner shrugged and grinned. 'Boss's daughter. Can't goof off. Gotta go. See you around, huh? Maybe we'll have a chance to wet a line together while you're here.'

'I'd like that,' I said.

I wandered out onto the porch, found an empty Brumby, lit a cigarette, and stared out at the lake. A few minutes later Tiny eased himself into the chair beside me.

'So,' he said, 'tell me what the Indians are up to.'

I summarized my conversation with Seelye Smith.

'The burial ground, eh? That's the key, then.'

I shrugged. 'Could be. That's the threat. Sue on the basis of the burial ground if you won't sell.'

'Well, I sure as hell ain't sellin'.'

'It could turn out that selling would be smarter.'

Tiny turned to look at me. 'This place is my life,' he said. 'What in hell would I do anywheres else?'

I nodded. 'Anyway, you're in good hands. Seelye Smith comes highly recommended. I liked him. He's smart and well connected. Nothing more you can do.'

'That makes me feel a little better,' he said doubtfully. 'Now, if Mr Rolando would just come strolling up the path with a big grin on his face, itchin' to tell us his adventures, I'd feel great.'

'Maybe he will.'

'Doubt it.'

Tiny and I rocked for a while longer, staring out at the darkening lake and swatting an occasional mosquito. After a bit of that Tiny got up and wandered back inside.

I decided to smoke another cigarette before I followed him.

The Maine woods are filled with night sounds – the shrieks and calls of birds, the rustle of the breeze in pine boughs, the slapping of gentle waves against shore-bound rocks. Human sounds grate the attuned ear, and the hiss I heard, while not loud, caused me to tense my muscles. Because it was a secret sound, the whisper of connivers. I stopped rocking and squinted into the dusk. Two figures moved down the path away from me and toward the dock. They walked slowly. Their heads were cocked toward each other as they whispered.

As they approached the dock, they came into full silhouette against the light reflected on the surface of the lake. I identified one of the men as Gib and the other as Frank Schatz. Both men carried what looked like duffel bags.

I watched as Gib climbed up into his plane and Schatz handed the bags up to him. Then Gib came down again. He and Schatz then scurried quickly away from the plane and disappeared into the shadows of the trees.

It took all of three minutes, all very innocent, and I wondered why I had tensed as I watched them. They had done nothing more suspicious than stow some stuff into the airplane.

Had Kenneth Rolando not disappeared from this place, I knew I would not have given it a second thought. I was imagining plots and conspiracies. Probably, if the truth were known, I was *hoping* for a plot or a conspiracy, some spice for the humdrum life of a middle-aged attorney.

Nuts, I told myself. *Act your age, Coyne.*

My cigarette had burned down to the filter while I'd been staring at Gib and Schatz. I stomped on it and stood up. I peered into the darkness and tried to listen for more intrusive human sounds. There were none.

I climbed the stairs to my room. After I got my things unpacked, I padded to the common bathroom at the end of the hall and took a leisurely hot bath, with a paperback addition of a John le Carré novel for company. By the time George Smiley had me thoroughly confused and the bath water had cooled down and I had toweled myself dry, it was after ten o'clock – late by Raven Lake standards.

I pulled on a sweatshirt and old corduroys, slipped into my moccasins, and wandered downstairs. The big room was empty of people. I went outside. From the porch I could hear a soft breeze soughing in the tops of the evergreens. A half moon had risen. I walked down to the water's edge and out onto the dock. The water slapped softly against the pilings. I sat on the edge, dangling my feet. I lit a cigarette and listened for the loons.

The laughter of the loon never fails to stir something in me. It's a long, eerie, hysterical wail, a primal shriek that reminds me of the sounds expected of professional mourners. It should properly be accompanied by the beating of breasts and the tearing of hair.

But it's just loon talk. It's the sound they make. I suppose it doesn't convey particularly morbid emotions to them. A way of saying, 'Howdy, there,' or, 'Lookin' like rain,' probably. Whatever it means, it always thrills me.

I sat there for about fifteen minutes before the loons finally rewarded me. There were two of them, far away up toward the northern end of the lake, and their cries came echoing across the water as they called and answered each other.

'I brought you something.'

I jerked around. 'Jesus, Marge. You shouldn't sneak up on a man like that.'

In the night light I saw that she was holding out a glass to me. I took it. 'Thanks. Pull up a seat.'

She sat beside me, her shoulder touching mine. She had a glass of her own. 'Let's have a cigarette,' she said.

We smoked and drank in silence. Marge was a comfortable sort of woman. Even though I hadn't seen her for three years, I felt that I knew her well. 'You want to talk?' I said.

I felt her shiver. 'No. Not really. I don't mean to disturb your solitude.'

'You're not. There's room for you in it.'

'Thank you for that,' she said. She rested her head against my shoulder for a moment.

We sat in silence sipping our drinks. I thought of telling Marge that I had seen Gib and Schatz skulking around on the dock, loading up the Cessna. As I thought it, I realized how silly it seemed. So I said nothing about it.

'So how's the lawyerin' business?' Marge said after a few minutes.

'It's a living,' I said with a shrug.

'Come on.'

'You're right. That wasn't fair. It's a damn good living, is what it is. I help people out, and they give me lots of money. I come and go as I please. I owe nobody money – or anything else. I've got it knocked.'

'But . . . ?'

I lit another cigarette. I took a deep drag and let the smoke ooze out of my nostrils in the way that used to drive Gloria, my former wife, absolutely crazy.

'You look like a goddamn criminal when you squint your eyes and do that,' she'd scream at me. 'You look like a rapist. You look like someone who'd mark people's faces with knives. Cut it out.'

Married people always know how to drive each other crazy. The mark of a successful marriage, I guess, is the restraint each partner shows. I rather liked letting smoke ooze and dribble from my nostrils. My marriage failed after about a dozen years. It follows.

'But,' I said to Marge, 'my kind of lawyering, however rewarding, however much good I can do for people, is about the most deadly boring occupation imaginable. I continue to do lawyering because a week of it buys me a week at a place like Raven Lake, and so far the quid has been worth the quo. But you know what?'

She smiled up at me. 'What?'

'Hardly a day goes by that I don't find myself wondering what I'm going to do when I grow up.'

She touched my arm, squeezed gently, and then drew her hand away. It was a wonderfully intimate gesture. It conveyed perfect understanding and empathy. I could have repaid that gesture in kind only by kissing her. I was briefly tempted.

After a few minutes, the loons wailed again, and it occurred to me that 130 years ago Thoreau might have sat near this place on an evening such as this one, listening to the ancestors of these same loons. I found the possibility of such continuity comforting.

'God, they're spooky,' Marge murmured.

'Mmm,' I said. 'It's territorial, I expect. They're saying, "This is our place."'

'Well,' said Marge, 'they're right. We're just visitors. They live here.'

She hitched herself closer to me so that our thighs touched. I resisted the impulse to put my arm around the shoulders of Tiny's wife. Instead, I shifted, moving a few inches away from her.

Abruptly, she stood up. 'Time to go in,' she said.

She held out a hand to me and helped me up. I stood there for a minute, close to her, looking down into her face. Then I nodded. 'Yes. Let's go in.'

Chapter Five

I was brushing my teeth when I heard the voices. It sounded as if they were coming from the hallway just on the other side of the bathroom door.

'Where have you been?' It was Marge, speaking in an angry whisper. The hard emphasis was on the word 'you'.

'Out.' Polly did not whisper.

'Keep your voice down,' Marge hissed.

'That's easy. I have nothing to say.' But Polly did whisper, and her voice came through the bathroom door like a cold wind through the chinks in a drafty cabin.

'You were with him again, weren't you?'

'Him?'

'You know who I mean.'

'No, Mother, I don't. Tell me who you mean.'

'Gib.'

'No, I wasn't with Gib.'

'Well . . .'

'I was with another man, actually. So what?'

'If you wake up your father . . .'

'Nothing wakes up my father. You can't wake up my father.'

I heard the unmistakable sound of flesh smacking flesh, and I had no trouble visualizing Marge's slap against Polly's cheek.

'Well, now, Mother.' Polly laughed.

'Don't talk about things you don't know.'

Polly laughed again, a cruel bark.

'You know how we feel about – about socializing with the guests.'

'Socializing. Very nice, Mother. I like it. Socializing.'

'You know what I mean.'

'No. Say what you mean.'

'Twitching your ass at them. I mean – I mean flirting with them. I mean – '

'You mean fucking them.'

I didn't want to be where I was, a captive of this conversation that I didn't want to hear. I couldn't just open the door, excuse myself, and pad barefoot to my room down the hall. I thought of flushing the toilet to let them know I was there, imprisoned in the bathroom. But it was too late for that. They would know that I'd already heard.

So I dropped the lid on the toilet and sat down to wait it out.

'Is that what you were doing?' Marge's voice had lost its anger. It sounded sorrowful.

'What if I was?'

'Oh, Polly . . . '

'Well? What if I was? Do we have rules about screwing the guests?'

'Honey . . . '

'How would you like it?' she said, her tone different now, a querulous little-girl voice. 'How would you like to be me stuck up here? Nobody my age, no television. Not even a telephone.'

'I understand, Polly. It's only for the summer.'

'It's only for the summer,' Polly's voice mocked. 'Do you know how long a summer is? And what about you, Mother. Do the rules apply to you?'

'What the hell is that supposed to mean?'

'What were you doing down on the dock?'

'Listen to me, little girl. What I was doing is none of your business.'

'It works both ways.'

'It does like hell.'

'You got something going with Brady, Mother? Hey, he's kinda sexy. Can't blame you. Does Daddy know?'

'That is enough.' Warning hissed in Marge's tone.

'I didn't want this conversation in the first place.'

'And it is ended. Just keep one thing in mind, dear daughter. If I catch you in the sack with one of the guests, I'll . . .'

There was a long pause. Then I heard Polly's whisper, soft and mocking. 'Yes? You'll what? What will you do?'

'Polly, honey . . .'

'I want to know what you'll do.'

'Nothing. Never mind. Go to bed.'

'Mother?'

'What?'

'Don't worry. I won't tell Daddy about Brady. This can be our secret. Isn't it nice?'

'Dammit, Polly!'

'Our own little mother-daughter secret.' Polly laughed softly. I heard a door open and close, and a moment later another one. I waited a minute and then gathered up my things and tiptoed down the hall to my room. The floorboards creaked. The door to my room needed oil. And when I sat on my bed, I discovered that the bedsprings were noisy, too. So much for my efforts at discretion.

I propped myself up in bed and opened my book. I tried to concentrate on George Smiley's efforts to root out the mole in his Circus, but after I'd read three pages, I realized I hadn't been paying attention.

So I turned off the light and lay there in the dark,

thinking about big salmon and smelling the moist piny aromas that wafted in through the open window of my room and listening to the night noises of the big Maine woods. I pondered only lightly the mysteries of parent-child relationships, but it was good enough. It put me to sleep.

The whine of an engine woke me up. Gray light seeped in through the window, and under the distant din of the engine I could hear the slow, rhythmic patter of raindrops on the roof over my head. I climbed out of bed and went to the window. It wasn't raining, but it had been, and the thick mist in the air had settled on the tall pines that arched over the lodge, gathering into droplets that then fell from their own weight onto the roof.

I checked my watch. It was a few minutes before six. Late, for me. I tugged on my jeans, pulled on my sweatshirt, shoved my bare feet into my moccasins, and went downstairs.

A fire roared in the big fireplace. The table had already been set for breakfast. I found an urn of coffee on a side table and poured myself a mugful. The sounds of voices and the clank and clatter of pots and pans came from the kitchen. I pushed open the door and was greeted by a powerfully evocative mix of aromas. Frying bacon and baking bread dominated.

'Mornin',' I called.

Bud Turner and Polly and Marge, each at a separate station in the big kitchen, all turned, smiled, and greeted me. Whatever had been going on between mother and daughter the previous night, they seemed cheerful enough this morning. I wondered if what I had overheard was a nightly occurrence.

I lifted my mug. 'Glad to have this. When do we eat?'

'Six-thirty,' said Bud. 'How you want your eggs?'

'Over easy.'

'How many?'

'That bread I smell?'

'Biscuits. Bacon, sausage, fried spuds, mince pie, too.'

'Two eggs, then. Want to save room for all the other good stuff.'

I took my coffee out onto the porch just in time to see Gib's Cessna begin to taxi through the mist away from the dock. When he got halfway across the lake, he turned and headed uplake. The whine of the engine increased its pitch, and as the plane accelerated, I could see it begin to bounce and skip across the ruffled surface of the water. It lifted, dropped, then lifted again, and this time it stayed up. I watched it climb and then bank around behind me until the forest at my back obscured it from my sight.

I was sitting on the steps, watching the lake, when Marge came out carrying a big dinner bell. 'Mind your ears,' she said, and then she clanged it several times.

'That ought to get them moving,' she said. 'Tiny's idea, the bell. He thinks it reminds the sports of summer camp, or something.' She sat beside me. 'I reckon you heard more than you wanted to last night. Sorry about that.'

I shrugged. 'I had hoped you wouldn't know I was there.'

'Well, I hope you don't feel bad. And don't take it too seriously.'

'I've got a couple boys. I understand.'

Marge rolled her eyes. 'You never had daughters. You're lucky.'

'Lucky. I agree.'

'Brady . . .'

I turned to look at her. She was staring out at the lake. I said, 'You don't have to explain.'

'What I mean is, what Polly said. That was just, you know, talk. Her anger.'

I nodded. 'Sure.'

'Tiny's a good man.'

'The best,' I said.

She rubbed her hands on the tops of her thighs. 'Looks like a good day for fishing. Soft, just a little breeze. Radio said it'd be cloudy, but the mist's gonna dry up. You going out with Woody?'

'Woody and Frank Schatz, I guess.'

'Mr Schatz left with Gib. That was the two of them just took off. You'll have Woody all to yourself.'

I remembered seeing Gib and Schatz at the dock the previous evening. Mystery solved. 'I didn't know Schatz was leaving today.'

Marge shrugged. 'Me, neither. Guess he wasn't having much fun. I suppose he arranged it with Tiny. Sports'll do that, now and then. Find this isn't what they bargained for. Anyway, we're bracing ourselves for Mr Rolando. The other Mr Rolando, that is. The brother. Gib'll be flying him in this afternoon. I think Tiny will want you around for that. Let me get you some more coffee. It'll be just another few minutes before breakfast.'

'Thank you,' I said, and gave her my mug.

She brought me a refill and went back inside. I sat there, sipping and smoking and nodding to the people who straggled up from their cabins to the lodge. Lew Pike and two other guides came along first. Then the two elderly couples, followed by the pedantic Mr Fisher and his bride. Woody straggled up alone.

'You ready for some serious fishin', Mr Coyne?' he said.

'You bet.' I nodded, rising to follow him inside.

At the door Woody turned to me. 'Maybe you can teach Mr Schatz somethin'. I sure ain't been able to.'

'He flew out with Gib a little while ago. It'll be just you and me.'

Woody frowned. 'Mr Schatz left? I thought he was gonna be here for a week.'

I shrugged. 'Well, he's gone.'

'Damn funny time to go. Before breakfast. It sure'n hell ain't like Gib to miss one of Bud's breakfasts.'

'You didn't hear the plane? It woke me up.'

'My little cabin's way down the end, set back from the lake. I expect the others heard it.'

'You don't bunk with the other guides, do you?'

Woody stepped away from the door. 'It's one of them traditions, I guess you'd call it. The Indians bunk separate. I'm the last Indian. So I got my own cabin. I like it that way.'

'That's pretty damn old-fashioned,' I observed.

He frowned. 'That's one way to look at it. Let's eat. I got a special place I want to try, now that it's just gonna be you and me.'

Woody and I took a broad-beamed twenty-foot canoe with a little four-horse motor up to the northern end of the lake. As Marge had predicted, the misty rain had stopped. A southerly breeze roughened the surface of the water.

A fifteen-minute run took us to the mouth of Harley's Creek. The rains of the past several days had swollen it enough so that a café-au-lait-colored tongue of current was pushing into the lake itself. Woody killed the motor and let our momentum drift us to the edge of the eddying water. 'We'll anchor here,' he said. 'Salmon should be coming from all over the lake. Lookin' for smelts. Good place. Been savin' it for you.'

Woody and I cast streamer flies into the currents. We let them sink for a few counts, then twitched them slowly back, and for more than an hour there was scarcely a minute when either Woody or I wasn't tied to a salmon. They hit the flies hard and tried to run to the deep water with them. We played them against the drag of our reels. When the big fish stopped running, they would turn and begin to leap, great silver arcs over the gray face of the lake, heads shaking, tails walking on the surface of the water.

Woody kept one fish, a fat four-pounder. He rapped it once on the back of its head with his wooden priest. 'Our lunch,' he said.

The rest of them we released gently by running our fingers down the leader to the spent fish where they lay finning beside the boat and carefully twisting the hooks from their jaws.

We figured we caught around a dozen salmon between us during that time, although we didn't count them. When we had cast without a strike for half an hour, Woody reeled in and said, 'That's it for now. They've headed back to deep water. They'll be back. We can go up the creek and try for trout if you want.'

'I want to save that,' I said. 'I want to spend one day alone. Probably tomorrow. For my soul. Up in the creek is where I want to do it. I'll bring my little rod and look for some beaver ponds.'

Woody nodded. I knew he'd understand and wouldn't take offense at my desire to fish for a day without him. 'Beavers've been workin' up that creek. Little ponds'll be full of trout. Good idea.'

We had lunch on the lakeshore. I gathered dry hardwood and dragged it to our campsite, where I hacked it into short chunks. Woody arranged the cooking fire. He stuck two forked sticks into the ground on either side of the depression he'd scooped out, where the coals would lie. Across the forked sticks he rested a lug pole, and from the lug pole he hung a wanigan stick. This had a nail in it on which the water pot for our coffee was suspended.

Woody grilled the salmon over the coals and fried up some potatoes and onions in a black skillet. We ate from aluminum plates.

It was, by objective standards, pretty bad. The salmon steaks could have been moister, and I would have liked a wedge of lemon to squeeze over them. The potatoes were undercooked. The onions were burned.

But sitting there on the pine needles, sniffing the woodsmoke and sipping the harsh coffee and gazing across the water with my eyes lazily unfocused, I thought it was the best meal I had had since – well, since the last time Woody had cooked for me.

'You haven't lost your touch,' I told him.

'Mr Schatz thought we should pack sandwiches.' Woody grinned. 'And bring a thermos of martinis. But, hell, he never helped gather wood, neither. He was all for shooting a pair of partridge we came upon. Said he was sick of salmon, if you can believe it. I mighta done it, too, if I had my pistol with me.'

'You'd take a game bird out of season?'

Woody shrugged. A home-rolled cigarette hung off his lower lip. A long ash had grown onto the end of it. 'It's different up here. The city people down in Augusta make the laws, but they're not our laws. Folks generally take what they need. No more. No less, neither. It ain't killin' for the fun of it. Hell, killin' ain't no fun, anyways. It ain't waste. It's what nature gives us, and we respect it. Local people, most of the guides, they're like the Indians that way. They know how it's supposed to be. It's always been that way for us. You know that, Mr Coyne. The Indians worship the animals and birds and fish that they eat. It's all part of the big circle.'

I nodded. 'But it's poaching.'

Woody picked the cigarette off his lips and flicked off the ash. 'That's white man's law. Indians don't even have a word for it.'

I sipped my coffee. Woody had brewed it by throwing a handful of grounds into a pot of boiling water, letting it bubble away for a long time, and then shoving the glowing end of a stick from the fire into the pot. This, Woody claimed, was an old Indian trick that sank the grounds to the bottom. In my experience either Woody did it wrong, or the trick was no good. There was nothing smooth or gentle about Woody's coffee. Stray grounds tended to get caught in my teeth, for one thing. But it beat the hell out of the sanitized, mechanized stuff that came out of the Mr Coffee machine back in my office.

Woody was staring off at the sky. His profile looked as if it had been carved out of a granite mountain. 'What happened to the other Indian guides?' I said to him. 'Seems to me that there used to be several at Raven Lake.'

He took a long time to answer. When he did, it was with a characteristic shrug. 'Fred, he died. The others got old. Went back to the island. Young ones, hell, they don't want to do guidin' no more. They want to play guitars and drink Scotch Whisky and knock up white girls. They're happy to take their hundred and forty bucks a quarter from the government and live on the reservation.'

'You mean Indian Island, the place on the Penobscot?'

He grimaced. 'Yup. You ever been there, Mr Coyne?'

I shook my head.

'Good,' he said. 'You don't see my people at their best

there. I hope you don't take this wrong. But the Indians sold out to the white men. First we let them take our land. Then, we tried to get it back, we let them buy us out cheap. We got some land back, a little money in trust, and a hundred forty dollars every three months. A goddamn insult. Nothin's changed. Indians still poor, livin' on the reservation, dyin' young. Drunks, most of 'em. Me, I don't take my money. And I don't live with my people. I'm not proud of 'em. I'm proud of my race, Mr Coyne, but I ain't proud of some of the people in it.'

'It can't be that simple,' I said.

'I ain't been to college,' he said, taking out his pouch and rolling another cigarette. 'But I know about what happens to people when they lose their pride. The Indians got lawyers and educated men working for them now, and maybe someday it'll make a difference.' He paused to lap the edge of the cigarette paper and stick it down. Then he took a stick from the fire and lit up. 'Anyways,' he continued, 'by my way of thinkin', a man's got to lift his own self up, and every time the government does it, it prevents a man from doin' it himself and makes it that much harder the next time.' He settled himself back on the ground and closed his eyes. 'I ain't bitter. I'm doin' what I like, and I'm beholden to nobody.'

The campfire died down. Our coffee mugs were drained, our cigarette butts ground out. I lay back on the warm earth and closed my eyes against the sun that had broken through the clouds. I savored the lethargy I felt in my limbs and felt their weight against the thin cushion of pine needles where I lay. I allowed my mind to drift. I dozed.

The sounds of Woody bustling about the campsite dragged me up from my sleep. He had taken the cooking utensils down to the edge of the water and was scouring them out with sand. I doused what was left of the fire and scooped sand over the dead coals. Then I lugged Woody's big wicker basket down to the canoe and handed it to him.

'Where's the burial ground?' I said.

'Up Harley's Creek a ways,' Woody answered, cocking his head at me. 'You gonna pay it a visit?'

'I thought I might.'

'Didn't know you had an interest in Indian heritage.'

I shrugged. 'I'd like to see it.'

Woody grinned. 'Spooky place. White men around here steer clear of it. They think it's haunted with the spirits of all the old Indians buried there.'

'What do you think?'

'It's a graveyard. Nice spot for one.'

'How do I find it?'

'Pretty hard to miss. You paddle the length of the lake, then up Harley's. You come to the place where the river divides, you beach your canoe and climb the bluff. Burial ground's at the top. It's a little hike up there. Not that far, but steep. Course, you can drive a truck within a hundred yards if you prefer.'

'I'll do it the Indian way,' I said. 'Fish for trout along the way.'

Woody nodded. 'Figured you would. That's why I told you how to find it. Figured you'd know how to respect the place.'

We finished loading the canoe. Woody took his seat in the stern, and I shoved us off.

'Want to try for some bass this afternoon, Mr Coyne?' he said, turning us with his paddle so our bow pointed out into the lake.

'Love it.'

We motored across the lake, and Woody paddled along the rocky shoreline while I cast floating deerhair bass bugs to the spawning beds that were visible as big, round sand-colored platters on the shallow bottom. I had crimped down the barbs on the hooks so that we could release any fish we caught without injuring them. The big females, heavy with roe, came boiling up from their nests to attack the intruders I cast there, and I caught and released smallmouth bass until my arms grew weary. Then I took up the paddle, and Woody fished for a while.

Around five o'clock Woody lifted his eyebrows to me, and I nodded. I'd had enough for one day. He cranked up the motor and pointed the canoe to the lodge.

We were unloading when Polly came down. I handed her my rods. Her eyes didn't quite meet mine, and it occurred to me that if Marge had figured out that I had overheard their little exchange last night, Polly probably had, too.

'Mr Rolando is here,' she said to me. 'Daddy wants you to meet him.'

'Sure,' I said. 'Soon's I get cleaned up.'

'No. He means right away. They've been waiting for you to get in.'

I shrugged. 'Whatever.'

We started up to the lodge. Polly said, 'Can I say something?'

'You don't have to,' I said. 'Forget it. I heard something last night I shouldn't have heard. None of my business. You don't have to say anything to me.'

'I want to say one thing,' she said. 'What I said about you. I didn't mean anything by it.'

'That was between you and your mother. Don't worry about it.'

She stopped and looked at me. 'Mean it?'

'Sure.' I held out my hand, and she took it.

'Friends?'

I nodded. 'Hope so.'

Chapter Six

Tiny Wheeler's office was a little cubicle partitioned out of the back corner of the lounge. The door was closed, so I rapped on it.

'Come on in,' yelled Tiny from inside.

Tiny's bulk was squeezed behind his desk. He seemed to fill the little room all by himself. His gold tooth glinted in a nervous grin.

'This is Mr Philip Rolando, Brady,' he said, gesturing to a man who was perched on a straight-backed chair. Rolando glared at me and didn't bother to stand up. He looked out of place in his dress shirt with a necktie loosened at his throat.

I held out my hand to him. He rose halfway out of his chair. 'Nice to meet you,' I said.

'Sure,' he grunted.

He was a stocky guy, with a thick neck and a military-style haircut. He had a jutting, aggressive jaw and heavy black brows from beneath which his flat gray eyes seemed to peer out at a hostile world.

I took the one remaining chair, which placed me nearer to Philip Rolando than I thought he liked. I had the impression that he and Tiny had been sitting across from each other for some time, Tiny grinning and Rolando glowering, and neither of them speaking, like a husband and wife waiting in an anteroom for their divorce proceedings to begin.

'Have a pleasant flight, Mr Rolando?' I said in an unimaginative effort to smash the glacier.

'Let's cut the bullshit,' he said. He leveled his ray-gun eyes on Tiny. 'Can we get started now?'

Tiny nodded vigorously. 'Sure. Now that Brady's here.'

'Good.' Rolando paused to select his words. When he spoke, his voice was as flat and colorless as his eyes. 'The fact that you think you need a lawyer tells me what I wanted to know, anyway.'

Tiny started to speak, but I interrupted him. 'It doesn't tell you anything. You're not a prosecutor, this isn't a court of law, and Tiny wants to cooperate with you. If your purpose is to level accusations here, then I suggest you climb right back into Gib's Cessna and go home. If you want to talk about what happened to your brother, then there's no need to be adversarial.'

Rolando's mouth moved. I figured it was his version of a smile. 'Good for you,' he said. 'You just earned your money.'

I saw Tiny begin to lean forward. I gave him a little shake of my head. I had actually seen him lose his temper only once, and that was when one of his guests had come back from a day on the lake with three limits of salmon lying dead in the bottom of the canoe. Tiny broke the guide's jaw and knocked several shattered teeth spewing in all directions with one blow of his big fist. It took two other large men in addition to myself to keep him away from the greedy fisherman. Except for that single incident, I knew Tiny Wheeler to be a placid, agreeable man with moderate tolerance for the shortcomings of others.

On the other hand, the guides told wondrous tales of the strength he could muster when aroused, and I knew he would not tolerate an insult to one of his friends.

Tiny sighed and eased himself back into his chair.

Rolando leaned forward and placed both hands flat on

the edge of Tiny's desk. 'All right,' he said. 'Okay. So tell me. What happened to Ken?'

Tiny lifted his bulky shoulders and let them fall. 'He just disappeared, Mr Rolando. I don't know what happened to him.'

'No trace of him, then?'

'Nothing. We looked. The sheriff was here.'

Rolando sighed and shook his head slowly. I read resignation in the gesture, but it fell short of sorrow. 'Start at the beginning, will you? Tell me everything from the time he got here.' He glanced at me. 'I'm not accusing anybody. Not yet, anyway.'

I shrugged and nodded to Tiny.

Tiny frowned and gazed up at the ceiling. 'Well, he came in with Gib about three Sunday afternoon. He was supposed to stay a week. He had no fishing gear with him, which is kinda unusual. Most of our guests bring their own gear. We have plenty, of course, but still . . . Anyhow, I put him in cabin six. That's a small one – it's where you'll be, if that's okay. We've left your brother's stuff right there. Keep thinkin' he's gonna show up. I asked him if he didn't want to get out on the lake for a few hours that afternoon. Hell, the salmon had been bitin' like snakes all week. Figured he'd have some nice fishin'. Told him I'd take him out myself. But he said no, he was tired, he wanted to grab a nap before dinner, which was okay by me. Funny thing was, he never did take that nap. I lugged his duffel down to his cabin, showed him where the outhouse was, and came back up here. Little while later I see him walkin' around. Not, like you might expect, sauntering, enjoying the air, lookin' at the lake, understand. More like he was searchin' for something. Went down to the dock, then around the cabins. Then he came up here. Asked if he could look at the register.

Hell, it ain't private or anything. I figured he just wanted to see all the famous people who've come here over the years.'

Tiny grinned and jerked his thumb at a mass of framed photographs hanging on the wall behind him, all of which showed Tiny posing with a string of salmon or a dead bear or whitetail deer hung from the pole in front of the lodge and shaking hands with men whose faces were vaguely familiar. They were invariably inscribed, 'To my good friend Tiny.'

'We've had senators, movie stars, couple big-league ball-players stay with us. They all had good sportin',' added Tiny.

'For Christ's sake,' said Rolando.

'Yeah, okay. Anyway, he spent a hell of a long time lookin' at our register. I didn't want to be nosy, see, so I stayed out of his way. But we were settin' up for happy hour, so I was around. I think he was actually takin' notes. It looked to me like he was writin' stuff down into a little notebook. Stuff from the register. Maybe not, but it looked that way to me.'

'Why would he be interested in the register?' I addressed the question to Rolando.

He glowered at me. 'How the hell should I know?'

'Maybe he was just interested in the famous people's autographs,' said Tiny. 'Like I told you, we've had – '

'Okay, okay,' interrupted Rolando. 'So what happened next?'

'I'm just tryin' to tell you everything I remember. So after he finished with the register I guess he went back to his cabin. I'm not sure. Maybe he had his nap then. He didn't show up for happy hour. He was the only one who didn't. Hell, everybody comes for happy hour, even kids, when they're here, and the teetotalers. It's the time when everybody swaps lies about how good the fishin' was and guides tell their favorite stories. I told your brother about happy hour. Everybody else was here.'

'Ken never was one for parties,' said Rolando. I caught his use of the past tense.

'Guess not,' said Tiny. 'He got here for dinner. Sat beside Lew Pike, I recall. My little girl, Polly, she was on the other side of him. Lew's a great talker, once he gets warmed up, but near as I could tell, Mr Rolando didn't talk to anybody. Oh, he was polite and all. I don't mean anything bad. Just that he seemed happy enough to eat and listen. After dinner I guess he went back to his cabin. Most everybody else hung around for a while. Usually after dinner some of the guides'll tie a few streamer flies over at one of the tables by the bar. The sports like to watch them do that. They can have another drink if they want, enjoy the fire, shoot the shit for a while, play a couple games of cribbage. We all go to bed pretty early. Nine, nine-thirty, the place is pretty well cleared out.'

'And was it that night?'

'Near as I can recollect. We like to get up with the sun, get out on the lake. Mr Rolando showed up for breakfast bright and early. Well, it wasn't bright, actually. Cloud got stuck here between the mountains. Not a hard rain but a kind of drizzle. Not anything that should keep a fisherman off the lake. But your brother, he said he thought he'd wait it out, see if the weather was gonna break. Hell, I figured it's his vacation, he can do whatever he wants. Still, he was payin' good money just to hang around. I told him I'd be happy to take him out. We could've gone for an hour, see what was bitin', but he said, no, he thought he'd wait. Said he was happy enough just to be here.'

Rolando folded his arms and cleared his throat. 'Get on with it, will ya?'

Tiny shrugged. 'I'm tryin'. I gotta tell it the way I remember it.'

'Okay, okay.'

'Anyhow, he hung around for a while. I noticed he went over and took another look at the register, which struck me as a little queer. Not likely there'd be any new names there since the last time he looked. I mean, unless Gib flies folks in, they don't come, and Gib was still here. Had been since he flew in with your brother. I recall, now that I think of it, that he asked me if there were more guests comin' in during the week. I remember that, because generally folks come in on the weekend. Friday, Saturday, Sunday – '

'I know what the hell a weekend is, for Christ's sake,' barked Rolando.

'Yeah. Right. Anyway, the thing was, we did happen to have a fella comin' in that day. Monday. Last Monday, that is. Gib was worried that he couldn't get out, what with the low ceiling and all. Gib said to me, I remember, that he could get up okay, but he wasn't sure if he could get down anywhere. I got on the shortwave and talked to Greenville, and they said it was okay down there.'

'There was somebody coming in that Monday?'

'Yep.' Tiny glanced at me. 'That was Mr Schatz,' he said to me. 'And he did come in. Late that afternoon. Your brother,' said Tiny, his voice softening, 'was gone by then.'

'Ken disappeared the morning before this Schatz arrived. Where's Schatz now?'

'He's gone. Left this morning.'

Rolando seemed to move this information around in his head for a minute before storing it away. Then he shrugged. 'Ken never did go fishing, then.'

'Nope. The last thing I saw of your brother, he was

sittin' out there on the porch, watchin' everybody load up the canoes and settin' off. Marge and Polly – that's my wife and my little girl – they were around. And Bud Turner, our cook, he was in the kitchen. You want, you can talk to them.'

Rolando shrugged. 'What else?'

Tiny shook his head. 'According to Marge, he hung around the lodge, here, then went off. Supposedly to his cabin. Marge and Polly usually go around to the cabins in the morning, bring clean towels, clean up a little. They didn't go to your brother's, figuring he was in there. He didn't come to the lodge at lunchtime. Most of the sports eat with their guides out on the lake, anyway, but Bud always leaves the makin's for sandwiches for anyone who comes back. See, Bud sometimes takes the truck down to town during the day for supplies. He didn't that particular day, but he often does. He can get down and back between breakfast and dinner if he leaves right after breakfast. We've got a couple four-wheel vehicles, and the lumber road's passable – '

'Ken,' interrupted Rolando. 'What about Ken?'

'What I mean is, we don't really have an organized lunch. Bud don't have to make lunch. Everybody more or less fends for themselves. So when your brother didn't show up, it wasn't like noticeable, really. When I asked Marge later, she said she hadn't seen him around. That's all I'm tryin' to tell you. It wasn't like there was anything to worry about, because you don't expect to see anybody at lunchtime. It's just Marge and Polly here. And sometimes me and Bud.'

'You don't need a lawyer, Mr Wheeler,' said Rolando.

'What do you mean?'

'You're quite a talker yourself. So far you've given me a lot of bullshit about what a great place this is. Fine. I accept that. I want to know how the hell my brother could disappear from such a wonderful spot.'

'We don't know that he did disappear,' I said.

'And when did you get here?'

'Yesterday.'

'Well, it's no wonder you don't know anything. I'm asking this man.' He jerked his head at Tiny.

'Well, Brady's right. We don't know. I couldn't tell you when he disappeared or where he was going or anything. Nobody saw him after he left the lodge. Probably seventhirty, eight in the morning. Whether he was in his cabin most of the day or went walkin' in the woods in the morning or what, I couldn't tell you.'

'When did you realize that he was gone?'

'Dinner. When he didn't show up, Polly went down to his cabin. Banged on the door. No answer. She came up and told me, so I went down, knocked for a while, called to him. Finally I opened the door and went in. He wasn't there. He wasn't anywhere around. Well, we ate, though I was worried at that point. Still, I didn't figure he was gone. Understand? You don't think like that. I mean, it just doesn't happen. But after dinner I asked around if anybody had seen him. I checked with everyone – the guests, the guides, Marge, Polly, Bud. Everybody. I guess Marge must've been the last to see him, and that was when he was out on the porch in the morning. So I got the guides together quiet like, so as not to upset the guests, and told 'em that Mr Rolando was nowhere to be found. They got into the canoes, took flashlights with them. Bud got into his truck along with Marge, and they drove up and down the roads, showing the light along the way. I stayed around here, you know, with the other guests. After a while the guides came stragglin' back in. Nobody had seen anything. So the next morning I raised the sheriff on the shortwave. He flew up that afternoon. We talked about bringin' in the dogs. No sense to it, though. It'd been raining for a long time.'

'Your new guest,' said Rolando. 'Your Mr Schatz. What time did he come in?'

Tiny frowned. 'Five, maybe. I guess it was a little hairy, but Gib got him in. About the same time we noticed your brother was gone.'

'But the sheriff didn't get in until the next afternoon?'

'He can't fly in the night, Mr Rolando. This is a lake, not an airport, for Christ's sake.' Tiny took a deep breath. 'Yeah, okay. I thought he might've gotten in earlier in the morning, but it was still socked in pretty good. Guys like Gib, they'll do it. Them bush pilots can do things like that. The sheriff's got cops flyin' for him. They don't take chances at all.'

'Look – ' began Rolando.

'I want to finish,' said Tiny. 'Since your brother turned up missing, I've had Bud Turner drivin' the loggin' roads every day. There's only so much we can do. The police know about it. Maybe they could do more. I don't know. Fly around in their planes. Maybe they could still bring in dogs. Maybe you should talk to them.'

Rolando slouched down in his chair and closed his eyes for a moment. When he looked up at us, I thought I detected, for the first time, a hint of sadness on his face. 'There's something you should know about my brother,' he said. He cleared his throat and stared at a spot on the wall between me and Tiny. 'Ken was no outdoorsman, it's true. But he was a tough son of a bitch. And smart. It is absolutely inconceivable that he would wander away and get lost and not find his way back.'

'Unless something happened to him,' I said, finishing what I assumed was his thought.

'Exactly,' said Rolando. 'So my question is this: what could have happened to him?'

Tiny shrugged and spread his hands, palms up.

'Your guess is as good as anyone else's,' I said. 'What I don't understand is why he came here in the first place. He wasn't a fisherman. Had no gear. He was alone.' I frowned at Rolando.

'I don't know. He didn't tell me. We've always been pretty close, but that doesn't mean he tells me everything. He just said he was coming here for a vacation. That's it.'

There was a thump on the door. I reached over and opened it. Marge stood there with a little tray bearing three cans of beer. She squeezed into the room and put it down on Tiny's desk. She glanced at me and Rolando, then said to Tiny, 'It is happy hour, you know. Be nice if you could mingle with our guests.'

Tiny nodded without smiling. 'Be out in a minute.'

On her way out Marge gave me a private grin and rolled her eyes in the direction of Mr Rolando.

Each of us took a can of beer from the tray. Rolando sipped tentatively at his, as if he suspected it might have been poisoned. 'Ken's reservation extended through when?' he asked Tiny.

'Sunday.'

'Okay. I'm going to stay here that long. That's okay, isn't it?'

Tiny shrugged. 'Sure. It's all paid for.'

'Good. And if you don't mind, I'd like to kind of have the run of the place. I mean, I'd like to talk to people, maybe have a guide to show me around, see what I can find out. Any problem with that?'

'I'd rather you didn't upset the guests,' said Tiny.

'I understand. But those who were here when Ken

disappeared – you wouldn't mind if I just asked them if they'd talked to him or if they saw him, would you? Maybe I can pick up something.'

Tiny glanced at me. I shrugged.

'I guess so. We've already done that, so it won't be anything new to them.'

Rolando sipped his beer again. 'I just want to feel that I've done all I can. You can understand that.'

Tiny nodded.

Rolando placed his beer can gently back onto the tray on Tiny's desk and pushed himself up from his chair. 'I've kept you long enough. I guess I came on a little strong. Sorry about that. It's kind of upsetting. I'd rather have somebody to blame. Understand?'

Tiny and I stood at the same time. 'No problem,' said Tiny. 'Whatever we can do.'

Rolando nodded, and we went out into the lounge, where happy hour was in full swing. Tiny grabbed my arm and held me back. When Rolando had moved out into the room, Tiny said, 'What the Christ is going on with that guy, anyway?'

'I don't know. His brother's missing. He's upset.'

Tiny shook his head. 'Somethin' ain't right. Can't put my finger on it.'

I shrugged. 'Doesn't look like he plans to sue you, anyway.'

'Like to see him try it.'

'No, you wouldn't,' I said.

His gold tooth glittered from inside his beard. 'You're right. I wouldn't. Still, I'm glad you're here.'

'Well, me too. I had good fishing today.'

I was listening for the loons again that night when Marge came down to the dock. She sat beside me, tinkling ice cubes in the two glasses she carried.

I lit a cigarette and handed it to her.

'Are you sure you don't mind?' she said. 'I keep thinking maybe you'd rather be alone.'

'I don't mind,' I said. 'I like it. But –'

'Polly, right?'

'Yes.'

'That's not your problem,' she said. She spoke in a low, private voice. The vast quietness of the lake at night seemed to call for that kind of respect. 'Brady, can we talk?'

'Sure.'

'I don't really have anybody I can talk with.' I started to speak, but she rushed on. 'No, not Tiny. Tiny's almost sixty-six years old. He doesn't know about teenage girls. He worships Polly. He wouldn't hear anything I'd say. I've tried. He walks away. It's my problem. Raising her has always been my problem.'

I thought of my own family. Gloria had raised Billy and Joey herself, too. That we were divorced didn't make me any less responsible than Tiny for the burden that fell on our wives. Oh, I conducted the requisite father-son sessions on subjects such as marijuana, condoms, and French homework as the need, typically hinted at by Gloria over the telephone, arose. I watched Billy play third base and Joey run the 440. I evaded those painful back-to-school nights, but so did a lot of resident fathers. I took my sons fishing. Billy went along dutifully. I had the feeling Joey really liked it.

I always mailed the child-support checks on time. I gave Gloria a little extra around back-to-school time. I bought my boys expensive presents for Christmas and their birthdays. Gloria, too. I was a marvelous provider.

And I missed it all. I missed the day-to-day stuff, the sulks and laughs and the silly times and the triumphs. I have no idea when Billy kissed his first girl or how Joey learned to drive a car. I never got to check their homework or make fun of their taste in clothes and music. I liked my boys very much. They seemed to be turning out real well. Gloria was doing a helluva job. I could take no credit whatsoever. I was proud of Billy and Joey. But I was not especially proud of myself.

'I'm hardly the best person to consult about child rearing,' I told Marge.

Her hand touched my leg. 'Right now you are. You're here. I just need someone to listen. You don't need to give me any advice.'

'I can listen.'

She shifted, edging closer to me. I felt the soft solidness of her hip against mine. 'I was nineteen when I met Tiny Wheeler,' she said softly. 'My parents dragged me up here after my sophomore year at college. It was supposed to be a family vacation. Togetherness. My father wanted to make up for all the years he hadn't been around. I was a city girl. I had boyfriends. I thought fish were slimy. They didn't even have waterskiing here. I pouted and sulked. But I ended up coming with them, of course. We didn't dare to rebel back then. Well, one day it worked out that Tiny guided me. Just me. The folks were off with another guide, for some reason. Probably they just wanted to get away from my bitchiness for a day. Anyway, Tiny paddled me around the lake, and I didn't talk to him at all, this forty-five-year-old backwoods hick whose grammar wasn't that good and who had a weird gold tooth. And he didn't try to talk to me, either. He just paddled, and I trolled a fly. I hooked a salmon, and it was exciting as hell, but I didn't let him know it.'

Marge sipped her drink thoughtfully. 'At noon he beached the canoe and went about making lunch. I sat on the ground, hugging my knees, still sulking, watching him. I noticed how strong he was and how gracefully he handled an ax and how efficiently he went about his business. He was in charge, confident, competent. He cooked our salmon, and we ate without even looking at each other. And after lunch, without either of us saying a word, we both took off our clothes, and he made love to me right there on the pine needles. And when my parents were ready to go home at the end of the week, I just stayed on. Tiny and I never did get church married, you know. Still, after all these years, I guess we're about as married as anyone gets. Common law, right? I've been here twenty-one years. Can you believe that? Tiny and I, we still don't talk much. Do you understand what I'm getting at?'

'I'm not sure,' I confessed.

'Not a day goes by that I don't wonder if I did the right thing. And now Polly . . .'

I nodded. 'You think she might do the same thing.'

'She comes on to the guests, Brady. I came here to get away. Now she wants to get away from here. You shouldn't use a man to get yourself away from things. I try to tell her. She won't listen.'

'I expect it's out of your control.'

'I guess you're right. Still . . .'

'You're blaming yourself, Marge. Isn't that what you're doing?'

'Yes. Shouldn't I?'

'No, you shouldn't. But you will. It's what parents do.'

There was a bitter edge to her chuckle. 'For some reason there's not much consolation in that.'

We finished our drinks in a silence that was finally broken by the loons uplake. Then we got up and went back to the lodge. Rolando was sitting on the porch.

Beside him in a rocking chair was Polly. I had the feeling that they had been watching Marge and me the entire time we had been sitting on the end of the dock.

Marge walked right into the lodge. I paused beside Rolando and Polly to nod and smile at them. Rolando nodded back at me. Polly kept staring out at the lake.

Chapter Seven

'I don't want a motor,' I told Woody as he helped me load up a canoe for my day of solitary fishing. 'I'm happy to paddle. I like to travel light and quiet.'

'Gonna play Indian, eh?' the old Penobscot grinned.

'I'll see what I can sneak up on.'

I shoved off from the sand beach, kneeling on the bottom of the canoe behind the middle thwart. For the first few hundred yards it was work, stroking with the paddle and feathering in the J stroke. The backs of my thighs burned, and I felt hard, painful knots on the fronts of my shoulders. But gradually I found my rhythm – stroke, feather, glide. The canoe knifed through the glassy water. The only sound was the faint hiss up at the bow where the canoe sliced through the water. I was in no particular hurry. The fish would be there, and the old Indian burial ground wasn't going anywhere. But I wanted to go fast, to step up the beat, so I could feel the air move across my face and savor that sense of power as the blade of the paddle pushed against the solidness of the lake.

I stopped paddling to glide up on a pair of mergansers that were diving and frolicking in the shallow water against the shore ahead of me. They let me approach almost into shotgun range before they dipped under the water and out of sight, and I wondered how they had become educated. Farther on, I saw a heavy swirl break the smooth surface of the lake. It could have been a bass, but I preferred to think it was a salmon. I unlimbered my fly rod and cast to it, but it didn't take. And I didn't actually care.

By the time I arrived at the mouth of Harley's Creek, I had worked up a healthy sweat. I nosed the canoe into the slow current and pushed against it. Soon I entered the channel where it cut through the big evergreen forest. The current flowed smoothly near the mouth of the river, where it narrowed before entering the lake. Then the river widened as the riverbed grew shallower, and the water bumped and eddied unevenly as it passed over submerged boulders.

I beached the canoe and pulled on the waders I had stowed up in the bow. I tied on a bushy Royal Coachman and waded into the riffles. The little Orvis rod was a wand in my hand. The currents surged around my knees. The gaudy dry fly bobbed and drifted, and then there was a quick burst of silver. I struck too late and felt just a momentary tug before the fly came free. I cursed, but not with enthusiasm. I felt too good to care very much about failing to hook a trout. I false cast a couple of times to dry out the fly and then set it down as soft as an autumn leaf on the water where it divided on an exposed rock. Again, the silvery flash of a trout. This time I didn't miss him. The brook trout tugged upstream, a poor tactic, since he had to battle both the tension of my rod and the force of the moving water. Soon he allowed me to lead him down to where I stood in the water. I ran my fingers along the leader and carefully twisted the hook from his jaw.

Without moving from that spot I caught half a dozen foot-long brook trout, brilliantly colored little bundles of muscle, with spots like drops of fresh blood on their flanks and flashes of orange like Baltimore orioles. Then I waded ashore and sat beside the canoe. When I lit a cigarette, I realized it was the first one I had had since breakfast. I held it in my fingers for a moment, staring at it. Then I scooped out a hole in the earth and crammed the butt into it. I stood up and ground it under my heel. I felt exhilaratingly virtuous.

I got back into the canoe and navigated the riffles, sticking to the light currents against the shore. Up ahead lay a broad, shallow stretch studded with rocks. I clambered out and, still in my waders, dragged the canoe upstream to the next pool. At that point the character of the stream became consistent: broad, deep pools alternating with shallow rapids. I didn't stop to fish. I knew that somewhere deeper into the woods the creek divided and at the top of the bluff was the Indian burial ground. I wanted to see it. Perhaps I'd fish some more on the way back to camp.

So I paddled through the pools and dragged over the rapids, and by the time I arrived at the fork, I found myself regretting my indulgences in Winstons and Jack Daniel's and renewing my resolve to amend my self-destructive habits. I beached the canoe and then dragged it entirely out of the water. It was only about eleven in the morning, but I was ready for the lunch that I had hastily assembled in Bud Turner's kitchen after breakfast. It consisted of half a dozen leftover breakfast sausages, a slab of Vermont cheddar, half a loaf of home-baked bread, and a canteen of icy lake water.

I munched on my cold lunch and watched a trout that was rising steadily against the opposite bank. A kingfisher swooped over the river, dived, missed, and flew up into a tree, chattering like an out-of-tune lawn mower. After lunch I shook a Winston out of the pack. I hesitated only an instant before I put it back. I didn't need it, I told myself.

I disassembled my fly rod, shucked off my fishing vest

and waders, and shoved them all up into the bow of the canoe. Then, out of habit instilled from fishing more populated spots in Massachusetts, I wedged the canoe up into the bushes and laid some balsam boughs over it. Then I began to climb the hill.

It wasn't exactly hands-and-knees going, but the slope was steep and the undergrowth thick, and I soon worked up my second healthy sweat of the day. I had just begun to persuade myself that the exercise was going to do me good when I felt the first dart jab into the back of my neck.

Out on the lake, one forgets about blackflies. In the heavy woods, where there is no breeze to blow them away, one cannot forget them. Blackflies have a special fondness for human crevices and orifices – ears, nose, mouth, among others of a more intimate nature. They enjoy crawling under pant legs and down shirt collars. They like to wander through human hair. And wherever they go, they bite. Mosquitoes plunge a tiny needle into the soft parts of human flesh. Blackflies bite. A thousand blackflies bite ten thousand times. I can tolerate mosquitoes. Nobody can tolerate blackflies. The Maine guides that I have known claim that blackflies will not bite pretty women. The truth is, perfume repels blackflies. The cheaper it is, the more effectively it repels, and the really savvy guides dose themselves until they smell like Times Square whores.

City sports bring expensive concoctions from L. L. Bean and wonder why their tawdry-scented guides don't seem to be bothered by blackflies.

I had brought neither perfume nor Cutter's. So I cursed and sweated, swatted and scratched, and by the time I got to the top of the hill, I decided my day had been irrevocably ruined. I paused there, waving my hand in front of my face like a windshield wiper on fast speed. One of the miracles of the natural world, which intrigued me at that moment, was the uncanny navigational system that directs blackflies to the insides of a man's underpants, where they find his tenderest, juiciest parts to munch on.

The top of the hill proved to be a round, relatively flat place, almost a mesa. I imagined with the fringe of undergrowth cut away it would give a broad panorama of the two tines of the forked river below – a classic Indian lookout.

I moved to the middle of the circular area. It was, I realized, gently mounded and unusually free of undergrowth. Some low-bush blueberry bushes were scattered here and there among mossy rocks. The area itself was perhaps fifty yards in diameter, enclosed by a square of four giant deciduous trees. It took me a moment to identify them. They were chestnuts, virtually extinct but somehow surviving up here. And the four huge trees were identical in size and shape. A quick fix on the sun told me that they had been planted at the four quadrants of the compass – due north, south, east, and west.

Inside the square of trees a ring of boulders had been laid out. They lay tumbled and moss covered now, but I wondered if one day they had formed a kind of Stonehenge up in this primeval spot in the Maine wilderness.

I stood in the center of the sacred circle, my feet, I had no doubt, atop the bones of generations of Penobscot Indians, and even this jaded twentieth-century urban cynic was awed. The Indians, I felt with conviction, had a greater right than the Wheeler brothers to claim ownership of this place. As I gazed around, my eye was caught by an alien shape and color half hidden behind one of the great chestnuts, a solid dark mass where all around were dappled greens and tans. I walked over to it, and I was almost close enough to touch it before I identified what it was.

Hung by her hind legs from a sturdy branch of the chestnut that grew on the east compass point was the carcass of an enormous cow moose. Her body cavity had been slit from sternum to pelvis and emptied, and it was wedged open with two sticks. Her throat had been sliced halfway through. A dark stain covered the leaves under the cow's upside-down body.

The sight didn't sicken me. I have spent enough time around sporting camps to grow accustomed to eviscerated game. I don't anthropomorphize animals. I like them. In many ways, I like them better than people. But they aren't people.

I have seen dead human beings. That sets my gastric system flip-flopping. But the blood of animals does not affect me the same way.

My reaction was a mixture of anger and disgust. I recalled what Woody had said to me the previous day – that folks in this part of Maine respect wild game, if not the laws that governments create to protect it, and they kill it in order to use it. This dead moose that I was staring up at had not been killed for sport or for a trophy, which, to me, is the worst possible excuse. She had been proficiently gutted and strung up out of the reach of bears, and she waited to be taken off for butchering. A big slab of dead meat.

But this cow undoubtedly had left a spring calf some-where, and that angered me. No one who respected wild game would kill a cow moose with a calf. Anyway, moose are great, noble creatures. They live a gentle vegetarian life. The death of this particular one struck me as a violation – a violation of the same natural law that some philosophers claim prevents men from wantonly killing each other.

But men do sometimes wantonly kill each other. And they kill moose, too. And if my feelings about it didn't add up to a coherent philosophical view, they did produce an unmitigated sense of disgust with my race.

I moved closer to the big bulk and touched her thick, oily hide. I put my hand inside the vacant body cavity. It was no longer warm. Killed, I guessed, by jacklight the previous night, or possibly even the previous afternoon. At the junction of neck and shoulder I found the wound. It was nearly an inch across, and triangular in shape. I probed it with my forefinger, pulling the hair away, and I could see that the skin had been sliced at the points of the triangle. An arrow wound, not a bullet.

'Don't turn around. Don't move. Don't say anything. Put your hands behind your neck. Real slow.'

The voice came from behind me. I obeyed it exactly. There was a spot between my shoulder blades that tensed as I imagined the arrow that had sliced through the hide and muscle and vital parts of the moose and how easily it might slip through my body.

'Good.' The voice was low, calm, and faintly familiar. 'Now. Down on your knees. Keep your hands where they are.'

I sank awkwardly to my knees and stayed there beside the dead moose.

'Okay. Now lie down. Keep your hands on your neck.'

I dropped down onto my stomach. I heard the man approach. He came slowly, cautiously, his feet light on the soft earth. Then his hands were patting at my sides and prodding my legs apart.

'Okay. You can sit up. Keep your hands where they are, and do it slowly.'

I rolled onto my side and sat.

'Oh, for Christ's sake . . . '

'It's you,' I said.

Philip Rolando held an ugly revolver in his hand. It had a short barrel, unlike a Colt Woodsman or other handguns popular among outdoorsmen, and a bore that looked about twice the size of a .22.

It was aimed at my belt buckle. Rolando let his hand fall to his side. Then he grinned. The bastard seemed to be enjoying it.

'What the hell are you doing here?' he said.

'What am *I* doing here? You pulled a gun on me, you son of a bitch. What are *you* doing here is the question.'

'Why, I'm out for a stroll in the forest primeval,' he said.

'Yeah. Bullshit. Did you kill the moose?'

Rolando cocked his head to the side and gazed at the upside-down carcass. 'Me? Naw. Look. I'm sorry if I scared you.'

'You didn't scare me, for Christ's sake. I have people point weapons at me all the time. What is that thing, anyway?'

Rolando held his gun up in front of his face and looked at it with what I took to be affection. 'Colt Python .357,' he said matter-of-factly.

'Right. That's what I thought,' I said. 'Well named. Think maybe you can put it away now?'

I fumbled for a Winston. So much for good intentions. I found my hands trembling, whether from fright or fury I wasn't sure, so I turned my back on Rolando so he wouldn't see them shake as I struck a match. When I turned back to look at him, the Python was out of sight, and he was frowning at me.

'Listen,' he said. 'Are you sure you're okay?'

I dragged deeply on the cigarette. It calmed me. 'Of course I'm okay. But you didn't answer my question. What in the hell are you doing here? I mean, it's a big woods. Plenty of room for both of us.'

He snorted through his nose, a humorless laugh. 'I'm looking for my brother. Decided to drive the back roads. Mr Wheeler was kind enough to let me borrow one of his four-wheel-drive trucks. The cook mentioned this burial ground, told me how to get here, and I figured, it's someplace, maybe appropriate that I should come here looking for Ken. The road's only a few hundred yards that way. There's a little path, even, that leads right in here.' He gestured back over his shoulder. 'So I parked the truck and followed the path. I came to this moose. Looks like somebody's going to come back for it. Anyway, I heard you coming. Do you know that you were talking to yourself?'

'I was probably cursing the goddamn blackflies.'

'Whatever. It sounded like there were two people coming, all the noise you were making and the conversation. So I hid in the undergrowth. I couldn't make out who you were. Waited until your back was to me. Then figured I'd confront you. Guess you didn't come for the moose, huh?'

'No. I just wanted to see the place, like you. Saw this shape hanging over here, decided to take a look.'

Rolando sat on the ground beside me. 'So do you think this has something to do with what happened to your brother?'

He shrugged. 'Supposing Ken stumbled on to something like this moose. And supposing whoever killed the moose happened upon him, the way I did with you.'

'You think some poacher is going to kill a man just because he found some illegally killed game.'

Rolando shrugged. 'It's one idea.'

'Actually it's happened,' I said. 'Wardens get killed. Up in these woods folks have a peculiar concept of justice, you know.'

'So I understand. Still . . . '

'Your brother wasn't a warden, was he?'

He frowned. Perhaps he noticed that I had used the past tense. 'Of course not,' he said.

'Because,' I continued, 'I understand that selling poached game is a pretty big business. Matter of fact, even the federal government has gotten involved. Game killed on national park land, for example.'

'This isn't federal land,' said Rolando.

'No, it's not. But the other thing is, taking game across state lines to sell it puts it in federal jurisdiction.'

'We're a long way from another state.'

'You said there's a road near here. A truck could load up with a couple moose, drive from here to a butcher, then to New Hampshire or Massachusetts in less than a day. I don't know what a man might get per pound of moose meat, but I'll bet this cow would dress out at six or seven hundred pounds of the most delicious eating you can imagine. Say even a couple bucks a pound. Two moose. That'd be way over two grand. Big money in these parts.'

'Big enough to kill a man for, maybe,' Rolando mused aloud.

'Maybe,' I said. 'Maybe somebody thought your brother was a warden. Wrong place at the wrong time. All it'd take. It's possible.'

Rolando was staring at the suspended moose carcass. 'Big sucker, isn't she?' he said.

I nodded. 'You'd think it'd take a bazooka to bring her down.'

He nodded. 'High-power rifle would do it, I guess.'

'An arrow got this one.'

'How do you know?'

I pushed myself to my feet and went over to the dead beast. 'Here. Look.'

Rolando came over, and I showed him the wound on the moose's neck. He prodded it with his finger. 'Looks like an arrow wound, all right.' He moved around to the other side of the animal. 'Look at this.'

I went to his side. There was another wound, virtually identical to the first. 'Went clean through her,' I observed.

'It's all muscle here. Tough gristle and hide. Takes a hell of a lot of power to send an arrow clean through. A strong man pulling a mighty bow, I'd say.'

I nodded. 'Smart, too, if you're a poacher. No gunshots to attract attention. I don't imagine it's that difficult to stalk a moose. They're not easily spooked. A well-placed arrow is just as deadly as a bullet.'

'Sounds like Indians,' said Rolando.

I glanced sharply at him. 'Indians aren't the only ones who hunt with bows. Matter of fact, I bet Indians don't hunt with bows at all anymore. They don't hunt for sport much. You ever see one of those modern compound bows?'

He shook his head.

'They're short – no more than four feet from tip to tip. Made out of space-age alloys. They've got gears and pulleys – wicked-looking contraptions, and they can really zip an arrow. Thing about them is, you can get about eighty pounds of thrust for only forty pounds of effort. And they're accurate as hell.'

He shrugged. 'An Indian could have one of those bows.'

'So could anyone else.'

We moved away from the hanging carcass and sat on the ground. I lit another cigarette. 'I had quit these things,' I remarked to Rolando.

'And I went and drew a gun on you. Blame me. Things like that put a man back on the weeds, I suppose. How long did you quit for?'

'Couple hours, at least.'

'Very impressive,' he said. He gazed up at the moose. 'Wonder who's doing the poaching.'

I shrugged. 'Could be anybody. With those logging roads, men could come from pretty far away. There's a lot of marshland around this place.'

He nodded. 'Well, anyway, I don't think I want to be here when they come back. I'm going to just mind my own business about this.' He stood up and brushed off the seat of his pants. 'You want a lift back?'

I shook my head. 'I've got a canoe stashed down the hill. I'll have to take it back. Not looking forward to another bout with the blackflies, I can tell you that.'

'See you later, then,' he said, and in a moment he had disappeared through the undergrowth.

I took one last look at the dead moose and tried to think of something appropriately reverential to do to pay proper respect to the sacred Indian place. I ended up swatting at a cloud of blackflies and plunging back into the undergrowth.

As I fought my way down the hill through the blow-downs and briers and blackflies, several questions nagged at me. Who the hell was this Rolando, and what was he really doing at this old burial ground deep in the Maine wilderness? Why did he carry a weapon – and, from the looks of it, a professional's gun at that? And who, for that matter, was his brother? And how was his disappearance – or death – related to a dead moose?

Who had killed the moose?

And what did any of it have to do with an offer the Maine Indians had made to Vern Wheeler to buy the Reven Lake sporting camp?

They all sounded like pretty good questions. I couldn't answer any of them.

When I nosed the canoe onto the sand beach, it was after five o'clock. Between the weariness of my muscles and the constellations of blackfly bites on several tender parts of my body, the only thing I wanted was a long cool bath.

But when I entered the lodge, happy hour was in full swing, and Tiny saw me and waved me over.

Happy hour seemed to have developed a singularly unhappy tone on this particular occasion.

Guests and guides had gathered into a tight knot by the bar. I sidled up beside Tiny, who handed me a bottle of beer and whispered, 'Little argument goin' on here.' Tiny seemed uncomfortable about it.

Woody was seated by the bar, his face granite. Rolando stood close to him, his chin outthrust and his eyes flashing. ' . . . anything I feel like saying. About Indians or Poles or Eskimos,' Rolando was saying.

'I didn't kill no moose,' muttered Woody.

'They've been goin' at it for a while now,' Tiny whispered to me. 'Mr Rolando came in, had a couple quick pops, and started shootin' his mouth off.'

'I didn't say you shot that moose,' said Rolando, his voice tense. 'I said that Indians don't respect the law.'

'That's just crap,' said Woody, lifting his eyes to stare hard at Rolando. 'And anyone who says it is full of crap.'

Tiny pushed his way toward the two men. He touched Rolando on the shoulder. Rolando whirled around. 'Get your goddamn hand off me.'

'Come on,' said Tiny. 'Let's change the subject.'

'It's okay by me. I said what I wanted to say.'

'Apologize,' said Woody.

'Aw, leave it,' said Tiny.

'The white man insulted me.'

'No apology,' said Rolando. 'And don't call me white man.'

Several people who had been listening chuckled at this. Rolando glanced around. He seemed to notice for the first time that there was an audience. After a moment, he smiled. Then he looked back at Woody. 'Look,' he said, 'I didn't mean anything personal, okay?'

Woody stood up. He was several inches taller than Rolando, and he stared down at the shorter man from a dignified height. 'Was that an apology?' he said.

'By Jesus, it wasn't an apology,' said Rolando. 'It was an explanation. Take it or leave it.'

Woody glowered at him for a brief instant. Then he pivoted and stalked out of the room.

Chapter Eight

I awakened the next morning, itching. I had blackfly bites between my toes, inside my ears, in my armpits. When I sat up in bed, I discovered stiff muscles where I hadn't known muscles existed. A day of paddling and hiking had taken its toll on my middle-aged body.

I dressed as quickly as I could and shuffled downstairs. Bud was up early, and I silently thanked him for the urn of coffee on the table in the room. I poured myself a mug and decided to take it down to the dock. I could watch for the swirls of rising salmon on the misty surface of the lake and wait for the sun to come up.

I padded onto the porch. The predawn air lay in a wet, gray opaque blanket of shadowy fog. The pewter face of the lake glimmered dully through the trees, a misty blur that mingled with the ground and the sky like a watercolor wash. Where I stood, it was still night. Everything was shapes and shadows. Back in the woods a few birds had begun to try out their morning songs.

I picked my way carefully down the steps, groping among the eerie, distorted shapes of tree trunks toward the lake, touching them as I passed.

I went down to the end of the dock. I sat on the edge, dangling my legs. The surface of the lake looked as if it had been layered with smoke.

Suddenly, almost at my feet, a large bass broke the surface. I could see it swirl and dart back under the dock where I sat.

I moved so that I was lying prone on the dock. I eased

my head and shoulders over the edge to see if I could spot the spawning bed under the dock.

Instead, I saw a man's hand. It was attached to an arm, which was attached to a body. The body was lying facedown in the water. It appeared to be unclothed.

I extended my torso as far as I could over the edge of the dock and found I could reach the hand. I tugged at it, and it floated readily to me. I managed to maneuver it out from under the dock, and as it emerged, I saw that the body was clad in pajama bottoms. It wore no top. That enabled me to see clearly the bloodless, puckered tricornered wound on its neck. A leech had attached itself alongside the wound.

I floated the body around the side of the dock to the sand beach. Then I jumped down from the dock and tugged it up out of the water. I rolled it over.

It was Philip Rolando, recognizable even though his face had swollen and turned pasty white after his now-still heart had pumped out his lifeblood into Raven Lake.

He wore a matching three-sided wound on the other side of his neck. Through and through from the side with an arrow.

I noticed also that a strip of his hair was missing. His scalp was strangely white. It took me a moment to recognize what had happened.

He had been scalped.

I stood quickly, revulsed by the realization. I hugged myself against the shudder that shook my spine. Then I sprinted back to the lodge, went inside, and shoved open the swinging door into the kitchen. Bud and Polly and Marge were there, creating what normally would have been inspiring aromas. But this time the good smells barely registered.

Marge turned and stared at me. 'Brady, what the hell . . . ?'

'Where's Tiny?'

'He's upstairs getting dressed.' She frowned. 'What's the matter? You look like you've seen a ghost.'

'Yeah, like that,' I muttered.

I went up the stairs and pounded on the door to Tiny's bedroom. 'Tiny, for Christ's sake, open up.'

It took him a moment before he pulled open the door. He stood there tucking in his shirt. His hair and beard were snarled, but he was grinning. 'Hey, Brady! What's up?'

'Phil Rolando's been killed.'

'What are you talking about?'

'He was floating under the dock. He's been shot with an arrow, it looks like, and he's been scalped. Get the damn sheriff here.'

'Jesus Christ,' he muttered. 'You're not joking, are you?' He shoved past me and bounded down the stairs. He was very nimble for a big sixty-five-year-old man. I hurried after him and caught up to him down on the beach next to Rolando's body. Tiny was staring at it.

'Holy shit,' he said. 'What are we going to do?'

'I already told you. Call the sheriff. Tell him someone's been murdered and that he'll need to bring whatever passes for a medical examiner up here. Don't let anybody near the body. Don't let anybody walk around out here. If I were you, I'd just tell the folks that there's been an accident and somebody drowned. And don't let anybody go out on the lake. I'm sure the sheriff'll want to talk to everybody.'

The next couple hours were a blur for me. I watched the sun come up and burn the fog off the lake from a seat at a table by a window inside the lodge. I drank coffee and smoked cigarettes. All the others had gathered inside, as Tiny had quietly asked. The folks talked among themselves in low, grim voices. Marge came over once and sat down across from me. We shared one of my cigarettes. We didn't talk. After a while she wandered away.

When the sheriff pushed open the front door to the lodge, everybody turned to look at him. He was a tall, stoop-shouldered, hollow-chested man in the gray years of middle age. Behind his round wire-rimmed glasses were small, watery eyes. He had caved-in cheeks and a wide, mournful mouth.

Tiny went to him, and the two of them muttered together in grumbly voices for several minutes. Tiny jerked his head in my direction, and the sheriff peered beady-eyed at me. Then he nodded to Tiny and came over to where I was sitting.

'Mr Coyne?' he said. His mouth barely moved when he spoke. He did not show his teeth.

'Yes.'

'I'm Thurl Harris. I'm the sheriff. You prob'ly already figured that out. Can we talk?'

'Sure.'

We went into Tiny's office. Harris sat behind the desk. I took the same chair I had used when Tiny and I had our discussion with Rolando.

'So you're a lawyer, Mr Coyne.'

It was a statement, not a question. I nodded.

'From Boston, huh.'

'Yes.'

'And you found the body.'

'Right.' I lit a cigarette.

'What can you tell me about this?'

'This is a tricky line of questioning, Sheriff.'

He cocked his head and smiled, showing his teeth.

They were terrible teeth – gapped, crooked, stained the color of tobacco juice. They were backwoods teeth. Rural, impoverished teeth. Thurl Harris's teeth gave away his origins. 'There's no reason to try to raise my hackles, Mr Coyne.'

I nodded. 'You're right. I'm sorry.'

'It's upsetting. So. Why don't you try to tell me what you can.'

I took a deep breath and explained to him what I'd seen.

When I'd finished he nodded his head sympathetically. 'How well did you know this Philip Rolando?'

'Just from being up here. He was looking for his brother, Ken. You know about his brother.'

'He's missing. Did you talk with Rolando at all?'

'Sure. When he got here, he wanted to know all about his brother. Tiny asked me to be there.' I lifted my hands and let them fall. 'So he asked about his brother. Natural enough. And I saw him again yesterday, out in the woods.'

'You went out with him?'

'No. I went out by myself.' I proceeded to tell Harris what had happened at the Indian burial ground.

'So Rolando was hiding by this dead moose, huh?'

'Yes. And he had a gun. A Colt Python .357, he told me it was. We talked about the possibility of his brother being killed by poachers. It seemed pretty farfetched.'

'And now this one is killed, too, with an arrow wound through the neck just like that dead old moose. What do you make out of that, Mr Coyne?'

I shrugged. 'If it had something to do with finding that moose yesterday . . .'

'Yes? What if it did?'

'Well,' I said, 'I was there, too. Do you understand?'

He smiled. It was a quick, automatic expression, a facial shrug, without any humor in it. 'I understand.' He stared at his hands, which were resting motionless on Tiny's desk. Then he suddenly lifted his gaze to my face. 'Did you kill him, Mr Coyne?'

'No.'

'Who did?'

I hesitated. I thought of the argument Woody and Rolando had had the previous evening. 'I don't know,' I said. 'But you'll hear about an argument Rolando had with the Indian guide. I can guarantee that Woody didn't kill him.'

'An argument, huh?'

I nodded. 'I came in on the tail end of it. Look, Sheriff. Woody's no killer. I'm sure of that.'

'Nobody's a killer, Mr Coyne.' He sighed. 'It seems to me that whoever killed that moose just might've killed our Mr Rolando. Wouldn't you say so?'

'It's a workable hypothesis, I suppose.'

'Of course,' continued Harris, 'if someone wanted to kill Rolando, the argument with the Indian and the story of the moose might've been just a convenience, if you follow me.'

'Pin it on Woody,' I said. 'Sure.'

Harris cocked his head at me. 'You're pretty sure the Indian didn't do it, huh?'

I nodded. 'Just from knowing him.'

'What do you make of the fact that this moose was at the Indian graveyard?'

I shrugged. 'Are you suggesting something?'

'Another reason for the Indian to be offended, maybe.'

'Not Woody,' I said. 'That wouldn't offend Woody.'

He leaned back in his chair. 'I value your opinion,' he

said. He sat forward again and peered at me. 'You okay, Mr Coyne?'

I shrugged. 'I guess so.'

'Good. Because I need your help.'

'Okay.'

'I've got a trooper out there by the body. I've got another one out in the big room there. The coroner will be coming by jeep. Should be here in an hour or so. There'll be some forensic guys along about then, too. In the meantime I need to talk with everybody here. I'd like for you to be present. Okay? Just so nothing comes back on us later, assuming we can come up with something. Do you follow me?'

'Makes sense,' I said.

'Good.' He got up and went to the door. The state trooper came over, and they whispered for a minute. Then Harris went back to his seat behind Tiny's desk.

And one by one he interrogated every person at Raven Lake Lodge. He had a gentle, almost apologetic way of doing it. He never raised his voice or leveled an accusation. And yet he seemed to treat every person as an equally likely suspect.

He queried them on their whereabouts the night the moose was probably killed. He learned that anyone could have walked the hundred yards or so to where the lodge trucks were parked and driven around the lake and back without being noticed. The keys were always in the ignitions. From the lodge nobody could hear them starting up. Anybody might have killed the moose.

But no one admitted doing that.

He asked them where they were the night of Rolando's murder. Some of them had been together. Most of the guests shared a cabin with at least one other person.

117

The guides, except for Woody, bunked together and could account for each other's whereabouts.

Woody readily admitted the anger he felt at what he believed to be Rolando's insult. He said he'd spent the evening in his cabin reading and fell asleep early. No, he didn't recall seeing anybody after he walked away from Rolando at happy hour. He missed dinner. He often missed dinner, he said. And no, by Jesus, he said, he never killed no cow moose in the springtime, this year or any year.

The newly married Fishers had been with each other. Mrs Fisher blushed when Harris asked what they had been doing, and her husband's Adam's apple bobbed.

The two older couples had played bridge by lantern light until midnight, when they went to bed.

Tiny and Bud and Gib had been together until they retired.

Polly admitted that she had seen Rolando briefly after dinner, but heedful of her mother's feelings, she had gone to bed early. Harris queried her closely, but she didn't have much to contribute.

The three guys from Boston said they played poker late in the cabin they shared. They had done quite a bit of drinking, they confessed. When they finally went to bed, they slept the sleep of the drunk. No one had seen or heard anything.

Everybody had heard Rolando and Woody argue. Although nobody reported it exactly the same way, all agreed that Woody had demanded an apology and had received none.

By the time the last person had been questioned, the coroner and a gang of other policemen had arrived, and the sheriff sent them off on a variety of chores. All the

118

guests and guides and other Raven Lake folks remained in the lodge.

Harris sat back and sighed. 'What do you think, Mr Coyne?'

'Anybody could have done it, really,' I said. 'Some of them don't have anybody to corroborate their story. Others – well, if it was the work of more than one person, then they could just be covering for each other. But there doesn't seem to be anybody with a sufficient motive to kill Rolando. Hell, nobody even knew the guy. He just got here night before last.'

'What about the Indian? He had a motive.'

'Not a motive to kill.'

He nodded. 'What about the missing brother?'

'Obviously he could have been killed, too.'

'Obviously.'

There was a knock on the door. Harris said, 'Yeah? What is it?'

A trooper pushed open the door and glanced at me. 'Thurl, we've found something.'

Harris said, 'You can come in.'

The trooper entered the room and stood stiffly in front of the desk. 'Shut the door,' said Harris. 'And sit down.'

The trooper did as he was instructed. He was carrying something in a big red handkerchief. He put it on the desk in front of the sheriff. 'We found this.'

Harris gingerly unfolded the handkerchief. I sat forward to look. It was a hunting knife. There was blood caked on the handle. The sheriff glanced sharply up at the policeman. 'Where did you find this?'

'In the Indian's cabin. The first place we looked. Logical, see? I mean, since the dead guy was scalped, you think about the Indian first, right?'

Harris nodded impatiently. 'Did you find anything else?'

The trooper glanced at me and then looked at the sheriff and grinned. 'Matter of fact, yeah. He had a crossbow under his bunk.'

'Did you look in the other cabins?' I said.

The trooper opened his mouth, but Harris quickly said, 'Don't look like there's a need, does there?'

I shook my head slowly back and forth. 'Are you kidding?'

Harris shrugged.

'Do you have search warrants?' I persisted.

'Don't need 'em. Tiny said we could look. They're his cabins. Right?'

'Jesus Christ,' I muttered.

Harris peered at me, then looked up at the trooper. 'Bring the Indian back in here.'

The trooper got up and left the room. Harris smiled carefully. 'Looks like we've got something here, after all, now, don't it?'

I shook my head. 'Not much.'

'You've got to admit, Mr Coyne, that the evidence is what you city lawyers would call compelling.'

'We city lawyers would call it circumstantial.'

'A couple of murder weapons – '

'You don't know that.'

' – and a big fight the night of the murder – '

'An argument, not a fight. A disagreement.'

'In my book,' said Harris, 'they add up to something.'

'In my book,' I said, 'they add up to a case of racial discrimination.'

'Oh, Christ,' he said.

'You better go carefully,' I said.

He smiled without showing his teeth. 'Oh, I'll sure be careful, believe me. I know how to be careful.'

A moment later Woody came into the room. 'Have a seat, please,' said Harris to him. Woody remained standing.

Harris shrugged. 'Explain his rights to him, Mr Coyne.'

'You,' I said.

Harris grinned. 'Wanna see if I screw it up, huh?'

'Right.'

He did it perfectly, then looked at me. I nodded and spoke to Woody. 'Do you understand all that?' I said to him.

He stared straight ahead and did not respond.

'Woody,' I said, 'you have been charged with a crime. You don't have to answer any questions. I recommend that you don't. I can serve as your attorney for now. If you want, I'll stay with you through this. Okay?'

He turned his head and looked impassively at me. Then he nodded his head once.

'Good,' said Harris. 'So you understand all your rights. But listen. If you'll just answer some questions, maybe we can clear this all up. What do you say?'

Woody neither spoke nor nodded. His face was stone, stolid and unyielding.

Harris shrugged. 'Do you recognize this?' He opened up the handkerchief and showed Woody the knife.

Woody gave no sign that he had even heard the question. He didn't glance at the knife.

'Do you own a crossbow?'

No response.

'Tell me again where you were last night.'

'He already told you that,' I said.

'He told me he went to bed early and slept all night. I want him to think some more about it.'

Woody made no reply.

'Did you kill Rolando?'

'He's not going to answer that,' I said. 'He said he didn't before. Look, Sheriff. Aren't you going to search the other cabins? What does the coroner say? This is very premature, I think.'

Harris ignored me. 'You are under arrest for this murder,' he said to Woody. 'Mr Coyne, do you want to come along?'

I touched Woody on the arm. 'Do you want me to?'

His seamed old face turned to look at me. I could read nothing in his expression. 'No,' he said. 'I know a good lawyer. An Indian lawyer.'

Woody, I hope you don't think . . . '

But he turned away from me to face the sheriff. He held his hands out in front of himself, palms together. Harris stood up and came around from behind the desk. 'I won't handcuff you,' he said. 'It's not necessary.'

He opened the door, and a moment later the trooper appeared. 'Take him down to the plane,' said Harris. 'There's no need to hold a weapon on him.'

Woody left, and the sheriff turned to me. 'I appreciate your help, Mr Coyne.' He held out his hand to me.

I did not take it. 'You've got the wrong man.'

'We'll see.' He shrugged and dropped his hand.

'I'm telling you. Woody didn't do it. It's obvious he's been framed.'

'Well, let's see, now.' He gouged at his ear with his forefinger. 'We've got a dead body, so I figure we've got ourselves a crime. We've got opportunity. Looks like we even got a couple weapons. Now, as for motive, I know for a fact that Indians'll do most anything when they think they've been insulted, and by God I've got a whole roomful of folks who'll attest to the fact that this Indian thought he got himself insulted. That's not even to mention the fact that this dead guy might've profaned a place the Indian thinks is sacred. I dunno, I think maybe I got enough to take the man in. We'll see what happens after that.'

'Have you investigated a lot of murders, Sheriff?'

He lifted his eyebrows. 'Have you, Mr Coyne?'

'I'm not a law officer.'

He smiled. 'Let's put it this way. I've investigated a hell of a lot of homicides. Not a deer season goes by but what we don't have six or eight fellas get themselves shot, mostly by someone else. Usually by their friends or relations. We investigate 'em all. So, yes, I guess I've had my share.'

'This is different.'

'Maybe.'

'That knife and crossbow could easily have been planted in Woody's cabin. And did it occur to you that somebody might scalp the man precisely to make people think an Indian did it?'

'Yes, it did occur to me. We've got some work to do, all right, and I surely do appreciate your reminding me of it, Mr Coyne. But just about now I've got to take my prisoner back to Greenville, so, again, I want to thank you for your help. I trust you can verify the fact that nobody's rights have been violated.'

'Yes,' I said. 'I can verify that.'

'Well, good.'

He turned and slouched out of the room. I stood in the doorway for a moment, watching him. Then I went out through the big room, where the people still mingled in little groups, talking in muted voices. I sat on a rocker on the porch and watched Thurl Harris's floatplane taxi out onto the lake and then take off.

Chapter Nine

I rocked and smoked and watched the lake and tried not to think about Rolando's dead and violated body or the look on Woody's face when Thurl Harris led him away.

The sports and guides wandered out of the lodge and made their way down to the water. I watched them load the canoes. One by one, the motors were cranked up, and they sputtered out onto the lake. They seemed subdued by what I felt would henceforth be referred to as the 'accident'. But they all went fishing.

After a while Tiny came out and sat down beside me. He carried a Styrofoam cup in one hand. He was working on a big chaw, which was lumped up in his left cheek. Now and then he spat into the cup. Marge came out. She stopped and looked at us for a minute. Then she shrugged and headed in the direction of the cabins.

'Helluva thing,' offered Tiny.

'Ay-yuh,' I said.

'Thurl let on to any of the folks what happened?'

'Couldn't very well avoid it,' I said. 'The man was, in his own crude fashion, trying to investigate a murder.'

'Damn!' he said with sudden vehemence. 'Vern'll have my ass.'

'He may be a little curious about the goings-on up here.'

'I dunno, Brady. Maybe we ought to sell the place, after all. I ain't cut out for this kind of shit. I like things simple.' He spat emphatically over the rail and out onto the pine needles.

'How long have you known Woody?' I asked.

He rocked for a moment. 'Hell, Woody came with the place. More'n twenty-five years.'

'You know him pretty well, then.'

'Yup. Guess I do. Course, Woody was never one to say much.'

'Ever see him mad?'

Tiny shook his head thoughtfully. 'Nope. Never.'

'Ever hear him speak badly of another man?'

'Use to accuse Lew Pike of cheatin' at cribbage, but that don't count. That was just part of their game. Couple times I recollect Woody sayin' somethin' about fellas who'd kill more fish'n they could use or try to get their guide to kill a deer on their tag. But those're things a man has a right to be critical of. I never heard Woody be spiteful or mean.'

I lit another Winston and thought fleetingly of my short-lived resolve to quit the damn things the previous day. 'Do you think Woody killed Rolando?' I asked Tiny.

'I suppose I do,' he said carefully. 'You never know what a man's thinkin' or what he's capable of doing. Least of all, Woody. Man always kept his own counsel. And he took bad at that insult last night, for damn sure. You missed most of it. Anyways, I guess Thurl Harris thinks he's got his man.'

'Thurl Harris,' I said. 'Beneath that dumb hick sheriff façade there lurks a dumb hick sheriff.' I scowled at Tiny. 'Do you know that the only place his men searched was Woody's room?'

Tiny cocked his head. 'But they found what they needed there.'

I slapped my forehead. 'You, too? Look. Did you give them permission to search the cabins?'

'Sure. Why not?'

'Why not? Because a man like Woody could get the shaft, that's why.'

Tiny shrugged. 'But if he did it . . .'

I stubbed out my cigarette and then moved the ashes around in the ashtray with the dead butt. Then I looked up at Tiny. 'I know what you're saying. I can't say I've got a better suspect. But Woody? How can that man seriously believe that Woody would be dumb enough to stow the murder weapons in his own cabin, just for one thing?'

'Unless he didn't care if he got caught. Look, Brady. I've been thinkin' about this. I've known old Woody for a good many years. Can't truthfully say I really know him, if you follow me. But we've been together. And I can tell you this. He's a prideful man. Most especially when it comes to his race. You can maybe insult Woody himself. But you oughtn't to say anything bad about Indians.'

'Woody told me that he had completely divorced himself from tribal matters,' I said. 'He even refused his allotment from the government.'

'Because they aren't living up to his expectations. He still takes pride in his race, if not the particular people in it. See what I mean?'

I nodded. 'I see what you mean,' I said. 'It doesn't convince me that Woody killed Rolando.'

Tiny stared at me sadly. 'You know,' he said, 'for a lawyer who's supposed to work with facts and all, sometimes you act pretty dumb.'

'I offered to defend him,' I said. 'He refused me cold. Said he knew a good Indian lawyer.'

'I thought he had nothin' to do with other Indians.'

I shrugged. 'Yeah. That's what he said. God! The look on his face in there when Harris told him he was under arrest. Cold as a rock. Proud and cold. And when he looked at me, it was as if I were the enemy.'

Tiny spat. 'Blood's thicker,' he said.

'I expected something different.'

'You were doin' him a favor. You wanted him to say thank you. You don't understand Indians, Brady.' Tiny stood up. 'Listen. Don't get hurt feelin's. You know as well as me that Indians are different. I ain't sayin' better or worse, but different. Push comes to shove, they stick together. Lissen. You wanna go fishin'?'

'My guide's off to jail.'

'I ain't proud. I've paddled city fellas before.'

'I don't think so,' I said. 'Thanks.'

Tiny looked at me for a moment. Then he turned his head and spit hugely over the rail. 'That's all right,' he said. 'I've got a lot of things to do, anyway.'

I sat there for a while longer, feeling drained of energy and wondering if I'd hurt Tiny's feelings. It took an effort of will to hoist myself out of the rocking chair. I wandered back into the lodge. The place was deserted. I noticed the big register book sitting open on a table against the wall. I remembered how interested Ken Rolando had been in it. I went over to take a look.

The most recent entry was the name 'Philip Rolando'. He gave his address simply as Albany, New York. Immediately preceding Rolando's was my own signature. The name before mine was Frank Schatz of Bayonne, New Jersey, the man who didn't like fishing. Philip Rolando had expressed brief interest in Schatz, I remembered. Reading backward, I saw several other entries before I came to Kenneth Rolando, also of Albany. I read all the entries for the season, wondering what the Rolando brothers might have been looking for. Nothing struck me as remotely interesting beyond the names of a couple of prominent Boston businessmen who had registered as

127

Vern's guests the first week in May. Vern's annual ice-out salmon fishing extravaganza.

If there was something in that register that would explain the disappearance of Ken Rolando and the murder of his brother, Philip, I failed to discover it.

I went back outside. I had begun to regret my decision to turn down Tiny's invitation to go fishing. But I didn't feel like fishing particularly, and I didn't relish the idea of being Tiny's captive in a canoe. He would expect me to be wise and comforting. I felt bereft of wisdom, and Rolando's murder – and, equally, Woody's arrest – had left me feeling needy of comforting myself.

I walked down the path toward the cabins, only half aware that I wouldn't have minded running into Marge. The cabins were all constructed of peeled spruce logs. Steel stovepipes jutted from the roofs. The cabins varied in design and shape and were set off one from the other in the grove of pines so each was assured a measure of privacy. The setup reminded me of the summer camp on the shores of Sebago Lake that I had attended as a boy. I remembered how homesick I had been.

I heard what sounded like somebody quietly gagging. I moved around to the front of the nearest cabin. Polly Wheeler was sitting on the steps. Her arms were crossed on her knees, and her forehead rested on her wrists. Her shoulders were shaking.

I went and sat beside her. She looked up at me.

'Oh, hi,' she said.

She snuffled and wiped her nose on her forearm. I pulled out my handkerchief and handed it to her.

'Thanks,' she muttered, and blew her nose extravagantly into it. Then she balled it up and gave it back to me. She combed her hair away from her face with her fingers, blinked her eyes, and tried to smile. Then she said, 'Aw, shit,' and I saw the tears rise into her eyes. 'Gimme that thing again.'

I gave the handkerchief back to her. She dabbed at her eyes with it.

'You're upset,' I observed brightly.

'Hey, no shit, Sherlock Holmes.'

I grinned. 'I've got this real powerful deductive sense.'

Her little smile looked as if it might stick.

'I'm not all that great at comforting distressed maidens, though.'

'That's not what I hear.' Her smile had become sly.

Several retorts came to mind. All of them would have sounded self-righteous and judgemental and stuffy as hell. So instead I said, 'You're upset over Mr Rolando's death.'

'Bingo. That's it. A Kewpie doll for the middle-aged man with the gray eyes.'

'Yes. Well, your reaction seems – '

'Melodramatic? Out of proportion?'

'Yes. Those things.' I shrugged.

'Hey, Mr Lawyer, I never had a person I knew get murdered and scalped before. Well, I suppose I should take these things right in my stride. I should be tough. Like my mother. Talk about tough broads. Or maybe I should just be dumb like my father. But, hey, what the hell. I'm just me.'

I nodded. There was nothing to say.

'I never saw a dead person before,' she added. 'But I went down there this morning and saw him.'

'I guess there'd be something wrong if it didn't upset you.'

She put her head down on her folded arms again and said something I couldn't understand. 'What did you say?' I asked.

She looked up. This time there was anger in her eyes. 'I said something nasty about Indians,' she said.

'Oh, I thought you mentioned the name Phil.'

'Well, I did.'

'You were on a first-name basis with Mr Rolando, huh?'

Polly leaned back and smiled. 'You gonna do my mother's interrogation routine on me now?'

'No.' I put my hand on her shoulder for a moment. Then I stood up. 'I'm sorry I bothered you. I guess you came here to cry in peace. I'll leave you.'

I started to walk away. 'No, wait,' she said. I turned to look back at her. 'I need somebody to talk to. Okay? I mean, I can't very well talk to my parents.'

I went back and sat beside her. 'They're good people, Polly.'

She wrinkled her nose, then tossed her hair. 'Sure they are. That's not it.' She narrowed her eyes. She seemed to be looking for something in my face. I couldn't tell if she found it. 'Look,' she said finally. 'I was with Phil last night. I lied to dumb old Thurl Harris in there.'

'But you told him you were with Rolando.'

'I told him I left early.'

'And that was the lie.'

'Hey, you are real sharp, know that? I slept with him, is what I did. It was about three when I snuck back into my room. Okay? See why I can't talk to Mummy?'

'What happened? Did he seem afraid? Any hint that he might've been in danger?'

'No. Nothing like that. Look. You're a nice guy and all, but I don't know why I should tell you any of this. I mean, you're my mother's friend, right? We should probably just forget it.'

'Suit yourself,' I said. 'But I won't tell anyone. I'm a very discreet person. That's the main thing I'm good at.

Maybe the only thing. Ask your uncle sometime. That's why he hires me. Discretion.'

'Uncle Vern does say you're a damn good lawyer.'

'He means I know how to keep my mouth shut.' I gave her a very serious look. 'Polly, listen,' I said. 'What happened between you and Rolando last night isn't what's important right now. But if you can tell me what he said – anything you can think of – it might help us figure out who killed him.'

'Old Woody killed him,' she said.

'He's been arrested. That doesn't mean he did it. I don't think he did.'

'Then who?'

'That's the question.'

She stared at me and then nodded. 'Can I tell you something?'

'Sure.'

'About me, I mean.'

I nodded.

'Here's how it works. I can't talk to my parents. About men, I mean. So I tend to talk to men about men. About how I feel about them. Does that make any sense?'

I shrugged. 'I didn't say I was smart. Just discreet.'

Polly grinned quickly. I noticed that she had violet eyes, a very unusual eye color, like young lilac blossoms. 'Mummy thinks I'm Gib's girl,' she said. 'She figures I'm sleeping with him. She doesn't like it, but she seems to accept it. And she's right. Gib and I are real close. We made love in his airplane once. When it was up in the air, I mean. You ever make love in an airplane?'

'Not once,' I said.

'It's different. Not that easy to, you know, get organized up there. It's crowded, the seats are small, all those instruments . . .' She looked at me and gave me a phony wide-eyed innocent smile. 'Anyway, Mummy doesn't know that – well, that I sleep around a little. But I do. What does that make me?'

I shook my head.

'You can say it,' she persisted.

'Probably,' I said, 'it makes you a normal woman. But I'm sure as hell no expert on women. I just have always figured they were pretty much like men. As a starting point, it's worked pretty well. Of course, I have learned that they're not exactly like men. And it's the differences that turn out to be what's important. It's taken me a long time to learn all that. Mostly by trial and error. Mainly error.'

'I don't understand any of what you just said,' said Polly. 'But I know that if you weren't being polite, you'd call me a nympho. That's the name for it.'

'You don't have to put a name on it.'

'Phil,' she said thoughtfully after we had been silent for a minute. 'He was a nice guy.' She was staring out through the pine trees at the glitter of the lake. Her voice was soft. 'So was Ken. Both nice guys.'

'Ken,' I repeated. 'Ken Rolando, you mean?'

'Yes.'

'You knew Ken, too?'

She tilted her head and made a tight line of her mouth. After a moment I nodded slowly. I guessed that she got to know him intimately.

'Yeah,' she said. 'I knew Ken. He wasn't here long. But I knew Ken real well. And I'll tell you this. If he and Phil were brothers, then I'm Joan of Arc.'

'Why? Why do you say that?'

'You met Phil, right? Dark, stocky, moody. Quick moving. Those eyes of his, always darting around. Ken – you never did meet him, did you? – Ken was the opposite.

He was tall and fair and kinda awkward. He had this shy kind of easygoing smile that really turned me on. And this funny, almost hillbilly sense of humor. Ken was like a big old St Bernard dog. Phil, he was a cat. They were nothing alike.'

'Brothers can be different like that. My two sons are opposites.'

She shrugged. 'It's more than that, even. I can't put my finger on it.'

'Did they talk about each other? Or their families?'

She nodded. 'Yeah, that's part of it. They didn't. Not at all. I asked them, you know, the usual questions. If they were married. Well, they said no, of course. But Ken, he might've been married. Ken, when he was here, he never talked about Phil at all. Never mentioned having a brother. But when Phil came up here, all he talked about was Ken. Not like he cared about him, exactly. Not like they had grown up together, had shared experiences or anything. Just how much he wanted to find him or figure out what had happened to him. There didn't seem to be what you'd call brotherly love there. At least it didn't seem that way to me. Oh, he kept saying he had to find out what had happened to Ken. It was Ken this, Ken that. Did somebody say something bad to Ken, he'd ask me. Who did Ken talk to up here? What did he do, where did he go, questions like that, over and over, the same questions asked a little different. Do you understand what I'm saying?'

I nodded. 'I think so.'

'It was an obsession with Phil. He really had to do this thing. Find his brother. It was all he was interested in.' She smiled quickly and looked away. 'Well, I mean . . .'

'Okay,' I said. 'I know what you're saying. So did Phil

have a theory about what might've happened to his brother?'

She shrugged. 'If he had a theory, he didn't tell it to me.' Polly cocked her head and stared up into the pine trees. 'He was funny, though,' she said. 'I mean, not on purpose. He didn't really seem to have much of a wit. Not like Ken. Ken was real witty. But Phil – he was strange. So serious. He'd say funny things in this serious way, and at first you'd think he had this dry wit, you know, like Lew Pike and some of those guides, and then you'd look at him and realize he was dead serious. He'd make you laugh – he made me laugh, I mean – and then he'd stare at you, not as if he was angry but more puzzled, when you'd laugh. Like, what did I say? Why are you laughing at me? Except he'd never say that. It was just his look. That damn dark scowl of his.' She shook her head back and forth a couple times. 'Oh, he was a sexy man.'

Polly didn't cry this time. She shifted her gaze to look at me. She touched my face with her fingertips. 'My mother thinks you're a sexy man.'

'I think she's a sexy woman. But that doesn't mean we have that kind of a relationship.'

'Why don't you? Maybe you should.'

'Come on, Polly.'

'That's what you mean by discreet, huh?' She shook her head. 'No. You're right. I'm wrong. I'm the one who's wrong.'

'I didn't say that.'

She laughed abruptly. 'He called himself Wyatt Earp. Asked me if I wanted to be his deputy. He said we'd ride into town and be a posse of two. We'd round up all the bad guys and find the one who killed Ken and – '

'Did he say that? The one who killed Ken? Did he say "killed"?'

Polly frowned at me. 'Yes. I mean, I think so. Sure. That's what he said. Because he said we were going to string him up. The bad guy, that is, not Ken. And instead it was Phil who . . . Aw, dammit. Here I go again.'

One tear popped out of each eye like eggs being laid. Large and round and perfectly shaped tears. They rolled down her cheeks in perfect synchrony with each other. She brushed them impatiently away with the back of her hand when they reached her jaw. 'I don't want to go in there,' she said, jerking her head at the door to the cabin. 'I'm supposed to go in and clean up.'

'This was Rolando's cabin?'

She rapped her knuckles on the step where she sat. 'Yes. This one.'

'Can't your mother clean it?'

Polly turned down the corners of her mouth. 'What am I supposed to say to her? "Hey, Mom, dear, I know that this cabin is the one that I'm supposed to do, but, see, I was in here just last night making love with the man who was staying in it, and he's dead, and except for the person who killed him I'm the last one to see him alive, and right now I've got his sperm swimming around inside of me, and it's a good thing I'm on the Pill, if you only knew, so how about if you cleaned up this cabin, okay? Don't mind the messy bed. It's just where Phil and I were rolling around. And those candles on the table, that was so we could see each other in the dark when we were lying there naked. He had a nice body, Mother. You'd have liked it. Dark and strong, and you should have seen how the shadows moved on it in the candlelight. Once I picked up a candle and held it over him as he lay there so I could examine him. He liked that. He was proud of his body, Phil was. So you can see why I don't want to go in there and clean up."' Polly arched her eyebrows at me.

'Did the police go in, do you know?'

She shrugged. 'I was up at the lodge, just like everybody else. I don't know.'

'So why don't you leave it for a day or two? You don't have another guest coming right in, do you?'

'No. It's rented for the week. Nobody'll be coming before Sunday. I guess you're right. I can do it tomorrow or the next day. I'll feel better by then.'

I touched her arm. 'You may not feel better for a long time.'

'Oh, I'll be okay. I'm feeling better already. Talking to you. It helps.'

'Good.' I stood up. 'Come on,' I said. 'Let's head back to the lodge. Let's get away from here.'

I held my hands to her, and she took them and let me help her stand up. Then she grinned at me and squeezed my hands before letting them go. 'You're a nice man,' she said.

'In an avuncular sort of way,' I added.

'If that means fatherly.'

'It doesn't. But close enough.' We started up the path toward the lodge.

'I can trust you, can't I?' she said after a moment.

'Sure. We're friends, remember?'

'Because if my parents ever find out . . . '

'Don't worry, Polly.'

'Or Gib, either. Gib's got a wicked temper.'

I stopped and held Polly by her shoulders. 'Polly, I will tell no one. Trust me.'

'Even my mother?'

'Especially your mother.'

'Because I know that you and my mother – '

'Your mother and I are friends. That's all.' I spoke quickly, interrupting her. Too quickly, I thought. Protesting too much, it sounded like, which was silly. I had nothing to protest against.

Polly grinned sideways at me as we resumed walking. 'Sure,' she said.

We walked slowly. When we came in sight of the lodge, she stopped. 'Why'd he have to scalp him?' she said.

'To make it look like Woody did it,' I said.

'And you don't think he did.'

'No.'

We started walking again. 'Why does someone like Phil have to die?'

'I know you're not asking me for an answer,' I said.

'Because there isn't one,' she mumbled. She looked up at me. 'He deputized me, you know.'

I shrugged.

'He called me Bat Masterson. Promised I'd always get my man. I thought at first he meant a little joke. You know, how a girl gets her man. But he never joked, like I told you. He meant get the man who killed Ken, get the bad guys.'

She started to sniffle. She wiped her nose on the back of her hand and smiled up at me through tear-sparkled eyes. 'Some joke, huh? He didn't get anybody. That old Indian got him first.'

Chapter Ten

The day after he had left with Woody as his prisoner, Sheriff Thurl Harris returned. We heard the drone of the plane while we were gathered around the big breakfast table in the lodge, eating beans and eggs and ham and biscuits fresh baked by Bud Turner.

'That'll be Harris's plane,' said Gib without looking up.

'How'n hell do you know that?' asked one of the sports from Boston.

Gib paused, his fork, with a hunk of ham impaled on it, poised in front of his mouth, and regarded the Boston guy balefully. Then he leaned toward Polly, who was sitting on his left, and whispered something to her out of the corner of his mouth. Polly glanced at the sport and then quickly returned her attention to her food. She was fighting a losing battle against the smirk that was storming her good manners.

'I say something funny?' said the sport.

'The sound of the engine, man,' said Gib.

The sport shrugged.

Tiny got up from the table and walked out onto the porch. He returned a few minutes later and resumed his seat. 'It's Harris, all right. He's taxiing in toward our dock. Expect he'll want to talk to some of us again.'

Most of us had finished eating and were sipping coffee when we heard the clomp of feet on the porch. Then the door opened, and Thurl Harris entered, looking even more gaunt and pale than he had before, if that was possible. Behind him stood two other men. One was the same cop who had flown the plane before. The other wore a pin-striped charcoal-colored suit that looked as if it had been custom tailored for a Neapolitan gigolo. This man carried a lightweight leather attaché case in his hand and, judging by the glare in his eye, a heavyweight chip on his shoulder.

'Ah, sorry to barge in like this,' said Harris to Tiny, speaking carefully, as I had seen him do before, so as not to show his teeth. 'Afraid we're going to have to bother some of the folks here with more questions.' He shrugged, as if it weren't his idea. He jerked his head at the nattily dressed man behind him. 'This here's Mr Danforth,' he added. Mr Danforth acknowledged the introduction by scowling.

'Well, for Christ's sake, Thurl,' said Tiny, 'at least pull up a chair and have some coffee. You boys are up early this mornin'.'

'Ain't got time for socializin', afraid,' answered Harris.

Danforth shifted his weight back and forth as if his legs were cramped. Then he spoke into Harris's ear.

The sheriff nodded. 'If you don't mind, we'd like to use your office again.'

Tiny shrugged. 'He'p yourself.'

Danforth whispered to Harris again. 'We wouldn't mind if you brang us some coffee,' the sheriff said, forgetting himself momentarily and showing his black-ened teeth.

Marge, who was sitting beside me, muttered, 'The urn's right beside you.' But Harris and Danforth had already disappeared into Tiny's office. The policeman remained standing awkwardly outside the door, as if he were on sentry duty.

Marge pushed herself away from the table and went

over to the policeman. 'Like some coffee?' she said to him.

'Sure would, ma'am.'

'Well,' she said, 'if you're not afraid those two men in there are going to escape, why don't you help yourself.'

The cop looked first confused, then grateful, and went over to the coffee urn.

A moment later Harris opened the door and pushed his head out of Tiny's office. 'Mr Coyne, would you mind coming in?'

'Sure,' I said.

When I got into the office, I saw that Danforth had taken the seat behind the desk. His attaché case lay atop it, unopened, suggesting to me that he carried it as part of his wardrobe – for decoration rather than for function. He rose as I entered and extended his hand to me. His smile was well practiced. 'Asa Danforth,' he said. He had a baritone voice that would sound great on television.

'Brady Coyne,' I replied.

'Mr Danforth is the district attorney,' said Harris, much as if he were introducing me to a monarch or a movie star.

'*Assistant* D.A.,' said Danforth with just the right note of humility and good humor. 'For now,' he added, twitching his eyebrows at me. 'Do have a seat, Mr Coyne.'

I sat as instructed. Danforth shook a pack of Kools at me. 'Smoke?'

I shook my head. 'I'm not trying to quit.'

He frowned. 'Come again?'

'If I were trying to quit, I'd smoke those things. I've got my own here.' I did not light a Winston at that time, as I normally would have done, no cue being too insignificant to call for a cigarette under ordinary circumstances.

But for some reason I didn't want this assistant district attorney to think he could make me smoke if he wanted to. It would suggest he had put me ill at ease, that I was acknowledging I was about to be the object of his clever and probing interrogation.

Hell, I was just being childish.

'Thurl says you were a big help to him the other day,' Danforth said, making a show of lighting his cigarette with a silver-plated butane lighter.

I nodded. He expected me to say something self-effacing. I decided not to.

He cleared his throat and glanced at Thurl Harris. 'May I be frank with you, Mr Coyne?'

'Up to you.'

'Yes. Well, all right, then. Thurl, here, tells me that you have expressed some reservations about the viability of our case against Woody Pauley.'

Danforth cleared his throat several times. He tapped his cigarette against the edge of the ashtray on Tiny's desk. I watched him without speaking. 'Well, Mr Coyne? How do you answer that?'

'It wasn't a question, Mr Danforth.'

'You don't think the Indian did it, he means,' said Harris.

I turned to the sheriff. 'I did understand what he said. Viability, reservations – tough words, but I got 'em. I'm just waiting for him to ask me a question. He said he wanted to be frank. Then, I suppose he was. At least he was trying to give that impression. I'm not sure why it was important that I witness his act of frankness, but I did. Now what?'

Danforth suddenly grinned. His teeth, in contrast to Harris's, were shiny and white and even. City boy's teeth. Orthodonture. Regular flossing. They would glitter and gleam on television. 'Do you think the Indian did it, Mr Coyne?' he asked.

'No.'

'Would you mind telling me why not?'

'No, I wouldn't mind. Would you mind telling me why you care what I think?'

'I'd be delighted,' he said. He showed me a bit less of those teeth. 'I care what you think because you are an experienced attorney, I am told. I rarely have the opportunity to work with a big-city lawyer with a degree from Yale, and one who has experience with homicide cases.'

'I didn't realize we were working together,' I said.

He shrugged. 'We're here together.'

'You checked up on me.'

'Routine,' said Danforth humbly.

I nodded. 'Good thing to do. The wonders of the computer age.'

'The wonders of the telephone, Mr Coyne. This is still the sticks up here, you know.'

'Whatever,' I said. 'Why don't I think Woody did it? Mostly, I know the man. He's not a murderer, in spite of how it might look. It seems pretty obvious to me that he was framed.'

Danforth arched his brows. 'Framed? Really?'

'Sure. Those weapons could easily have been planted in his cabin.'

'What about the argument?'

'So they had an argument. That's why whoever killed him decided on Woody to set up. It's too pat. I'd expect an experienced lawman to see that.'

'Experienced lawmen,' said Danforth, 'know that things most usually turn out to be exactly the way they appear to be.'

142

'The commonest things most commonly happen,' I said. 'But in this case a frame-up is what it appears to be.'

Danforth nodded thoughtfully. I glanced at Harris, who looked a bit puzzled, his lips pinched tightly together.

Danforth stubbed out his Kool. 'Was Mr Pauley a poacher, Mr Coyne?'

'Woody? I seriously doubt it.'

'Do you have any idea how he felt about poaching?'

'Yes. I do.' I finally lit a Winston and slouched back in my chair.

'Well, come on,' said Danforth.

'Have you asked Woody that question?'

'Mr Pauley's lawyers have advised him not to talk.'

'Good advice.'

'Are you afraid that answering my question would incriminate Mr Pauley, Mr Coyne?'

'I'm afraid that anything might incriminate him. That's why we lawyers routinely advise our clients not to talk to district attorneys.'

'Mr Pauley, may I remind you, is not your client. And you are an officer of the court.'

'I surely appreciate the reminder,' I said. 'May I ask you a question?'

Danforth's eyebrows twitched, whether from amusement or nervousness, I couldn't tell. 'Ask away, Mr Coyne.'

'Who did Woody secure for counsel?'

'Boggs and Kell,' he said promptly, as if to demonstrate how questions ought to be answered.

'That an Indian firm?'

He nodded. 'Yes. Pretty big one, actually. They don't normally handle criminal cases. But, of course, this one has the potential for being a big case.'

'For all concerned,' I observed.

Danforth grinned. 'Fair enough. Big for all of us. Which is why I'd appreciate your views on Mr Pauley's attitude toward poaching.'

'You couldn't use anything I'd say. Inadmissible. Hearsay. Why bother?'

'Humor me, Mr Coyne.'

I stubbed out my cigarette, then leaned toward Danforth, resting my forearms on the top of Tiny's desk. 'Instead of hearsay, let me give you some conclusions. Equally inadmissible. Okay?'

He shrugged.

'Okay,' I continued. 'Woody Pauley is an Indian. His values come from a different cultural heritage than ours. How he feels about what we call poaching is not, therefore, a simple question. Understand that poaching is a crime created by white men in order to regulate a major industry. Indians don't think of hunting as recreation or sport or business. In their culture, hunting is simply how they survive. It's not good or bad. It's living. Animals are worshiped. They are essential. They exist to be killed, but only as needed. To Indians, these are not chosen values, things to be believed in or not. These are facts. Do you understand what I'm saying?'

'That was a pretty speech,' he said, glancing at Thurl Harris. Then he cocked his head at me. 'Of course I know what you're saying, Mr Coyne. You're saying that Indians might very well be poachers, that they do not respect – hell, they don't even acknowledge – laws that regulate hunting. They hunt what they want when they want, and the hell with the law.'

I sighed and leaned back. 'If you insist on being obtuse – '

His hand slammed onto the top of the desk. It startled me, which was the effect he wanted. 'I am not being obtuse,' he said, spacing out each word. His voice turned soft, a lawyer's trick for commanding attentiveness. 'I am being legalistic. That is my job.'

'Obtuse and legalistic aren't all that different,' I said mildly.

Danforth shrugged. 'He could've killed that moose,' he said.

'Okay, I'll play your way,' I said. 'Woody would not refrain from killing an animal because the season was closed. That's what you want me to say, isn't it?'

He nodded. 'Go on.'

'He would kill an animal for food. For himself, for his family, for his tribe. Regardless of the season. But for no other reason. And he would never kill a cow moose in the spring. Moreover, he wasn't hungry, he had no family, and he had separated himself from his tribe. Anyway, you didn't arrest him for poaching, did you?'

Danforth snorted. 'He would kill an animal for money,' he said, a fact, not an opinion.

'Nope. Not Woody.'

'The crossbow Thurl found in his cabin. It was his. Mr Pauley's. Does that surprise you, Mr Coyne?'

'It would surprise the hell out of me if Woody killed a moose with it. Hell, I'd be more surprised if he killed that moose than if he killed Phil Rolando.'

Danforth grinned. 'My point is that it wasn't planted there.'

'It could've been taken from him, used, then returned. Or it may never have been used at all. You can't do ballistics on crossbows. No way to prove that the crossbow was the murder weapon, is there?'

'And,' he went on impatiently, 'the knife was his, too. We have established that. The blade had been wiped clean, but there were traces of blood on the handle.

Human blood. Same blood type as the deceased. Notice, Mr Coyne, I didn't say it was Philip Rolando's blood. Same type, though. So. We have two possible murder weapons that belonged to the suspect. We have a motive, whether you agree or not. Aside from the argument, I mean. The poached moose, I mean, possibly shot with a bolt from the suspect's crossbow and gutted out and strung up in a place where local folks are afraid to go. Rolando, I understand, accused the Indian of poaching that moose. I'm tempted to believe that he struck a nerve there. Mr Pauley killed that moose. He killed Rolando not just because his pride had been insulted but also because Rolando was going to turn him in for poaching. We've got ourselves a case here, Mr Coyne. I believe we do.'

'You don't need to convince me.'

'I'd like to,' said Danforth with a professional smile.

'It's a lousy case, and you know it. It'll never get past a probable-cause hearing.'

'I've got a week,' he said with a shrug. 'That's why I'm here. This is a very important case.'

'Politics. Sure.'

He shrugged again.

I stood up. 'I don't think there's much more I can tell you,' I said. 'But I'm glad I had the chance to talk with you. It's been very reassuring.'

'Well, thanks.' He half rose in his seat to extend his hand to me.

'Yes,' I went on. 'It's reassuring to know that the prosecution case is so totally inept that no court system in the land would allow Woody to be put on trial. I feel much better having talked with you.' I walked out of the room without waiting for Danforth's reaction. I wished I had as much conviction as I expressed. In fact, I had to admit, Danforth's case against Woody didn't look that bad.

Tiny was still sitting at the big dining table, along with Gib and Lew Pike and a couple of the other guides. Most of the guests had dispersed. I assumed that Marge and Polly and Bud were in the kitchen. I went over and sat at the table.

'So what's going on in there? They got the goods on old Woody?' Lew Pike, who had known Woody for at least twenty years, grinned at me. He hadn't put his teeth in yet.

'They wish they did,' I said, pouring myself a mug of coffee. 'That's what they're here for. To get the goods on Woody.'

'That so?' said Pike. He snuffled loudly. Then he grasped his coffee mug and poured some of its contents into the saucer it had been sitting on. He put down the cup, lifted the saucer with both hands, and bent his mouth to it. He blew across it and then slurped noisily from the saucer. When it was empty, he belched softly and murmured, 'Ahh.'

'They really think they have a case against Woody?' said Gib.

'They've got a lot of circumstantial stuff,' I said, sipping my coffee. 'In my opinion, nothing solid. What about this Danforth, anyway?'

'Young up-and-comer, I hear,' said Tiny. 'They're talking about him for Congress down in Bangor.'

'Ivy Leaguer,' added Gib. 'Harvard. Then Cornell law. Turned down a couple Wall Street offers to come to Bangor in the district attorney's office.'

'Well, it looks to me as if he expects to make some political hay at Woody's expense,' I said.

147

Gib nodded. 'It's got all the makin's. Plenty of head-lines in this one for the guy who plays it right. Pretty interesting type murder. Not that many corpses turn up scalped these days, man. And you've got yourself an Indian to put on trial, which'll please the hell out of every white person in the state of Maine, save for a few of them liberal Boston types down in Portland.' Gib nodded again. 'Such a nice case that it don't much matter whether he ends up winning it or not. Every redneck in the state figures if you're an Indian, the government'll protect you, anyhow. That's all Danforth's got to say if he loses. "What in hell do you expect, man?" he'll say. "Everyone knows he did it, but you can't get justice out of an Indian. Government give 'em land, let 'em get away with murder. If it was a white man, he'd have been sent to prison. If you don't like it, all you gotta do is vote for me."' Gib sat back and smiled. 'That's how it is. A real nice case for Mr Asa Danforth, win, lose, or rainout.'

Tiny shook his head, and Lew Pike smiled toothlessly. 'By Jesus, you're right, Gib,' said the old guide. 'They give them Injuns our land, they let em shoot our animals, and they tell 'em they don't have to go to jail.' He slurped from his saucer, then crinkled his eyes. 'But I'll be god-damned if I'll vote for a pansy who wears pants so tight you can see which side his balls are hangin' on.'

When Thurl Harris stuck his head out the door a moment later, he saw the gang of us sitting at the dining table, slurping coffee, smoking, and rubbing the tears of laughter off our cheeks. He cleared his throat. 'Ah, Lew Pike? Mr Pike?'

Pike turned his head and looked over his shoulder at Harris. 'Yup. That's me.'

'We'd like to talk with you, please.'

'Why, shore,' said Pike. He stood up, then leaned

toward those of us who were seated at the table. 'I'm gonna check him out. See if it's left or right. I'll let you know.'

He winked at us, showed us his gums, and shambled into Tiny's office. When he emerged fifteen or twenty minutes later, he was still grinning. He came over to the table and whispered 'left' to us and walked out of the lodge, chuckling to himself.

Danforth and Harris interviewed all of the guides and others who lived and worked at Raven Lake one at a time. I studied the faces of the interviewees as they emerged from Tiny's office. The guides were all smiling. I assumed they had inspected the cut of Asa Danforth's trousers to verify Lew Pike's observation. Gib's face was blank when he came out, and he went directly down to his plane. Polly looked pale. I suspected she had told Danforth the truth about her last evening with Phil Rolando. Marge wasn't in there long, but when she came out, she looked grim, although she did manage to give Tiny and me a wink before she went back into the kitchen. Bud Turner rolled his eyes at me as he walked out of his session.

They saved Tiny for last and kept him in there for a long time. When they finished with him, the three of them came out together, nodding and smiling. Tiny shook hands with Danforth and Harris. I was alone at the table, glancing through an old issue of *Field & Stream*. Tiny came over and slapped my shoulder. 'Want to go out on the lake this afternoon?'

'Sure,' I said.

'Meet me in an hour at the dock,' he said, and went out into the kitchen.

Harris and Danforth and the cop chatted for a moment outside Tiny's office, and then they headed for their plane. They ignored me. They seemed very confident. I wondered what they thought they'd learned.

I went out onto the porch to watch their plane take off. Then I climbed the stairs to get my fishing gear together.

Chapter Eleven

The next morning after breakfast Bud Turner mentioned that he was taking the truck to Greenville for supplies. I asked him if he'd mind company. He allowed as how he didn't mind.

'You oughta see them big trucks, all loaded down with long logs, speedin' over these roads,' Bud remarked after we had gotten under way. 'They go sixty, seventy miles an hour. They sometimes don't make the turns. Go rollin' right down the hills, ass over teacups. Fellas tend to get killed doin' that. You don't wanta meet up with one of them trucks goin' the wrong way, tell you that.'

The crude roadways had obviously been engineered for a single purpose: to get logs out of the forest on big trucks. They had been hastily bulldozed out of the woods. They were just wide enough for one vehicle – rock strewn, eroded, and unimproved, with big mounds of boulders and loose earth piled alongside. After each particular section of forest had been lumbered, the roads fell more or less into disuse. The route from Raven Lake to Greenville was no exception. It passed through shallow creek beds and clung precipitously to the sides of hills. The roadside was a tangle of uprooted trees and boulders.

Behind the seat of the cab of Bud's truck hung a gun rack. It held a short lever-action rifle and a battered twelve-gauge pump-action shotgun.

'That rifle's a nice Marlin .30-.30,' Bud commented when I turned to look at his guns. 'I've got that old Remington pump loaded with bird shot.'

'What for?'

Bud grinned sideways at me without taking his eyes from the rutted roadway.

'You keep them loaded?' I persisted.

'Hell, yes. A gun ain't no goddamned good if she ain't loaded.'

I shrugged. It was illegal, but that was irrelevant. All the good old boys in Maine kept loaded guns in their pickups.

Bud had brought along a big stainless-steel Stanley thermos full of strong coffee, and he and I sipped from it as well as we could in the bouncing truck. It took us nearly three hours to reach Greenville. I felt as if I had spent a week on the back of an unbroken horse.

When we pulled into town, Bud said, 'Where do you want to go?'

'Do you happen to know where the lawyers Boggs and Kell have their office?'

He thought for a minute. 'Same building as the hardware store, if I ain't mistaken. Up on the second floor. I recall seein' the sign. I can drop you off there if you want.'

I told him that would be fine, and we agreed to meet at one-thirty at the little restaurant a few doors down from the lawyers' office.

A narrow flight of stairs led up to a tiny hallway. There were two doors. One appeared to be a closet. On the opaque glass of the other, neatly painted letters announced, 'Boggs and Kell, Attorneys-at-Law'. I tested the knob and then went in.

The door opened into a tiny waiting room in which a single desk, a magazine-littered coffee table, and two straight-backed chairs managed to seem crowded. Behind the desk sat a swarthy middle-aged woman whose dark hair had been braided and wound onto the top of her

152

head in an intricate crown. A brown cigarette smoldered in an ashtray at her elbow. It smelled like burning cowflaps. A paperback book was propped up on her desk in front of her.

'Help you?' she said. Her tone suggested that she resented my intrusion and that it would be just fine with her if she couldn't help me at all.

'I'm looking for Mr Boggs or Mr Kell,' I said. 'Either one would be fine.'

'Either one of 'em ain't here,' she said, her tone almost mocking me. She picked up the evil-smelling cigarillo and puffed at it.

'When do you expect them?'

'I don't.'

'Are they gone for the day? I don't have an appointment, but I hoped . . .'

She stubbed out her butt. 'They don't work here, mister. They're never here.'

'But the sign . . . ?'

She sighed, as if it were terribly obvious. 'The sign says Boggs and Kell. I know that.'

'Then . . .'

'But Mr Boggs and Mr Kell themselves, they're in Bangor. Always. They don't come here. But this is their office.' She lifted her heavy black brows at me, as if that explained it.

'Like a branch office, is that it?' If she intended to test my patience, I intended to pass her test.

'Yes. Like that.'

I glanced at a doorway behind her, which appeared to lead into an inner office. 'Well, is there a lawyer in?'

'Mr Stack's in, sure.'

'Is he busy?'

'Doubt it.'

I took a deep breath. 'Do you suppose I could see him?'

She squinted at me. She had high cheekbones and dark eyes. I realized that she must have been an Indian. Pocahontas in her middle years, wheezy, worn out, and going to flab. 'Who are you?' she said.

I handed her one of my business cards. She scrutinized it carefully, then peered at me as if she were comparing the words on the card with the evidence of my appearance. Apparently what she saw satisfied her. 'I'll have to tell him what it's about,' she said almost apologetically.

'Tell him it's about Woodrow Wilson Pauley.'

She arched her eyebrows. 'You from the DA's office or something?'

'No. I'm on his side.'

She shrugged, sighed, and pushed herself back from the desk. She waddled to the door and went in without knocking, closing it behind her. A minute later she emerged. 'You can go in if you want,' she said as she wedged herself into the chair behind her desk and picked up her book.

I went in. The man seated at the desk looked as if he might have posed for the old Indian-head nickel. All he needed was a feather in his hair. High cheekbones, aristocratic nose, finely etched mouth, and thick black hair tied at the nape of his neck in a short ponytail. He wore a dark green chamois shirt and well-worn jeans with a thick leather belt. He stood when I entered. He was about my height. He had the physique of a basketball player, slim hipped and wide shouldered. He looked quick and dangerous.

He came around from behind his desk and extended his hand. 'Will Stock, sir.'

'I'm Brady Coyne,' I said. 'I appreciate your seeing me.'

154

He flapped his hand toward a chair. 'Have a seat. Tell me what I can do for you.' His voice was higher pitched than I expected, but years of education had worn all the rough edges off his syntax.

I sat, and he retreated to his desk chair. 'This isn't official business or anything like that,' I said.

'Yes. Dolores said you were on our side.'

'I'm a friend of Woody Pauley. I was told that your firm is handling his case.'

Will Stack struck me as a man who would consider a smile a sign of weakness and who would consider weakness the worst of all traits. He was young, no older than thirty, and very solemn. 'Boggs and Kell are handling it, yes. Not me personally.'

'I was there when the murder took place,' I said. 'I've talked with the sheriff and the assistant district attorney. They are trying to put together a case against Woody. Fabricate, I should say. I don't think he committed any crime. I'm convinced this whole thing is trumped up. I don't know why. Anyhow, I wanted to offer my help.'

Stack picked up a pencil from his desk and rubbed his forehead with the eraser end absent-mindedly. He stared at the ceiling for a moment. Suddenly his gaze focused on me. 'Why?' he said.

'Why do I want to help? Because I think he's innocent. And because he's my friend.'

'What makes you think we need help?'

I shrugged. 'Everyone can use a little help.'

'Especially Indian lawyers.'

'I didn't mean that at all,' I said. 'I – '

'Let me tell you a story, Mr Coyne,' said Stack. 'Several years ago, when I was in law school, some members of my race went to Plymouth, Massachusetts, on Thanksgiving Day. They have ceremonies there, you know. Descendants of the *Mayflower*. Daughters of the American

155

Revolution. They dress up as they imagine people dressed in 1620. Some people dress up like Indians. So we went there to make a peaceful demonstration. Symbolic. Pretty obvious. Trying to make some points about Indian rights. Many were Mashpees, who, as you may know, have made some substantial land claims in Massachusetts.' He paused and stared at me.

I nodded. 'I'm familiar with the cases,' I said.

'There were some women dressed like Pilgrims, or whatever they were. White women. One of them came up to me. She was very angry. Clearly we were spoiling her Thanksgiving celebration. Know what she yelled at me?'

I shook my head.

'She said, "Why don't all of you go back to where you belong." That's what she said.'

I shrugged. 'All races have their share of ignorant people.'

'Mr Coyne,' said Will Stack, 'we are competent to handle Mr Pauley's case. Indian lawyers can practice the law. We have to pass the same bar exam as white lawyers. So I hope you won't be too offended if I suggest to you that you should go back to where you belong.'

I stood up. 'Okay,' I said. 'Fair enough.' I put my hands on the top of his desk and leaned toward him. 'But,' I said, 'you better not fuck up Woody's defense out of some misguided sense of ethnic pride. Where I come from, we take all the help we can get, and we don't much care if the people who give it to us are green, pink, or purple.'

Stack stared at me expressionlessly. 'Where I come from,' he said calmly, 'we have a pretty good idea of who really wants to help. But thanks, anyway.'

I took a deep breath, decided not to say the next thing that came to my mind, and walked out of Will Stack's office. Dolores didn't look up from her paperback as I slammed out of the place.

The two-minute walk down the street to the restaurant where Bud and I had agreed to meet calmed me down. It was about noon, and the tables and booths were filling up with patrons. It was an interesting mix of guys in work boots, blue jeans, and colored T-shirts, and men and women wearing business suits and lugging briefcases. I stood inside the doorway for a few moments. A skinny woman of indeterminate age wearing a stained white uniform muttered, 'Help yourself to a table,' on her way by. I spotted one against the wall and took it.

I opened the menu that was propped up between the salt and pepper shakers. Standard fare – a variety of hot lunches and sandwiches. The special for the day was 'home-style meat loaf'. I wondered what other styles of meat loaf there might be.

The same skinny waitress appeared at my table. Her name, according to the pin stuck on to her uniform over her left breast, was Vera. She had a pencil poised over her pad and a grimace of concentration on her face. 'He'p ya?'

'How's the meat loaf today?'

She shrugged. 'Same as most days. Your basic meat loaf. Ain't fancy.'

'I'll have it. What goes with it?'

'Mashed potato. Green beans. Salad. Coffee. Dessert. The usual.'

'Sounds fine.'

'You want a beer or something?'

'No. Bring me some coffee. And tell me. Is there a pay phone here?'

She jerked her head backward. 'There. Outside of the rest rooms.'

I spotted it, an old-fashioned booth, complete with folding door. Just what I wanted.

The service was almost instantaneous. The meat loaf was delicious. Vera brought me a wedge of apple pie with a big slab of cheddar cheese on top for dessert, and I lingered over my third cup of good coffee and a couple of Winstons while the restaurant gradually cleared out. Then I went to the phone booth, gave the operator my credit-card numbers, and rang Seelye Smith in Portland.

His receptionist or clerk or whatever he was – the handsome kid named Kirk – told me that Mr Smith was unable to come to the phone just then. I told him to say it was Brady Coyne calling long distance and that I'd wait. He hemmed and hawed. I told him I guaranteed Seelye would have his ass if he didn't put me through right away. He told me to hang on. He called me 'sir'.

'You've gotta excuse Kirk, Mr Coyne,' said Smith when he came on the line. 'He takes his responsibilities seriously.'

'Wouldn't have it any other way,' I said.

'Glad you called,' he said. 'Been wanting to talk to you. I've done some snooping. Interesting. You know the Indian lawyers who're trying to buy Raven Lake?'

'Yes?'

'Looks like they're fronting for somebody.'

'You mean the Indians don't want the place for themselves?'

'Right. From there it gets murky. But I can tell you this. It's out-of-state interests. Private.'

'And probably not all that legitimate,' I said.

'Probably not.'

'And,' I said, 'these private, out-of-state, not-that-legitimate interests, they don't want anybody to know

158

who they are and what they're up to. That's why they've got the Indians fronting for them.'

'Exactly.' Smith sighed. 'Which so far they've been successful at.'

'So far.'

'Yeah. But I'm still trying.'

'Who are the lawyers?'

'Firm out of Bangor. On the up-and-up, so far as I know. Boggs and Kell.'

'No shit.'

'Huh?'

'Maybe it's a coincidence,' I said, and I told him about the murder at Raven Lake and Woody's arrest and my unproductive visit with Will Stack. Smith interrupted me several times, asking for clarification and details. I could tell that he was a good lawyer.

When I finished my recitation, Smith said, 'Well, of course, it could be coincidence. Matter of fact, if I were a betting man, that's where I'd put most of my money. Boggs and Kell are one of the big firms. Probably the biggest in Bangor. Still, getting stonewalled like you did by this Stack this morning, maybe there is a connection. What do you make of it, Mr Coyne?'

'Hell, I don't know. Only thing is, if the murder is somehow related to this group trying to buy the lodge – and Boggs and Kell handling the real estate offer and then defending old Woody certainly seems to suggest a relationship – '

'That,' said Smith, 'would be significant.'

'What do you know about the district attorney who's prosecuting the case, this Asa Danforth?'

'Very ambitious young man,' replied Smith promptly. 'I knew him when I was working for the state on the original Indian litigation. He was one of those who wanted

159

to fight it down to the wire. Big defeat for him when the state lost. He's been trying to recoup ever since.'

'By prosecuting Indians,' I said.

'Sure. That's how he saves face. He's had some success at it, actually. Made something of a name for himself – not to mention some points with the Republicans – by promoting the idea that the Indians are irresponsible, greedy, and lawless and that the state – and, by extension, Asa Danforth himself – was right all along not to cave in to their demands and that the feds blew it. It's a very popular position hereabouts. Anti-Indian, antifed, is Danforth's platform, dressed up just a little.'

'Makes it easy to see why he might want to build a case against Woody.'

'Yes. Not that it's good law enforcement, although he hasn't got that bad of a case, from what you say. At any rate, it sure as hell is good politics.'

I paused for a moment. 'It would be very interesting to find out exactly who wants to buy Raven Lake,' I said.

'I'm still trying, Mr Coyne.' He hesitated. 'Listen. Don't feel too bad about the lawyer. Your Mr Stack, there. He's just a flunky. Doing what he's told. I expect that he got the word from Bangor to refuse all comment on the murder case, that's all. Which isn't that bad of an idea. The rest was just rude manners. Nothing you could have done.'

'I could have slapped him with my glove,' I said.

Seelye Smith and I agreed to keep in touch. I would try to call him again in a few days.

I disconnected, got the operator back, and called Vern Wheeler in Boston. He answered the phone himself, as I knew he would, since I was one of the few people who had been given access to his private line.

'How they bitin'?' he said.

'Excellent, Vern. Just like snakes.'

'We've been havin' some troubles, I hear.'

'You hear correctly.'

'Tiny called the other day. Hard to believe, old Woody killin' a man.'

'Hell, Vern. Woody didn't kill anyone.'

'Well,' drawled Vern after a moment, 'I guess that's a matter of opinion, now, ain't it?'

'I know you're not asking me for a dissertation on the law,' I replied. 'It's a trumped-up case, Vern. Woody was framed, and the DA up here is taking it down the line.'

'That ain't quite the way Tiny told it, Brady.'

'I thought you knew Woody.'

'You letting your feelings for the man color your view of the facts?'

'Nope. Something coloring your view, Vern?'

'Nope. I just figure, they arrest a man, they gotta have something.'

'Oh, they've got something. Enough to arrest him. But not enough to convict him. In my, ah, learned opinion. As an attorney, not a friend.'

'I do respect your opinion,' was all Vern said.

'Tiny says he's about ready to sell the place,' I continued. 'He's fed up with the trouble, he says. Figures the murder, the disappearance of the other guy, that they'll ruin business.'

'Yeah' – Vern sighed – 'that's what he told me, too. You think he's serious?'

'I can't tell. He's not joking, I can tell you that. Maybe he's just down. He'll snap out of it.'

'Selling the place might not be such a bad idea at that. Though I can't believe Tiny really means it.'

'He's discouraged. He'll come around.'

'Doesn't sound like you're having that much fun, Brady,' said Vern. 'Why don't you come home?'

'Tell the truth, it's not exactly what I bargained for. The fishing's been pretty decent. But I've done a hell of a lot more lawyering than I counted on. Still, I've got a feeling Tiny would like me to hang around a while longer.'

Vern paused, then cleared his throat. 'Far as I'm concerned, you don't need to stay. Tell me. What've you found out about these people who want to buy the place?'

'Talked with Seelye Smith. Checked up on him, too, as promised. Impeccable reputation. I like him. Trust him, too. He says the Indian lawyers are working for an un-named third party. Out of state. Private. He's trying to track down who they are and what their game is. It's the same Indian firm that's defending Woody, by the way, which may or may not mean something. Anyhow, Smith's okay. You're in good hands.'

'Yeah, maybe,' said Vern. 'Listen, Brady. Why don't you come home. Tiny can take care of himself.'

'Well, if I'm costing you money . . .'

He laughed. 'That's not it, and you know it.'

'Think I'll stay a while and hold Tiny's hand, then.'

'That's fine. Up to you.'

'I'll give it a few more days. Mainly because the fishing's been pretty damn good.'

'Hey, fish all you want. Drink all my Jack Daniel's. Enjoy yourself. And don't worry your head about old Woody.'

I promised Vern I'd be in touch if anything else happened. I thought of calling the office and checking with the answering service. Then I said the hell with it. This was supposed to be a vacation, not that it was exactly working out that way.

I returned to my table to wait for Bud Turner to take me back to the lake.

Chapter Twelve

'You're looking a bit glum, my friend,' said Marge that night as she eased herself down beside me on the end of the dock. I had my back against one of the pilings and my knees drawn up to my chin.

'I am thinking,' I intoned. 'I am being contemplative. I am pondering the wonder of it all.'

'Oh,' she said.

'Death and transfiguration. Being and nothingness. War and peace. That sort of thing.'

'I brought you some medicine.' She tinkled the ice in the glass. I took it, sipped, and sighed.

I jammed two cigarettes into my mouth, lit them both, and handed one to Marge. She hitched herself close to me, and I could feel her shiver.

'I'm really sorry about all this,' she murmured. 'You came up here for some fishing and relaxing. Now all this.'

'I went to Greenville with Bud today. Talked to Vern. He suggested I go home.'

She put her hand on my knee and didn't speak.

'I told him I thought I'd hang around a little longer.'

'I'm glad.'

'But, see, I can't do anything. I don't even especially want to do anything. But here I am. That is what I am trying to contemplate.'

'You do blather,' she whispered. I turned to look at her. She was staring out across the lake. In profile she looked remarkably like her daughter. I touched her hair, and she turned to face me. Her eyes sparkled in the darkness. I realized she was crying.

'Hey, look,' I said. 'I don't . . . '

She shook her head impatiently. 'Shh,' she said. 'Don't pay any attention to me.'

I shrugged. 'If you want to talk . . . '

'That's not what Vern pays you for, Brady.'

'What the hell. It's after five. I'm on my own time.'

She hugged her legs. 'Anyway, there's nothing, really. I mean, you know about Polly. She's been a perfect angel for the past couple of days, by the way.'

'Since the murder.'

'Yes. It seems to have put things into some kind of perspective for her.'

I nodded and didn't comment. Marge apparently did not suspect Polly's involvement with the dead Mr Rolando, and I certainly wasn't going to be the one to tell her.

'Then, of course, there's my husband,' she said.

'This I don't think I want to hear about,' I said quickly.

'I really think he's ready to sell the place,' she said. 'First he talks about staying open all year. Now he's ready to sell. Brady, if we left this place, I don't know what I'd do. I don't think I'd go with him. It would be like starting a new marriage. Tiny Wheeler and Raven Lake are all one person. Do you know what I mean?'

I shrugged. 'Look . . . '

'No, listen to me. Please. I can't imagine living with Tiny in some condominium in Sarasota or Phoenix or San Diego or something. When I committed myself to Tiny Wheeler, it was a commitment to a way of life, not just a man. I can't separate the two. It scares me.'

'He feels responsible for everything that's happened. I imagine Vern doesn't make it any easier for him.'

'Vern has never made anything easy for Tiny.'

'Have you told Tiny how you feel?'

'He knows.'

We fell silent. I hadn't heard the loons since I had been out there, a fact that deepened my morose frame of mind. Marge poked me and said, 'Gimme another one of them cigarettes.' I did, and we smoked quietly, staring at the shiny purple surface of Raven Lake.

'You want to go fishing tomorrow?' she said after a while.

'Sure.'

'I'll take you. Tiny's flying out for the day.'

I hesitated. 'You think it's a good idea?'

'What, you mean with my husband gone?' She laughed, a genuine laugh that sounded good. 'Would it matter? Listen, Counselor. I'm a registered Maine guide, okay? It's one of the things I do. I do it damn well, matter of fact. I'll show you some salmon. Deal?'

I grinned at her in the darkness. 'Okay. Deal. Where's Tiny going?'

She paused before answering. Finally she said, 'I don't ask, he doesn't say. It happens now and then. He tells me he's going to be gone for the day. He and Gib, they fly out after breakfast. They're back before dusk. They don't bring back supplies. They don't take any guests out with them or bring any back in.'

'And this makes you suspicious.'

Her laugh was low, deep in her throat, cynical, wry, and it made me uncomfortable. 'I am not naïve, Brady,' she said.

'And I am, huh?'

'Yes, you are. For a lawyer it's pretty unusual. It's a lovable trait.'

I harumphed my disagreement but didn't say anything.

'I don't suspect,' she continued. 'I assume. See, that's the difference between us. You're naïve. You assume the best. Innocent until proven guilty. That stuff. Well, not me. Tiny has a lady friend. It's pretty evident. It's kinda cute, actually. A couple of days before he leaves to see her, I can tell it's coming. He gets tense. Becomes polite and considerate of my feelings. Out of character. Then, when he figures he's got me softened up, he announces, and it's always when there's other people around so we won't really be able to discuss it, he says, "Oh, by the way, honey, I'll be flying out with Gib tomorrow, just for the day. Business, you know." And when he gets back he's – he's cordial, formal, very proper with me, as if I were an important stranger.' She snorted a little laugh through her nose. 'As if I had no idea what was going on.'

'I wouldn't jump to conclusions,' I said lamely.

'Jump? Shit. It took me a year to figure it out. I didn't jump. I took many small, careful steps. Anyway, it doesn't matter one way or another. He'll be gone tomorrow, and we'll go fishing, and then you can tell me whether Woody's any better at guidin' than me.'

The summer sun burned away the morning mists and beat down brutally on the lake. By eight o'clock, when breakfast was over and Gib and Tiny had taxied away from the dock in Gib's Cessna, the temperature had already reached eighty. No breeze relieved the heat. Raven Lake was a mirror, except in the coves, where thermal tricks sucked the air gently across the top of the water, corrugating its surface.

I lugged my fishing equipment down to the dock. Marge had maneuvered the canoe around to the side, where we could load it easily. I handed the gear down to her. A big wicker basket sat on the dock. I had to use both hands to lift it.

'What's in here, the anchor?'

She grinned. 'Just lunch stuff. You'll see.'

'A basketful of skillets, then.'

I eased myself into the canoe and cast us off from the dock.

'Lousy day for fishing,' said Marge as she shoved us off toward the middle of the lake with a strong thrust of her paddle. 'Salmon'll be down deep.'

'Maybe we should just concentrate on the bass,' I said.

'We'll catch us some salmon,' she said. 'Just have to work a little for them. Good guidin'll make the difference. I know a place.'

I was nestled in the bow, facing backward for the run downlake. Marge sat in the stern to run the motor. She wore a plain cotton shirt with the sleeves rolled up over her elbows, short cutoff blue jeans, tennis shoes without socks, and a man's felt hat, with the brim pulled low over her forehead.

She gave the engine rope a yank, and it sputtered to life. Then she turned to face forward, hunched in what looked like a familiar position, her left elbow cocked up behind her to handle the steering and her right arm resting casually across her smoothly tanned thigh. She squinted her eyes against the reflected glare of the sun and smiled at me. She mouthed something to me, which was lost in the roar of the outboard motor. I thought she said, 'Tallyho!' I responded with a grin and a thumbs-up sign. She rolled her eyes, and I knew I had misunderstood her. I shrugged apologetically. She shook her head in mock disgust.

After a ten-minute run she cut the motor. The sudden absence of engine noise was startling, and we drifted for several moments without speaking, unwilling to destroy the silence.

Marge took up a paddle and steered us to a spot perhaps a hundred feet from shore, off a point of land. 'There's a ledge that runs out here,' she said softly, respectful of the quiet. 'Drops off quick on either side. We'll anchor on top of it, and we can cast parallel to the dropoff. Salmon like to lie here on a day like this.' She took bearings from the shore, grunted her satisfaction, and let the anchor over the side, paying out line through both hands. 'There,' she said, as the line went slack. 'Perfect.'

She took a couple of half hitches with the anchor line onto a thwart. Then she picked up her fly rod. 'You gonna fish, Counselor, or are you gonna sunbathe?'

'Gonna fish.'

'This is Woody's place.' She stripped line off her reel and begun to cast. 'He took me here once. Day like this. Rest of the lake was dead far as salmon were concerned. We done real good that day,' she drawled in a poor imitation of Woody. 'Everyone else got skunked. So we agreed. Neither of us'd show it to anybody else. It was our place. Mine and Woody's. I don't think he'd mind if I shared it with you, though.'

'I'm not so sure,' I said.

'Brady?'

'Yes?'

'You don't think Woody killed that man, do you?'

'No, I don't. Do you?'

She stared at the lake thoughtfully for a moment. 'I want to,' she said finally. 'It makes me feel like a traitor, but I want it to be Woody.'

'I think I understand.'

'See,' she continued, 'in my heart I don't believe it.

But if it wasn't Woody, then it was someone else, right? And if it was someone else, that frightens me. Because that someone else . . .'

'Sure.'

'They're still here,' she finished. 'That's why nobody wants to say that Woody didn't do it.'

I nodded. There was nothing more to say.

We fished hard for more than an hour without a strike. Marge cast comfortably and accurately, and she didn't seem to tire. Once we saw a dimple on the surface of the water, maybe eighty feet away, equidistant from Marge and me. It could have been a tiny baitfish. Or it could have been a monster salmon, sucking in a floating insect.

She glanced sideways at me from under the brim of her hat. 'My fish,' she said.

'Like hell,' I replied. We both took aim at the disappearing rings. It was a long cast for a fly rod, maximum distance for a strong caster with properly balanced equipment. I dropped my streamer fly on the edge of the nearest widening ripple. Marge's landed five or six feet beyond mine, almost a bull's eye.

The fish, whatever it had been, ignored both of our flies.

'That,' I said, 'was one helluva cast.'

'For a woman, you mean,' she said.

'That is not what I meant, and it is not what I said.'

She shrugged, but I could see her smile as she turned away from me.

A few minutes later Marge muttered, 'Hey, there. Little tipdipper, huh? Come on, big fella.' An instant later she cried, 'Ha!'

Her rod bowed as something strong and heavy began to rip the line from her reel. She held the rod over her head with both hands, using a finger of her left hand to increase the drag of the reel. When she turned the fish, it bolted toward the surface and leaped high out of the water.

'A noble fish,' I commented.

Marge grunted, too deep in concentration to respond.

She finally brought the spent salmon alongside the canoe. I reached down with the long-handled net and scooped him out. 'Five and a half pounds, easy,' I said, extending the net to her so she could remove her fish.

She used the mesh of the net to help her grip the fish behind his gills. She twisted the fly gently from the corner of his mouth and then jerked her head at me. I lowered the net into the water and flipped it over, releasing the big salmon.

Marge sat there in the stern of the canoe, panting and grinning. Her forehead glistened with perspiration. 'Imagine living in a city,' she said. She reached over the side of the canoe with her hat, scooped it full of water, and replaced it on top of her head. The frigid lake water cascaded down the front of her, soaking her shirt and plastering it to the front of her. It made her breasts stand out against the wet fabric. She wore no bra. I could see how the cold water had hardened her nipples.

'Wow!' she breathed. 'That is some cold.'

'A pretty piece of angling,' I observed.

'Mmm,' she said. 'Ready for some lunch?'

'Aye, aye, Skipper.'

She hauled up the anchor and paddled us to shore. She beached the canoe, and I climbed out and held it steady for her while she moved down the length of it. She put her hand on my shoulder to brace herself as she stepped out.

Our luncheon site was a sandy little spit of land. Several tall pine trees shaded us from the high sun, but the place was exposed enough to allow what there was of a breeze to waft through, cooling us and clearing away the blackflies.

I went on a firewood search while Marge unloaded her basket and moved some rocks together for the fireplace. When I returned with a big armload of wood, she had already set out on a blanket a plate containing a pleasing arrangement of three different cheeses and crackers. She held two goblets of wine in her hand.

She passed me one of the glasses. 'To this place,' she toasted.

'Amen,' I murmured.

'You just sit tight, now,' she told me after sipping her wine. 'I'm gonna make you a lunch the likes of which you have never tasted on the shores of this or any other lake.'

She built a big fire, and we sat away from it while it burned down to coals. By then the wine bottle was nearly empty. 'Don't worry,' said Marge. 'I brought another.'

She fished it out of the basket and handed it to me, along with a corkscrew. I twisted out the cork and refilled our glasses. Marge removed a big black skillet from that seemingly bottomless basket. She set it atop the rocks over the coals. She put in a whole stick of margarine. After it had begun sizzling, she tossed in three or four garlic cloves. When their aroma burst forth, she removed a small cooler from the basket. From it she took out a plastic bag that was filled with small white Y-shaped pieces of meat. 'Kept 'em on ice,' she said as she dropped them into the skillet.

I leaned forward and frowned. I couldn't tell what she was cooking. She noticed and grinned. '*Grenouilles,*' she said.

I shrugged.

'*Coscie di rana.*'

'*No hablo,*' I said.

171

'Frogs' legs. Caught 'em myself last night.'

'Delicious,' I said. 'Love 'em.'

She splashed some wine into the skillet, lifted it by its handle, and rocked it back and forth, mingling the juices. Then she used a long-handled fork to turn them over.

She dove back into the cooler and came out with a small bunch of asparagus spears. 'Catch them last night, too?' I said.

'Had Bud bring 'em back from Greenville. They're in season. Native and fresh.'

She stirred them frequently, and after a couple of minutes she announced, 'Chow time.'

She handed me a plate from her basket. Real china. I held it while she loaded it up with frogs' legs and asparagus. Then I held her plate for her so she could serve herself.

Finally, she brought forth a round loaf of hard bread. She broke off a piece and handed the loaf to me.

I topped off our wineglasses. We clicked them together. Our eyes met over the rims. Marge was not smiling. 'To good food,' I said.

'To this day,' she answered somberly.

We ate slowly, talking little. It was the kind of meal that deserved to be savored and contemplated, and it took a conscious effort of will to restrain my appetite and normal gluttonous approach to dining.

We sat cross-legged on the blanket, side by side, plates balanced on our laps, needing more than two hands apiece to steady the plate, manipulate a fork, hold a glass, and maneuver a chunk of bread among the juices of the meal.

When we had finished, I poured more wine into our glasses. 'That,' I proclaimed, 'was elegant.'

Her eyes stared into mine. 'I wanted it to be memorable.'

I grinned. 'Frogs' legs! Damn!'

She stood up abruptly. 'Gotta clean up,' she mumbled, turning away from me.

She scraped the little frog bones into the coals, which crackled briefly into flames. Then she gathered the dishes and the skillet and took them to the water's edge. I doused the fire and then dropped onto the blanket, lying back on my elbows.

She returned a moment later, wiping her hands on the fronts of her thighs. 'Any wine left?'

'A little.'

She knelt beside me and found her glass. I sat up, filled it, and lay back again.

She lifted it to her mouth, watching me. 'Brady?'

'You want a cigarette?'

She frowned, then shrugged. 'Sure.'

She sat back on her heels while I lit cigarettes for us. She took one from my hand and puffed at it quickly. 'Listen,' she said.

'No,' I said. 'I think . . .'

She reached over and placed two fingers gently on my lips. 'Shh,' she said. 'Don't talk, for once. Listen. Okay?'

I rolled my eyes and nodded.

'You are thinking I brought you here to seduce you. Right?'

I shrugged.

'Well, it's true. I did. And you are thinking that I am trying to recapture something that happened between me and Tiny Wheeler twenty-odd years ago. You don't have to say anything. You aren't all that dumb. So you've got this whole scene psyched out, being a smart city lawyer and all. And you're Tiny's friend and Vern's attorney, and

173

the last damn thing you need is to get messed up with this horny country wife who's been neglected for too long, but you're too much of a gentleman to straight out turn me down, because you don't know how to do it without doing something bad to what's left of my dignity, probably not being accustomed to turning down an easy lay in the first place. Am I making any sense here?'

I nodded.

'Well, good. And you're thinking that this broad who just turned forty must need piles of reassurance that she's still attractive and sexy, and you'd really like to find a way to give her that without getting otherwise involved. And you're pretty damn sure that if we stripped down and coupled right here by the lake, we'd end up getting involved, knowing the horny broad in question as well as you do. So you're figuring you've got two alternatives. Wanna hear them?'

'Sure. I guess so.'

'I was gonna tell you, anyway. The first one is, give in, do it, and damn the torpedoes, which you'd like to do – I think – right?'

'Yes,' I said. 'What's the other alternative?'

'The only other thing is to act like a real shit so I'll get pissed off and you won't have to spurn me because I'll spurn you. Have I got it?'

I smiled and shook my head slowly. 'You're actually way ahead of me. But, yeah, that's about it, Marge.'

'And I'm way ahead of you,' she said, 'because I knew all that a long time ago. Before today, even.' With her forefinger she dug a little hole in the ground and shoved her cigarette butt into it. Then she took mine from me and did the same. She turned to face me. She put a hand on my chest and pushed me so that I lay flat on my back. She knelt beside me, her bare legs against the side of my chest, and placed her hands on either side of my head. She bent so that her face was only inches from mine.

'You,' she said softly, 'you think this is a big moral issue.' I could feel her breath cool on my face, the sweetness of the wine mingled with the acid smell of tobacco. 'It's not, my friend. This has nothing to do with Tiny. You're worried about Tiny. I know that. He's your friend. Okay. He's my husband. So Tiny is my problem, not yours. This isn't a moral thing, Brady Coyne. It has nothing to do with anything or anyone else. It's just you and me.'

'Look,' I said.

'No,' she said. Her mouth lowered itself onto mine. It was a soft kiss, tentative, a mere brushing of lips, quick, instinctive, and then a flicker of tongues. Abruptly she moved away. She sat back on her heels, smiling.

I rolled up onto one elbow and made a big show of searching for a cigarette. I found my pack behind where Marge was squatting. I snaked my arm carefully behind her to avoid touching her. Then I did what I usually do when I don't know what I really should do. I lit a cigarette.

Which goes a long way to explaining why I smoke too much.

I avoided looking at Marge for as long as I could. When I finally shifted my eyes to her, I saw that she had stopped smiling.

I took a deep breath. 'Jesus, Marge.'

She narrowed her eyes and thrust her chin at me. 'You gonna say something about the fickleness of women? Got a smartass comment to make, Counselor?'

'I certainly know better than to make generalizations about women,' I said. 'Because every time I make one, I get taught that it's wrong. I will tell you one thing, though.'

'And what is that?'

'If seduction was your aim, lady, consider it an unmitigated success.'

She stood up quickly and turned away. I sat there puffing stupidly at my cigarette and watched her walk down to the lake. She held her shoulders rigid and barely moved her hips. I figured I'd said the wrong thing again.

Chapter Thirteen

Happy hour, as Tiny called it, had already begun, and I was rocking on the porch when I heard the distant whine of Gib's Cessna. Lew Pike was perched up on the railing by my feet. Somehow he managed to chew tobacco, drink beer, and tell stories all at the same time, which I found remarkable.

'That'll be Gib,' Pike drawled without turning or otherwise missing a beat in his tale, which had something to do with a porcupine that had acquired a taste for leather boots.

Several minutes later the plane skidded down and taxied up to the dock. I watched idly as Gib bounced out and made fast to the dock. Then Tiny climbed out. The two of them sauntered up the path toward the lodge.

They both nodded at Lew and me as they went inside. Moments later Gib came back out. He stood there, holding a drink in his hand, waiting for a pause in Lew's seemingly interminable story, the point, I gradually discerned, being that no goldurn porcupine could outsmart ol' Lew Pike, by God.

'Got a minute, man?' said Gib to me.

Lew spat dismissively over the rail. I gestured to the rocker beside me. 'Sure. Have a seat.'

'Been sittin' all day,' said Gib. 'Want to take a stroll?'

I shrugged and got up. 'Why not?'

I nodded to Pike, and Gib and I wandered down to the lake. A light breeze had sprung up, finally cutting the heat of the day and fluffing up the surface of the water.

Gib stared out at the lake. 'Been thinkin',' he said. 'Might be needin' help. Lawyer-type help.'

He turned to look at me. I nodded. 'What's the problem?'

He squinted, then shook his head. 'Don't want to talk about it just now. Thing is this. Would you mind flyin' down to Greenville with me tomorrow?'

I frowned. 'I suppose I could do that.'

'Oh, I'll pay you, man. I'd expect to do that.'

'Don't worry about it,' I said. 'I'd like a hint, though.'

'Rather not.' He tried to grin, but there was too much tension in his face, and it came out a grimace. 'Better to wait. Sorry to make a mystery out of it. You'll understand.'

I shrugged. 'I'm glad to help you. But tell me one thing, at least. Does this have anything to do with the murder? Do you know something?'

He didn't answer. Instead, he walked out onto the dock. I followed him. He lifted his drink and emptied it into his mouth. He swallowed, murmuring, 'Ahh,' then tipped the ice cubes out into the lake.

'You've been comin' here for a long time, haven't you?' he said.

'A long time.'

'Pretty friendly with Tiny.'

'Yes.'

'And Marge, too, huh?'

I cocked my head at him. I wondered if he suspected something. But his face seemed blank. I nodded.

'But it's Vern Wheeler who pays you.'

'Right.'

'Me, too.' He nodded his head a couple of times. 'First loyalty's to Vern, ain't it?'

'I guess. It's all the same.'

178

Gib shook his head. 'Nope. That's wrong. First loyalty's to yourself. Ain't that so?'

'What are you getting at?'

He smiled quickly. 'I'm in a little trouble, man, to tell you the truth. Guess maybe you figured that out. Got some business I need to straighten out. I'll feel better, you bein' with me. We can leave right after breakfast, if that's okay with you.'

'That's fine,' I said. 'But I have to tell you. It's not a good idea to have mysteries with your lawyer. Sure, I figured you were in trouble. If people didn't have trouble, lawyers would be out of business. It would be best for you to tell me what's going on. Trust me.'

He said nothing. He frowned at me for a moment before evidently making a decision. Then he turned and started back toward the lodge. I caught up to him and grabbed his shoulder. He stopped and stood there, saying nothing, gazing with infinite patience up into the tops of the pine trees.

'You're making a mistake,' I said.

He sighed and slowly turned to face me. 'It ain't you that I don't trust, man. Leave it lay right there, okay?'

I started to object. Then I changed my mind. I nodded, and together we trudged up the dark path.

Before bed that night I went down to the dock to check on my loons. There was a figure hunched out on the end, silhouetted in the moonlight reflecting off the lake's face. It was Marge.

I stopped in the shadows and watched her. She was hugging her knees, resting her cheek on top of them and staring out at the lake. She looked fragile and lonely, sitting out there on the rim of the wilderness, and I recognized in myself a powerful impulse to run out there

179

and gather her up in my arms and carry her off as she had suggested, full steam ahead and damn the torpedoes.

And, of course, damn my friendship with Tiny.

And damn whatever good opinion of myself I still held.

Marge seemed to feel that for me it should only be a practical problem, a matter of logistics and measurable consequences, a sort of utilitarian conundrum that could be solved by constructing the right equation and plugging in the right quantities for the constants and the variables. After all, she was the married one. It was, therefore, according to her calculus, she and she alone who confronted the moral issue. To cheat or not to cheat. Her question, not mine, which, she said, she had solved to her own satisfaction.

She had it wrong, of course. I didn't expect I could explain it to her. I didn't believe she wanted to hear it. And it would do no good to tell her how close I came to damning the torpedoes and damning the last shreds of my own self-respect out there on that sandbar. Should I tell her how powerfully I wanted her? Should I try to explain the distinctions among what I want, what I care for, and what I love? Perhaps we could discuss the definition of infidelity. One American statesman believed that the dirty thought was the moral equivalent of the dirty deed, in which case both Marge and I were already guilty as charged, so why not salvage the fun out of it?

I hesitated. It might be easier to turn around, return to the lodge, and read John le Carré until I fell asleep.

Equally easy: go tell her she misjudged me. My lust was powerful, my ethic weak. Then we could sneak off into the woods like a pair of adolescents and tear at each other's clothing.

I would, of course, do neither. I would attempt something civil. I slapped a smile on to my puss and strolled out to the dock.

I sat down beside her. She looked up at me and smiled. She handed me a glass. 'I anticipated you,' she said.

'That's real nice,' I said, accepting the drink. 'Cigarette?'

'That's what I came for.'

I held my pack of Winstons to her, and she plucked one out. Then I stuck one in my mouth. I held the lighter for her, cupping it in my hand. In the flicker of the flame I saw that she was staring at me.

I lit my own cigarette, inhaled, and sipped the bourbon she had brought me. 'Heard the loons yet?' I asked.

She nodded. 'They're wailing tonight,' she said. 'You ever notice the difference in their calls?'

'Never paid much attention,' I said. 'I just like to hear them.'

'They have three distinct calls at least. There's the wail, like tonight. Then there's the yodel. And the tremolo. All different. They mean different things. At least to each other.'

'You learn a lot, I guess, living in the woods like this.'

She smiled and waved her hand in the air. 'Naw. I read that somewhere. Tell the truth, I can't tell a wail from a yodel from a tremolo. They all make me shiver.'

At that instant, as if to confirm what she said, I heard from far uplake the eerie, laughing cry of a loon. It drifted down the lake toward us, sounding closer than it was over the water, and a moment later came an answer. Back and forth they went, and for several minutes Marge and I sat there in awed silence, listening.

They stopped abruptly, as if they had been frightened. Marge chuckled, low in her throat. 'Sometimes I feel as if I could understand what they're trying to say. Their loneliness. They need to have a whole lake to themselves.

You know, something else I read. The only real enemy of the loon is man. Did you know that?'

'I might have guessed,' I said. 'It's true for a lot of creatures.'

'Including man his own self,' said Marge. Still staring out at the lake, she said softly, 'I'm real sorry about today, Brady. I put you in a tough spot. It wasn't fair.'

'Don't worry about it.' I reached over and touched her hair.

'I hope it doesn't change anything.'

I let my hand fall to her shoulder. I hugged her quickly, then let go. 'It doesn't.'

She turned to look up at me. 'I'll take you fishing tomorrow if you like. Promise not to seduce you.'

'I'd like to. I can't.'

'Why not?'

'Gib asked me to fly down to Greenville with him.'

'What for?'

'I don't know. He wouldn't tell me. Just said that he needed a lawyer.'

'That's pretty strange.'

I shrugged. 'Probably pretty straighforward. Something to do with his licence, or his plane. Maybe an insurance problem. Maybe he got some girl in trouble.'

Her head jerked around quickly. 'It better not be my girl.'

'I'm sorry.'

'Forget it,' she said. 'I wasn't being serious.' She sipped her drink. 'How long will you be staying here?'

'I don't know. A few more days, I'd guess. I'll see how Tiny feels about it.'

'I'm not anxious for you to leave.'

'I'm not, either. Not that I'm doing anybody any good staying.'

She shook her head. 'You're doing me good. Hey . . . Brady?'

'Yes?'

'Kiss me, huh?'

'They can see us from the lodge, Marge.'

She stood up and hugged herself. I stood beside her. 'You're right,' she said. 'Of course. Someone might see us. They're probably watching us. Even in this big wilderness, this big empty lake, people are watching . . .'

She found my hand and squeezed it. 'I'm just a silly old broad. Lonely as those damn loons. Please don't think badly of me.'

We walked slowly back to the lodge, careful not to touch each other.

My sleep mechanism is set on a hair trigger, and all it took to awaken me the next morning was a faint rustling noise outside my door. The objects in my room were silhouettes. The window was a gray rectangle, emitting the half-light of dawn. I curled up fetally, facing away from the window, but it was no use. Once awake, I could not go back to sleep.

I rolled onto my back and stared up at the ceiling. Then, with a great effort of will, I sat up on the edge of the bed. I hoped it wasn't too early for coffee.

I dressed quickly in the chill of the room. As I reached to open the door, I noticed a piece of paper on the floor. I bent and picked it up. There was pencil writing on it, but it was too dark in my room to read. I took it back to the bed and switched on the light.

The brief message had been painstakingly printed. 'Mr Coyne,' it read, 'I chickened out. I'm sorry.' It was signed: 'Gib.'

I read it again, but Gib's note did not reveal anything

new to me. Last night he had evidently intended an act of courage. This morning he had decided against it. The only constructive question I could formulate was: Why had he bothered to confess his cowardice to me?

I folded Gib's note and tucked it between the pages of the thick le Carré novel on the table beside my bed. Then I went downstairs. The big coffee urn had begun to awaken. It grunted and belched, but the red light signaling that it had completed its task had not yet blinked on. With a sigh I wandered out onto the porch, feeling decidedly incomplete without a mug of java in my hand.

I sat in a rocker. I had, I mused, spent a great deal of time at Raven Lake this trip rocking and staring at the water and pondering unpleasant puzzles.

Out in the middle of the lake, a ribbon of water was riffled by the breeze that blew down the length of it. The cove in front of me lay flat calm. Wisps of morning mist sifted up from its surface and dissipated instantly. Gib's plane rocked gently by the dock. Half a dozen canoes lay overturned on the beach like the silvery husks of some giant variety of bean.

As I watched, I saw Gib step down from inside the plane onto one of its pontoons. He disengaged two lines and tossed them up onto the dock. Then he climbed quickly back into the plane. Abruptly the silence of the predawn was shattered as the engine of the Cessna coughed once, then roared into life. A moment later it began to creep out toward the center of Raven Lake.

Wherever he was headed, Gib had decided that he didn't need me with him.

As I sat there rocking and watching the plane slide across the water, a voice beside me said, 'Coffee, Mr Coyne?'

I glanced up. Bud Turner was grinning down at me

through a day's stubble of black beard. He held out a mug of coffee to me.

'Hey, thanks,' I said. 'Join me?'

He moved around and took the rocker beside me. 'Just for a minute,' he said. 'Can't leave Marge and Polly alone too long in there. They start snipin' at each other, they'll burn the bacon.' He gazed out at the lake. 'Gib's off early.'

'Mmm,' I murmured, sipping gingerly from the steaming hot mug.

'He alone?' said Bud.

'I don't know. Just saw him get out to untie the plane. Couldn't see if anybody was in there with him.'

I lit a cigarette, the first, always the best one of the day, inhaled, sipped, and rocked, following the plane's progress. It advanced perhaps five hundred yards, and then it turned to face uplake so it could take off into the headwind. Then Gib's Cessna made a higher-pitched sound, as if it were running more quickly. Then I heard the whine of the engine change its pitch. The plane lurched forward. It plowed through the water, and I could see it gradually rise up on its twin pontoons so that it skimmed across the surface. It lifted momentarily, dropped, and then seemed to skip like a flat stone.

It was the sound of the engine that caused me to sit forward. A cough, a hesitation, and then it all happened at the same time: the nose of the plane dipped, the tail lifted, the entire machine jerked and pivoted and seemed to rise up onto a wingtip. Etched into my brain was the image of Gib's Cessna doing a cartwheel from wingtip to wingtip, but that was an illusion, a memory trick, because the explosion came at the same instant, so that it was impossible to remember whether the plane blew up

185

before or after it began to bounce and the wing broke off and the nose buried itself in the water.

A sudden, silent burst of orange light, like a midday sun, surrounded by a ring of black smoke, widened and then burst into a pillar of soot. The sound of the explosion came afterward, like an out-of-synch old movie, traveling slower than the picture across the water. When it arrived, it came in waves — first a single, low-pitched 'crump' and then the boom-boom-boom, like a bass drum, pulsing ever more rapidly across the water until it all melted into a long, slow descrescendo.

It ended abruptly. One moment the plane was skipping across the lake, nearly airborne. The next instant there was nothing there. Just the awful silence that follows an unexpected, ear-shattering noise.

'Good Jesus,' whispered Bud.

I sat there, rigid, staring out at the placid lake. A minute later Marge and Polly came rushing out onto the porch, and then Tiny joined us. We stared at the surface of the water, and all we could see was the absence of Gib's airplane and the tranquil beauty of Raven Lake at dawn.

'What the hell was that?' said Tiny.

'Gib's airplane. She blew up,' said Bud. 'Just blew to hell up. Looked like she might've hit a snag.'

'There's a hundred feet of water out there in the middle,' said Tiny. 'How in hell's it gonna hit a snag?'

Bud shrugged. 'Must've hit something.'

'It looked to me as if it blew up first,' I said. 'It didn't look like it hit anything to me.'

'Anybody with him?' said Tiny.

'I don't know.'

I turned around. Marge and Polly had gone back inside.

Gib, I remembered, had been Polly's guy. At least one of them.

I continued to sit there while guests and guides came rushing up to the lodge, talking in excited voices.

'Hey, I heard an explosion.'

'Airplane blew up out on the lake.'

'Gib got killed.'

'Anybody else?'

'Sounded like a goddamn bomb.'

People ignored me. I ignored them. I sat there, smoking, sipping my coffee. I was an island of calm in a sea of chaos. But my mind was swirling with possibilities.

Possibility one, and the most likely, was that I had witnessed a tragic accident. Gib had hit a floating log or had maneuvered near a shoal and collided with the subsurface rock. Or his fuel system leaked and ignited inside the engine.

Possibility two, which would never have occurred to me had I not received a note from him shortly before the explosion, was that Gib had killed himself. His note, his reference to 'chickening out', had been a suicide message, then. For a man like Gib it would be the perfect way to do it – racing across the top of the water in the plane he loved.

What was missing from this was the motive, which I might have learned had he told me why he wanted me to go to Greenville with him.

The third possibility I liked least of all, but given all the events that had occurred at Raven Lake in the week that I had been there, I was forced to concede its feasibility. Gib had been murdered. Somebody had cut his fuel line, perhaps. I knew too little about engines to speculate on the particular method. Perhaps the intention had been for him to take off, then achieve altitude far above the vast Maine forest before his engine failed so that he would spin to earth far from anyplace where he would be seen or his body found for a long time.

Or maybe it had occurred exactly as planned, in plain sight and in the middle of the lake, where it would be witnessed and described as an accident and where all evidence would conveniently sink to the rocky bed of Raven Lake under a hundred feet of water.

A motive for murder, like one for suicide, Gib had chosen not to share with me.

While I sat there rocking, I saw two of the guides go down to the water, lift a canoe, flip it right side up, and slide it into the water. Then Lew Pike appeared, lugging an outboard motor. He climbed into the stern and crouched there, securing the motor to the transom. Then they shoved off.

They chugged out toward the middle of the lake. I watched them as they circled around slowly out there. The sputter of their four-horse Evinrude reminded me, by contrast, of the earlier throaty roar of the Cessna.

They stayed out there for nearly an hour. Then they came back. They tied up to the dock, climbed out, and trooped up to the lodge. They all nodded to me, and I said, 'Find anything?'

'Nothin',' said Pike. 'Not a goddamn thing.'

After a while, Marge came out with a fresh mug of coffee for me. Her face was red and stained from crying. She accepted my empty mug in exchange for the full one she handed me. Then she stood there for a moment, staring dolefully down at me. Without speaking, she turned and went back inside.

It took me a minute to interpret her look. Then I remembered. I had told her that Gib had asked me to fly out with him. I could have been on that plane with him. I could have been killed. That was Marge's thought.

And then it became my thought, and I had to press my elbows close against my ribs to control the shudder that suddenly shook my body. I sighed deeply a couple of times. It helped.

A little while later Tiny came out and sat beside me. 'Jesus Christ, anyway,' he said, sighing.

'Amen.'

He glanced sideways at me. 'Marge said you were going to go with Gib today. Good thing you changed your mind.'

'I didn't. Gib decided to go without me, that's all.'

Tiny rubbed his bushy beard with the open palm of his big hand. 'Like maybe he knew something was gonna happen to him, huh?'

I shrugged. 'I don't know. I haven't figured it out.'

'Most likely an accident.'

I nodded. 'Most likely.'

'Still . . .'

'I've been wondering myself.'

'Gib and the Rolando boys,' said Tiny.

'Did you call the sheriff?'

He nodded. 'Got ol' Thurl on the shortwave. He said he supposed he'd get here sometime today, but what in hell did I expect him to do, and I told him how the hell should I know. I was just tellin' him what had happened like I was suppose to, goddammit. So he said he'd call the FAA or the CAP or some damn thing or another. Asked me if it looked like an accident or what. I told him I had never seen a plane get itself blowed up before. Hell, I didn't see this one, neither. So just how in hell did he expect me to tell whether it got itself blowed up acciden-tal or on purpose. Thurl allowed I wasn't a shitload of help. I told him I wasn't specially tryin' to help, just tellin' him what happened, and anyway, you and Bud saw it. Expect Thurl might want to talk to you.'

'I've never seen a plane blow up before, either.'

'Poor li'l Polly's pretty shook up,' Tiny said softly. 'She and Gib were kinda sweet on each other, I think.'

'That right?'

Tiny nodded. 'He was a good fella, Gib. Dependable. Good company. Vern found him for us some years back. Gib did all our flyin' for us. Most camps, they depend on the services, take whatever they can get, but Raven Lake had its own pilot. Gib did other work now and then. But he was always ready for us when we needed him. And we did need him to make this place go. Gonna be hard to replace him. More and more, I keep thinkin' we oughta sell this place, let someone younger'n me worry about it.'

'That's a big step, Tiny.'

He sighed deeply. 'Yep. Big step. Don't know how Marge'd take it.'

He glanced sharply at me, and I wondered guiltily what Tiny suspected. Then I wondered why I felt guilty about it.

Tiny gazed out toward the lake. 'She ain't the easiest woman in the world to talk to sometimes. Least for me she ain't. She talks to you some, I know. That's good. I'm glad she got somebody more her own age. Guess I'm just too goddamn old. On different wavelengths, seems like. Her and my little girl. I dunno, maybe it's just women in general. You seem to have the knack, Brady. What's the secret?'

'Women?' I laughed. 'I know absolutely nothing about women. I'm the last person on earth you should ask.'

He shrugged. 'Don't suppose it's important, anyway.

'Cept now they're both so shook up, and I don't know what to say to them.'

'The closest I can come to wisdom on the subject,' I said, 'is, when you don't know exactly the right thing to say to a woman, it means you shouldn't say anything.' I shrugged. 'Not that it's done me a hell of a lot of good.'

Tiny grinned and lifted his bulk out of his rocking chair. 'Got me another problem here. Guests need to be flown out, new guests flown in. Gonna have to get me to Greenville and see if I can't scare up a new pilot. I dunno, Brady. Seems kind of . . . ' He waved his hand around as if he hoped to snatch the word he wanted from the air like a pesky mosquito.

'Disrespectful?'

He shrugged. 'Yeah. I guess. Me worrying about business and poor Gib blown all to hell and gone out there. Lew and a couple of the boys, maybe you saw them, they went out in a canoe. Couldn't find a damn thing. Sorta hopin' we might find Gib out there still alive. Nothing. Wind blowin' down the lake at a pretty good clip now. Anything that'd float must be down the foot of the lake by now.' Tiny put his hand on my shoulder. 'Glad you're here, Brady.'

'I am no help whatsoever.'

He squeezed quickly, smiled, and went inside.

Something Tiny had said had pricked my mind, and it took me a moment to recall what it was. Then I remembered. Marge had told Tiny that I was planning to fly out with Gib. If Tiny knew, others might have known, as well. Gib may have told somebody. Tiny may have passed along the information. Perhaps everybody had known, well before Gib taxied out onto the lake, that I was supposed to be going with him.

If that was so and if the explosion of Gib's Cessna had

been produced by sabotage, then there was one terrible conclusion I had to recognize: Gib's fate might have been intended for me, too.

Worse, it could have been intended for me, with Gib the innocent bystander.

The idea was like a smooth, opaque stone, and I turned it over and over in my mind, rubbing its soft, rounded contours, staring into its blurry surface, trying to determine its exact shape and dimensions. Maybe Gib had known who murdered Phil Rolando. Maybe he was flying out to report what he knew and wanted me along for moral support. Then he realized he might be endangering me, so he decided to go alone. If somebody blew him up, it was to keep him quiet. Whoever it was might assume Gib had shared his knowledge with me.

Now I was still alive. For all the murderer – if there was one – knew, I still had that knowledge. That thought did not soothe me.

A further thought. If Gib had been murdered, odds were that it was the same person who had murdered Rolando. And it couldn't have been Woody.

Then who? I tried to catalog the possibilities. Start with Tiny. If he ever found out that Phil Rolando had slept with his daughter, that might do it. For that matter, it would give him motive to kill Ken Rolando, too.

Marge. Same thing. Marge of the sweet, soft kiss. She could murder for Polly's sake. Maybe.

Gib was off the hook. Unless he had killed himself in his plane, the act of a conscience-stricken man who had murdered his girlfriend's lovers.

Or Polly herself, acting on some weird, adolescent, neurotic love-hate motive, some imagined or real slight. Jealousy, maybe.

I tried Bud Turner and Lew Pike and the other guides

and found no motive. But plenty of opportunity. Likewise the guests.

One thing I now believed: Woody's innocence was beyond question. Gib had been murdered, and that murder was linked to Rolando's.

Gib had been Polly's lover, just like the Rolando boys. There was a link. It brought me back to Marge and Tiny. And Polly herself.

I stood and stretched. I had been sitting and rocking for too long. All the blood had drained out of my head and had pooled in my backside. I was thinking foolish thoughts. Gib's death had probably been an accident. Happened all the time, small planes crashing in the bush. Gib himself had told me that when I had flown in with him. All the rest was nonsense.

I became aware of the growling in my empty stomach. I needed breakfast. Just as I put my hand on the door handle, it pushed open toward me. I stepped back.

Polly Wheeler came out. She looked somber but dry-eyed. Her face was pink, as if she had just scrubbed it. 'Brady,' she said, 'I hoped I'd find you here.'

'I'm here,' I said, smiling at her. 'How are you doing?'

She shrugged, as if that were not the important question. 'Look,' she said, 'I've really gotta talk to you.'

'Okay.'

'It's about Gib,' she said. 'Something he told me. Last night.'

Chapter Fourteen

'Now I know exactly what they mean by the kiss of death,' said Polly as we wandered away from the lodge. She scuffed her sneakers in the pine needles and kept her eyes averted from mine. 'I am the kiss of death. Literally.'

'You were with Gib last night?'

'I was, as you put it, with him. Yes. And now he's dead. Just like Phil. And Ken, too, I guess. What's the matter with me?'

I assumed she was being rhetorical, so I didn't tell her that I didn't believe she ought to feel guilty or that she was indulging in a classical *post hoc ergo propter hoc* fallacy. Just because one event follows another doesn't mean that the first caused the second.

Come to think of it, I wasn't sure that there was no connection.

Polly and I followed the winding pathway among the tall pines until we found ourselves down where the cabins were clustered, and as if we had planned it ahead of time, we ended up sitting on the front step of the cabin where first Ken and then Phil Rolando had stayed.

I lit a cigarette. As an afterthought, I held the Winston pack to Polly. She shook her head. 'You mentioned something Gib said to you,' I reminded her gently.

She nodded slowly. 'How well did you know him?'

I shrugged. 'Just from flying in the other day, really. Nice guy.'

'Yes. A very nice guy. Gib is – was – what I imagine my father used to be like when my mother met him. A

194

real man. Independent. Good at things. Quiet, strong. Know what I mean?'

She looked up at me. I nodded.

'He told me he was leaving today. That he might not be back for a while. He was saying good-bye, I realize that now. But that's not really the way it seemed. He had something important to do. Important for him. For his conscience.'

'Did he mention what it was?'

She smiled thinly. 'No, not exactly. Gib could be more indirect than anybody I've ever met. But I figured this much out from what he said. I can't remember his words or anything, but it had something to do with flying to Canada.'

'He was flying to Canada today?'

She motioned impatiently with her hand. 'No, he had been flying there. What he was going to do today was related in some way to those trips to Canada. What he had been doing there.' She looked up at me and shrugged.

'Something illegal.' I made it a statement, not a question.

She nodded. 'He didn't say so. Not in so many words. But, yes, I think so. He said you were going with him today, and he was going to explain it all to you in the plane. He said he needed a lawyer.'

'Did he mention anybody else, somebody who was involved in this Canada business?'

'No. He didn't mention anybody at all.'

'Nothing about Phil Rolando?'

'No.'

'Or Ken?'

She shook her head.

'Did they know each other?'

'Gib and Phil and Ken?' She shrugged. 'Not especially, as far as I know. I mean, just the way you knew Gib. He flew them in here. Gib flew everybody in here. People always felt they knew Gib. He was like that. But, no, I don't think . . .'

She touched her face with her fingertips and looked away from me. I said, 'Polly.'

'I know. You think Ken and Phil were up to something illegal. Like smuggling in dope or something. Working with Gib. I don't know. Maybe they were. But I don't remember ever seeing Gib with either Phil or Ken while they were here, and I don't think any of them ever mentioned the other one to me. But what's that worth, anyway?'

'I don't know.'

'Do you think that what happened to Gib – do you think it was . . . ?'

'Murder? Do you?'

'Yes.' She nodded several times, as if to reassure herself. 'And I'll tell you why. Because Gib was a very careful pilot, and he took good care of that airplane. He wouldn't have an accident. I used to tease him. I said he cared more about the damn plane than he did about me. Know what he'd say?'

I shrugged and smiled.

'He'd say, "Right." He was kidding, I suppose. I mean, I could usually tell. There was like a little glint in his eye. But he wouldn't smile, even when I'd tickle him and bite his ear. You could not make that man smile if he didn't want to. He really would never admit that he liked me more than that dumb old airplane. Dammit . . .'

I gave her my handkerchief, and she blew her nose in it. 'He knew all about stuff floating on the water that he might hit. He had the sharpest damn eyes you ever saw for seeing things on the water. And where he was out there this morning, there are no rocks or anything. He knew the lake. He didn't hit anything accidentally, I promise you.'

'I thought about engine trouble,' I said.

'All I can tell you is that he used to say that that engine was the only thing that kept him from crashing to the ground. If the engine died, he died. He said it wasn't love, it was survival. Can I tell you something?'

'Sure.'

Her eyes brimmed, but she looked intently at me. 'Gib was really afraid of flying. Isn't that dumb? I mean, that's how he made his living. It was his life. What he loved most was being up there, like he said, alone and free. He always said how good it was to know how you're going to die. He'd say that nothing ever bothered him, because he knew how he'd die, and it made things real simple. Take care of the plane and stay alive. So maybe it wasn't exactly fear but, like, respect for the danger of it and knowing that any time might be the time he was going to die. He told me that whenever he took off, he always wondered if it would be the last time. He was probably thinking that this morning.'

She smiled bravely and blinked back her tears. I patted her arm.

'You do think he was murdered, then,' I said.

'Don't you?'

'I don't know.'

'Somebody's murdering people around here.'

'You've got a point there.'

'Unless . . .'

'Unless what?'

She shook her head. 'It's dumb. But I was thinking. He

197

could have – you know, if he saw a big log or something in the water – I mean, he would see it, but . . . '

'You think he might have done it on purpose, you mean.'

She twitched her shoulders. 'Only because of how he seemed last night.'

'Guilty, you mean.'

She nodded.

'Was he the kind of man who'd kill himself?'

She made a flip-flopping motion with her hand. 'Really, no. At least I wouldn't have said so. He thought about dying more than most people, I think. Like every time he went up in the air, which usually was a couple of times a day. But it was more like fatalism. He was ready to die. But I don't think he wanted to. It's just that, last night, the way he seemed . . . '

'How late did you stay with him?'

'Oh, not late at all. Actually, we just took a walk. I got in early. I've been trying, ever since Phil, you know, my mother . . . '

I nodded. Then I gestured at the cabin at our backs. 'Have you cleaned up in there yet?'

She shook her head. 'Don't tell my mother. I just haven't had the courage.'

'So far as you know, it's just the way it was the night Phil Rolando was killed, then?'

'If I didn't clean it, nobody did. It's my responsibility.'

'Can we talk about the last time you saw him?'

'Phil?'

'Yes.'

'I told you everything.'

'Can we go over it again?'

She shrugged. 'I guess so. There's not much to tell. We made love. We had candles. He talked about getting the guy who killed his brother.' She looked at me and shrugged again. 'What do you want me to say?'

'I don't really know. About getting whoever killed Ken. What did he say about that?'

'Just that he was going to get him. That he and I'd get him and string him up.'

'Like Bat Masterson, you said.'

She smiled. 'Wyatt Earp, actually. It was so – it seemed childish. Silly. He deputized me. He was going to pin that phony badge on me, but I didn't have any clothes on, see –'

'What badge?'

She smiled quickly. 'He had this make-believe badge. I thought I told you.'

'I don't think so.'

'Well, it's dumb, anyway. He put it on my breast in its little leather holder, and –'

'What did it look like?'

'Jesus, Brady. What difference does it make? It was just a game. We were laughing about it.'

'Tell me about the badge, Polly.'

She sighed. 'It was in the drawer of the bedside table. He reached across me, opened the drawer, and took it out. And he put it on my breast, like I said, and he said, "I hereby deputize you an officer of the law." Like that. Then we laughed, and he put the badge back into the drawer.' She arched her eyebrows at me. 'You want to know what it looked like?'

'Please.'

She frowned. 'A star, I think. I mean, I didn't exactly examine it. But it was a star. Not a shield.'

'Did it have a circle around it?'

She nodded slowly. 'Yes. Yes, I think it did. A star with a circle around the outside of it.'

'And you assumed it was a toy.'

'Well, sure. It was all a joke, anyway.'

'I suppose it was,' I said. 'Can you remember anything else?'

'About the badge, you mean?'

'About anything Phil said that night.'

She stared off toward the lake, which glimmered through the trees. 'I know you're trying to help,' she said softly. 'And I know it was me who asked to talk to you. But I don't like thinking about it. I told you everything. About Phil and about Gib. I feel responsible. I really do. I know that's irrational. I can't help it. But I'll feel that way until I know what really happened to them. Can we – can we not discuss it anymore?'

I put my arm across her shoulders and hugged her. 'Sure,' I said. 'End of conversation. If you want to talk again, look me up. Okay?'

She nodded and smiled. Then she reached up and kissed my cheek. 'Sure,' she said. 'And thank you.' She stood up and pivoted to face me. She reached up with both hands to fluff her hair. It was pure seductiveness, the more so because I sensed that it was done without conscious calculation. She posed that way for a moment, hipshot, her breasts thrusting against the front of her blouse, her fingers in her thick hair. 'Well,' she said, 'are you coming?'

'Not just yet,' I answered. 'You go ahead. I'll be along in a minute.'

She smiled quickly. 'Okay.'

I watched her walk away. I waited until she was out of sight before I stood up and turned to try the door to the cabin. It was unlocked. I pushed it open.

The cabin that Phil Rolando and, before him, his brother, Ken, had stayed in was similar to all the others at Raven Lake – a single room, furnished spartanly. There were no electric lights, no indoor toilet facilities. This, as Tiny often reminded me, was the way the city sports seemed to prefer it.

Against the right wall as I entered twin beds jutted into the room. 'Beds,' Tiny had once told me, 'are important. You don't skimp on the beds. No matter how primitive the sports pretend they want it, by Jesus they better sleep well or they don't come back. Good box spring, good mattress. That and good food are more important than good fishin' for most folks.'

Against the back wall stood a ceiling-high wood cabinet with two doors. On the left was a stove and an untidy stack of firewood, with a few chairs arranged around the flat hide of a black bear that had seen better days.

One of the beds was neatly made. An open duffel bag lay on top of it. The other bed had been slept in. The covers were thrown back, as if someone had leaped out in a hurry.

I went over and sat on the unmade bed. Beside it lay a pair of moccasins and the rumpled top of a pair of striped pajamas. Rolando's, I assumed. He was barefoot and topless when I found him floating under the dock. On the table beside the bed was a windup alarm clock, a small pile of change, a wristwatch, a flashlight, and the stubs of a pair of candles set into simple glass holders. I picked up the watch. It was a Seiko. It looked expensive. I found no inscription on the back.

I opened the single drawer in the table. Aside from a small scattering of what looked like mouse turds, it was empty.

I moved around to examine the contents of Rolando's duffel bag. If the police had been in there ahead of me, they had treated Rolando's belongings with unusual respect. I would have expected to find his stuff strewn all over the room. Instead, everything was more or less neatly packed away – several changes of underwear, half a dozen pairs of socks balled up together, blue jeans, a sweater, a sweatshirt, two neatly folded flannel shirts, one dress shirt in cellophane.

In the bottom I found a leather toilet kit. I unzipped it. Razor, toothbrush, toothpaste, a can of Rise shaving cream, English Leather after-shave, dental floss, a wooden hairbrush, a bottle of nonprescription cold capsules, a bottle of generic aspirin, and a well-squeezed tube of Preparation H.

I emptied each pill bottle. To my inexpert eye and taste, each contained exactly what it purported to contain.

Having emptied the duffel bag, I held it upside down over the bed and shook it. No badge fell out. Nor did I find a wallet or a lethal-looking Colt Python .357 revolver.

For that matter, no plastic baggies full of cocaine fell out, either. Or big wads of high-denomination bills.

I got down on my hands and knees to look under the beds. Under the unused one I found a small leather suitcase. I slid it out and placed it on the bed. Its contents essentially duplicated those of the duffel bag. I looked at the labels of the undershirts and compared them to those that were in the duffel bag. Those in the suitcase were large. Those in the duffel bag were medium.

So the suitcase probably had belonged to Ken Rolando. Polly had said he was taller than his brother. But I found no identification in the suitcase.

It made no sense to me that these two men should travel with no identification whatsoever. No initials on the luggage. No inscription on the watch. No papers, no wallet. No badge.

Polly had been quite definite about Phil Rolando's badge.

It took only a modest application of intellect for me to deduce that Rolando had hidden some things. If I could find them, I might learn why he had hidden them.

I lit a cigarette and sat on the foot of the bed. I could slit open mattresses and pillows, pry up floorboards, and in general trash the place the way television spies do when they're searching for secret documents.

Or I could open the doors to the wooden cabinet. Which I did. And found it completely empty.

I tried to imagine what Rolando might have been thinking. Had he wanted to secrete his possessions against a careful, professional search, then I had no chance. But if he simply had taken the precaution to put things out of the sight of casually prying eyes, such as those of Marge or Polly when they came around to tidy up, that was a challenge I felt up to. And if he had hidden his badge after Polly left him the night he died, then it was likely his hiding place was somewhere in this room.

My eye fell on the wood stove. It was small, dull black, cast iron on stubby legs. I went over to it and unlatched the front-opening door. A cloud of wood ash burst out at me. I went back to the bedside table and got Rolando's flashlight, returned to the stove, and shone the light inside. The ash lay thick in the bottom. It probably hadn't been used since the cold spring evenings, more than a month ago.

I picked up a stick of kindling from the stack beside the stove and poked around in the ashes. I prodded something solid. Squinting my eyes against the billowing dust, I reached in and pulled out a plastic bag. It had been knotted. It was too dusty for me to see what it contained. I undid the knot.

Two wallets. Two thin black leather folders. Two weapons – one was indeed a Colt Python .357 revolver. The other one was a big-bored automatic.

The black folders fell open to reveal identical silver badges. Five-pointed stars surrounded by a circle.

Both Rolando men had been, as I suspected, U.S. marshals.

One wallet contained a variety of credit cards, licenses, and other documents belonging to someone named Kenneth Sadowski from Albany, New York. The second had ridden in the pocket of one Philip Genetti. Also of Albany.

Polly was right. The Rolando brothers hadn't been brothers.

Nor had they been Rolandos.

But they had both been federal marshals, and I knew enough to realize that the job of federal marshals is to chase down fugitives. It hadn't changed since the days of Wyatt Earp and Bat Masterson.

Of course, I reminded myself, U.S. marshals had every right in the world to take fishing vacations in the Maine wilderness.

But I doubted that they routinely traveled under assumed names when they went fishing. Nor did they normally disappear or get themselves murdered and scalped while on vacation.

I returned the items to the plastic bag, knotted it, shoved it back into the wood stove, and pushed the ashes over it with my hand. Then I closed the door to the stove.

I stepped back and brushed my hands on my pants. A thick film of wood ash lay on the pine-plank floor. I picked up the corner of the bearskin and dragged it back and forth over the dirty area. When I slid it back to its original spot, the floor looked reasonably clean.

I went over to the bed and repacked the duffel bag and

the suitcase. I slid the suitcase under the bed. I left the duffel bag where I found it.

I stepped back and stood by the door. To my eye, the room looked exactly the way it did when I had first entered. I went back outside, closed the door, and sat on the step.

What had I learned? A U.S. marshal named Kenneth Sadowski, but calling himself Rolando, had come to this place. On business, I had to assume. Within a couple days, he disappeared. Tiny Wheeler dutifully notified the man he assumed was the missing man's next of kin. A brother, he was supposed to believe, but in reality probably Sadowski's partner. This second man, whose real name was Philip Genetti, came to Raven Lake, claiming to be concerned about his missing brother. Shortly thereafter he was fatally wounded in the neck with an arrow, scalped, and dumped into Raven Lake.

I also knew that sometime earlier the law firm of Boggs and Kell had tendered an offer to Vern Wheeler to purchase the lodge and all the land that went with it. This, I concluded, just might not be an unrelated fact.

Then my friend, the Indian guide named Woodrow Wilson Pauley, was neatly framed for the murder of Phil Genetti, aka Phil Rolando, the U.S. marshal. And who should take Woody's case but the law firm of Boggs and Kell.

Then an airplane exploded in the middle of Raven Lake. The pilot was killed. Gib had seemed to both me and Polly Wheeler to be a man burdened with a guilty conscience. He wanted me to go with him on his airplane, to help him with what he called 'lawyer-type' problems. Polly thought he had been doing something illegal in Canada.

As far as I knew, nobody else possessed all of these seemingly separate pieces of information.

Except, probably, the murderer.

I got up and went back inside the cabin. I reassured myself that I had left behind no evidence that I had searched the place. I wasn't sure why I wanted to disguise it. But I did realize two things.

I didn't know who I could trust.

And I was in over my head.

Chapter Fifteen

Midafternoon that same day the police seaplane buzzed overhead and splashed down in the middle of Raven Lake. Tiny and I walked down to the dock to watch it taxi in.

A bulky state trooper climbed out first and made fast. Then Thurl Harris, the sheriff, slouched out, followed by Asa Danforth, the assistant district attorney. Danforth wore a dark green blazer identical to the ones they give the winners of the Masters' golf tournament every year. Otherwise, he didn't look much like Jack Nicklaus.

We shook hands all around and headed up to the lodge. 'So how's the fishin' been?' Harris said to Tiny as we walked.

'Good. Damn good, Thurl. You oughta try it sometime.'

'Keep meaning to. Like to get some of them salmon. I would.'

Tiny and Harris chatted in that vein until we entered the lodge. At that point Danforth took over. 'We want to talk to whoever saw the accident,' he said to Tiny.

'That'd be Brady, here, and Bud Turner. They were the only ones.'

'Who's Turner? I don't remember him.'

'Our cook. He and Brady were out on the porch when it happened. Far as I know, no one else saw it.'

Danforth glanced at his wristwatch and frowned. 'Well, let's go to it. We'll use your office.'

Tiny shrugged, and Thurl Harris followed me and Danforth into Tiny's little cubicle. We sat as we had the previous time, with Danforth behind the desk and Harris and me side by side in the straight-backed chairs.

'Tell me what you saw, then,' said Danforth without preliminaries.

'First,' I began, 'I had a conversation with Gib last night. I was going to fly out with him this morning, but – '

'Just tell me what you saw, please.'

'If I say something else, you will instruct the jury to disregard it, is that it?'

He waved his hand. 'You can say whatever you want, Mr Coyne. But first, describe the accident, will you?'

I did, as well as I could. When I finished, Danforth said, 'Would you say that the explosion came first?'

I shook my head. 'It all happened so fast . . . '

'Or did the plane flip and then explode?'

I hesitated and closed my eyes. All I saw was that orange flash and the cartwheeling airplane, caught in a still frame in my mind's eye. 'I think the explosion came first. But I'm not sure. It all seemed to happen instantaneously, do you understand?'

He nodded. 'It exploded first, then.'

I shook my head. 'I'm not sure.'

'It makes a difference, Mr Coyne.'

'I know.'

'If it exploded first, then he didn't hit a snag or something. We can surmise that the engine was the cause. If he flipped first, then we would assume he hit something and that was what caused the explosion.'

'Which,' I said, 'would make it an accident.'

'Either way it could have been an accident. I just want to know what kind of an accident.'

I sat forward. 'Listen. Don't forget that there has

already been one murder up here. Quite likely two. This could be the third.'

Danforth fussed with the knot in his tie. 'I know of one murder,' he said carefully. 'We believe we know who did it. He is nowhere near hear. And there is a missing person.'

I shook my head. 'This doesn't change your opinion on Woody, then?'

'Not at all.'

I took a deep breath and let it out loudly. 'I believe Gib intended to fly to Greenville this morning to talk with the sheriff.' I glanced at Thurl Harris, whose face revealed nothing. 'I believe Gib knew something about Rolando's murder. Maybe about the other Rolando's disappearance, too. He asked me to go with him. To give him legal counsel. I believe he was killed so that he couldn't talk.'

'You believe,' said Danforth.

I smiled. 'Yes, I do.'

'That's interesting, Mr Coyne. And with beliefs as firm as those, you must also have a belief as to who this murderer is. So let's have it. Who did all these killings? Who arranged for this airplane to explode this morning?'

'I have no idea whatsoever.'

'I don't suppose you'd care to speculate.'

'Right. I wouldn't.'

'Is there anything else you think I should know?'

I thought of telling him about the true identities of the men who called themselves Ken and Phil Rolando. I decided to hold on to that information until I could make some sense out of it. It was irresponsible, I knew. Irresponsible, as an officer of the court, not to be forthcoming with any information relative to a felony. Irresponsible to allow my feelings for Danforth to cloud my professional judgement.

The hell with it. I didn't like Asa Danforth. I didn't trust him. And I wanted to talk with Charlie McDevitt before I talked to anybody else. Charlie would give me hell. I deserved it. But Charlie could help me make sense of it all, and I'd be damned if this abrasive power seeker Danforth was going to climb into political office on my back.

'No,' I told him. 'That's it. That's all I know.'

Danforth spoke to Harris. 'Get the other one, the cook, in here, then.' He lifted his eyebrows at me. I took that as a dismissal. I stood up. 'Appreciate your help, Mr Coyne,' said Danforth, flashing me his well-practiced smile, as polished as the buttons on his Master's jacket.

I tried to think of a suitably sarcastic rejoinder. Finding none, I walked out without saying anything.

I took up my favorite Brumby rocker on the porch, and I was still there a half hour later when Harris and Danforth came out of the lodge, accompanied by Tiny. They stopped beside me, and Danforth looked down at me. 'Thanks again for your help,' he said.

In the intervening half hour, I still hadn't come up with a reply. I lifted my hand. 'Anytime,' I said.

Tiny walked with them down to the dock. I got up and went inside. Nobody was in the dining room. I found Bud Turner in the kitchen.

'What did you tell them?' I said.

Bud grinned crookedly. 'Same as you, I imagine. Gib's plane blew up.' He shrugged. 'They didn't seem that interested.'

'I had the same feeling.'

'They want it to be an accident,' said Bud.

'What do you think?'

'Oh, I s'pose it was an accident, all right. What else could it be?'

210

'You know.'

'Ah, hell, Mr Coyne. They got old Woody put away somewheres. He's the only one killing folks around here.' He lifted his eyebrows at me, and I nodded. I didn't agree with him, but neither did I care to discuss it.

'When will you be driving into Greenville next?' I asked him.

'Two, three days, I guess.'

I frowned.

'You need to get to town?'

'Yes, I do.'

He nodded. 'That's right. You were flyin' out with Gib this morning, weren't you?'

'Yeah. Listen, Bud –'

'Let me talk to Tiny. No reason I couldn't go down a couple days early. I've got a feelin' that until he finds somebody who can drive airplanes in here, we're gonna be doin' a lot of truckin'.'

'I'll speak to Tiny myself, if you want.'

'No problem,' said Bud. 'Check with me after dinner.'

I wandered out of the kitchen, wondering if there was anyone at Raven Lake who hadn't known that I was scheduled to be on the airplane with Gib.

It was easily arranged, and after breakfast the next morning Bud and I climbed into his pickup, bound for Greenville. Turner had just got the engine going when Fisher, the young man with the Adam's apple and the blushing bride, came running to the truck.

'Hey, wait,' he huffed.

Turner leaned out of the window. 'What's up, Mr Fisher?'

'Are you headed for town?'

'Ay-yuh.'

'Well, I – that is, Mrs Fisher – we'd like a ride.'

Turner shook his head. 'Sorry. No room. Tiny'll have another plane up for you in a day or so.'

Fisher's young face beseeched Bud Turner. 'You don't understand. My wife won't fly. She – she heard the explosion. And there was Mr Rolando who got murdered. She's in our cabin now crying her eyes out. She's petrified. I have to get her out of this place.'

'I can't take you in the truck.'

Fisher looked at me. 'Why not? He's going.'

'Mr Coyne works for Mr Wheeler.'

Fisher's shoulders slumped. 'Oh.'

'Sorry,' said Turner.

Fisher shrugged and turned back to the cabins. His first marital conundrum. I silently wished him luck. 'We could have put them in the back,' I said.

Bud Turner shook his head. 'Tiny wouldn't like it. Dangerous. Roads're too rough. No way to treat the sports.'

'They haven't been treated all that well, anyway,' I said.

Turner grinned and put the pickup into gear.

The crude logging road cut a dark, cool tunnel through the thick forest. The tangled blowdown along the roadside looked as if it must harbor fierce animals. It reminded me of a film I had once seen in which a pair of men traveled by canoe into the headwaters of the Amazon, seeking its source. These Maine woods seemed equally trackless and hostile, and I was grateful for Bud's nonchalant company and comforted by the presence of his rifle and shotgun in the rack behind us.

'One of these trips I gotta have this thing tuned up,' he observed, breaking a comfortable silence between us. He drove the twisting, rutted road easily, one elbow cocked out the window, drumming on the roof with his fingers to a tune that played in his head. 'Hear that?'

'Hear what?' I asked.

'Listen to the engine. There. Hear it? Keeps missin'.'

I focused on the sound of the truck's engine. 'I can't hear anything,' I said.

'Plugs all fouled up. Hate like hell to have her die out here. Long ways from triple-A tow trucks.' He grinned sideways at me.

I tried to listen more attentively. The closer I listened, the worse the engine began to sound to me. I could hear the pings and wheezes, coughs and burps. It sounded like an old man gasping for breath.

Or perhaps it was the power of Bud's suggestion. I couldn't tell.

He coasted to a stop. 'Gotta take a look,' he said to me. 'You just sit tight.'

He yanked up the emergency brake, opened the door, and climbed out, leaving the engine idling. Then he reached behind the seat and came out with a long-handled screwdriver. I stayed in the cab while he went around to the front and lifted up the hood. After a moment he called to me, 'Slide over, there, Mr Coyne, and give her a little gas.'

I did. Then he yelled, 'Okay. Ease off now.'

He played with it for a minute or two, making the engine race and then slow down. 'Turn her off now,' he told me. I obeyed.

He came back and reached in behind my seat. 'Gonna try somethin',' he said. He found a small wrench and returned to the front of the truck.

By the time we had been sitting still for five minutes or so, the blackflies and mosquitoes found me, and I was swatting and scratching and swearing under my breath when Bud stood to the side and said to me, 'Okay, Mr Coyne. Try and start her up.'

I turned the key and gave it a little gas. It chugged, sputtered, and died.

Bud frowned. 'You flooded it.'

'I'm sorry.'

He ducked under the hood, then reemerged. 'Try her again. Keep your foot off the accelerator.'

I did as instructed. The engine caught, and Bud revved it from under the hood. Then he slammed down the hood and came back. I slid over to the passenger side. He stowed his tools behind the driver's seat and climbed in. 'Sounds a little better, huh?'

I nodded doubtfully. 'I guess.'

But by the time we had traveled another mile or so, it became apparent that something was wrong under the hood. There was a rhythmic screeching sound, as if raw metal were scraping across raw metal. Bud gripped the steering wheel with both hands, and he drove hunched forward, a frown cutting deep creases into his long face.

'Well, shit, anyhow,' he finally muttered. He stopped the truck and got out again. He left the engine running. The screeching sound subsided into a faint whisper. But it was still there.

Bud took the screwdriver around to the front and once again lifted up the hood. I remained in the truck, feeling useless.

A minute later he came around to my side of the truck. 'Want to come out here and give me a hand?' he said.

'Sure.'

I climbed out and followed him to the front. 'Let's try something else,' he said. He leaned in and pointed into the innards of the engine. 'Look here. See this little screw?' I bent in beside him. He handed the screwdriver to me. 'Hold this here. When I tell you, rotate it a quarter turn clockwise. Okay?'

I nodded. I fit the business end of the screwdriver into the slot. He went around to the cab of the truck. 'Okay, now,' he called. 'Give her a little slow twist.'

I did, and the engine raced. The screeching noise was deafening.

'Okay. Back her off, now,' he yelled over the din.

He came back and stood at my shoulder. 'Keep her there, now, Mr Coyne. Gonna do one more thing.'

I was leaning awkwardly into the truck. The heat from the struggling engine caused sweat to burst from the pores in my forehead and trickle into my eyes. I didn't dare try to wipe my face, because I didn't want the screwdriver to slip.

I believe that in addition to the standard five senses, there is a sixth. Perhaps it's sensitivity to another person's electro-magnetic output. Maybe it's a subconscious sensitivity to the odor of someone's rush of adrenaline, or possibly we can detect subtle changes in air pressure as another moves into our personal space.

Maybe it really is extrasensory perception.

Whatever it is, I felt it suddenly as I crouched under the hood of Bud Turner's truck, and it caused me to duck away reflexively, just as a big Stilson wrench whistled past my ear and smashed against the front of the truck. I stumbled to the ground and rolled awkwardly away.

'Damn!' muttered Turner and he came at me, the heavy tool raised over his head.

I scrambled to my feet as he swiped at me again. I staggered backward and fell against the mound of boulders and earth at the edge of the road. The wrench was heavy enough to cause Turner to lose his balance momentarily as he followed through with his swing, and it gave me enough time to scramble over the boulders and duck into the thick undergrowth beside the road.

The land sloped acutely away from the road, a precipitous drop of a hundred yards or more. It was grown thick with scrub pine and birch saplings and brier, all interlaced with the uprooted old trees and big rocks that a bulldozer had shoved down the slope when it cut the logging road into the side of the hill.

I crawled, slid, and stumbled down the slope. Get away from Bud Turner. Get deep into the jungly forest. I could think only of escape. I barely felt the briers and the broken stubs of old trees catch and rip my clothes, scratch and gouge my face and arms. Saplings slapped my flesh. Sweat burned my eyes. I fought blindly, panicked, through the thicket until I reached a narrow, fast-moving stream at the foot of the incline.

'I'm comin', Mr Coyne,' Turner yelled. 'Might's well just give her up, because I'm comin'.'

I tried to run along the edge of the stream. My foot slipped on a mossy rock, and my bad knee cracked against it. 'Oh, damn!' I managed to shout before the pain came. My stomach convulsed. I lay there, gripping my knee. Blood seeped through my torn pant leg. I crept to the edge of the stream and eased my leg into it. The chill of the frigid water created a different pain, one I could bear, and when I pulled my leg out, it had grown numb.

I started to stand when a noise behind me caused me to crouch down, motionless. 'No use, Mr Coyne,' came Turner's voice. The report of his rifle and the thud of the .30 caliber slug spinning into the trunk of the fallen pine beside my head came at the same instant.

There was a thick maze of fallen trees in front of me. First on hands and knees and then flat on my belly, I scrambled under it. I heard Turner crashing through the brush behind me. Once I heard him curse, and I assumed he had fallen down.

I emerged on the other side of the blowdown. To my left ran the stream, burbling gaily through the forest. On the far side of the stream the trees grew tall, and the undergrowth, deprived of sunlight by the high canopy, was sparse. To my right the slope rose sharply back to the road through the tumbledown that had been shoved there by the bulldozers years before. I grabbed a sapling and hauled myself to a standing position. My knee throbbed. Gingerly I put my full weight on it. It hurt like hell. But nothing was broken. It would, if I insisted, support me.

Turner's rifle cracked again, over my head I heard the thwang of a deflected bullet. I figured he was guessing at my position, trying to panic me into showing myself. If he had seen me, I didn't think he would miss me that badly.

I inched my way carefully up the sharp incline, keeping low and quiet, hoping Turner would misguess my route. I wanted to get back to the road ahead of him.

Turner made no effort to hide his position. As a result, he moved faster than I could. I had fifty yards on him, I judged. If he stuck to the streambed rather than following me up hill, I'd be all right.

'You're a dead man, Mr Coyne,' he yelled. He fired again. By the sound of the rifle's report, I could tell that he hadn't aimed close to my direction.

Silence and stealth, I told myself. I pulled myself up the hill, slithering over fallen tree trunks, crawling on my stomach through the brush, moving as quickly as I could without making any noise. I came to the ridge where earth and big boulders had been piled. On the other side of the ridge lay the road.

To crawl over that mound to the roadside, I would have

to expose myself momentarily. A chance that had to be taken. I took a deep breath. I had to hope that Turner wouldn't be able to see me from where he was, or if he did see me, that he wouldn't be able to get a clear shot at me.

The pile of earth was taller than I. It was covered with pine needles, fallen brush, and forest debris, but underneath the earth was loose and soft. It was too steep to walk up. I had to climb, hands and knees, finding grips with toes and fingers.

I had nearly reached the top when my foot slipped. A large rock broke loose and crashed down the hill behind me.

This time he had me in his sights. The bullet screamed off a rock next to my left shoulder. Rock splinters bit into the side of my head. I heard Turner quickly lever another round into the magazine of his deer rifle. He was close behind me. I could hear him wheezing and cursing under his breath.

I heaved myself over the ridge and skidded onto the roadway. Down the road was Bud Turner's truck, its hood standing open like the gaping maw of a hungry animal. It was less than a hundred yards away. I stood up. My injured knee buckled for a moment. I slammed it with my fist. Then I began to hobble toward the truck, holding my knee with my hand as I went. Once I fell. I scraped my face on the road. I managed to stand. The truck was only a few yards from me.

Another shot and the slug careened off the hard-packed dirt beside my foot. I lurched for the truck and pulled myself into the cab through the open door on the driver's side. I glanced back. Turner was sliding down the mound of earth into the roadway, waving his rifle as he struggled with his balance.

I grabbed the pump-action shotgun from the rack and slid across the seat and out the door on the passenger side. Turner had told me he kept both guns loaded. I pumped a shell into the magazine and thumbed off the safety. I crouched beside the right front fender and rested the shotgun on the edge of the truck.

Turner was coming up the road, his rifle held in front of him at port arms. When he was thirty-five or forty yards away, he stopped and dropped into a kneeling position. He aimed right at me. 'Put her down, Mr Coyne. Put her down or you're dead.'

I was dead either way. I knew that. My only choice was whether Turner would shoot me or whether I should allow him to devise a more creative means for my death. The image of the puckered tricornered wound on Phil Rolando's neck and the strip of flesh sliced from his scalp intruded into my thoughts.

Turner would have trouble explaining what happened to me should I be found with a rifle slug in my chest. He might, however, be able to devise a plausible truck accident, from which he managed to escape miraculously just before the gas tank went, should I allow him to take me.

'You're going t have to shoot me,' I yelled. I kept the shotgun pointed at him.

'Suit yourself, then,' he said. He tucked the rifle against his cheek. We were close enough that I could see him squint as he aimed. The open bore of the rifle stared into my eyes.

The blood was pumping so loudly in my head that I scarcely felt the recoil or heard the report of the twelve-gauge and the simultaneous crack of Turner's .30-.30. But I heard the hot spinning slug buzz past my ear. And I saw Bud Turner leap into the air and fall on to his back.

And then I heard him moan.

I moved cautiously out from behind the truck, shotgun at ready. But I saw instantly that Bud Turner was no threat. He lay curled fetally on the road, covering his face with both hands. The rifle lay well beyond his reach.

I stood beside him. He was whimpering like a baby. Blood stained his shirt and his hands. 'I can't see,' he whined. 'You blinded me. You shot out my eyes. Good Jesus, help me.'

I put the shotgun down and knelt beside him. 'Sit up,' I said. 'Let me see.'

I helped him into a sitting position. Then I pried his hands away from his face. It ooozed blood. Blood seeped in little rivulets down his forehead and off his chin. It gathered in pools in his eye sockets. I took off my shirt and dabbed at Bud Turner's face. He jerked away. 'Oh, God. That hurts.'

'Shut up and sit still,' I said. 'Let me see what the damage is.'

The blood had not yet begun to coagulate, so I was able to wipe it clean. His face had been pocked with about two dozen number-nine pellets of bird shot. The pellets were so small and the distance from which they had been shot so extreme that most of them were visible, embedded just under the skin. Around each of them a drop of blood oozed up as quickly as I could wipe it away.

But his eyes had been spared, I figured, because of the way he had been hunched behind his rifle when I fired.

'You're all right,' I said to him. I stood and picked up the shotgun. Then I grabbed his rifle and flung it into the woods. I pumped another round into the shotgun's magazine. I tossed my shirt to Turner. 'Wipe off your face and get up,' I said.

'It hurts, man,' he moaned. I jabbed him with the gun. 'Okay, okay,' he said. 'I'm gittin'.'

He wiped his face again. This time the blood welled up from each tiny wound slowly and coagulated there. He looked as if he had a bad case of chicken pox. He put his hands to his face and touched it carefully here and there with his fingertips. 'I gotta see a doctor,' he said.

'It's a long walk to Greenville,' I said, 'with a truck that won't go.'

'I can fix the truck,' he mumbled. He approached the truck slowly, his legs wide apart. He walked like an old man who had messed his pants. He kept putting his fingers to his face. When he got to the truck, he bent under the hood. I held the shotgun on him. Then he straightened up. 'It's okay now. It'll go fine.'

'What was it?'

'I wedged a stick in there so's it'd rub against the fan belt. That's all.'

'To give us an excuse to stop.'

He nodded.

'Okay,' I said. 'Climb in. You drive. While you drive, you can talk.'

'I got nuthin' to talk about.'

He got behind the wheel. I went around and slid into the seat beside him. I kept the shotgun across my lap. My finger was curled on the trigger. The bore pointed at Turner's stomach. 'I wouldn't make a sharp turn or hit a bump too hard,' I said conversationally. 'I got the safety off, here.'

He glanced down at the shotgun. 'Jesus, you don't have to point that thing at me, Mr Coyne.'

I shrugged. 'You're a dangerous man, Bud. A killer. I've got to be careful. Nobody would blame me if you happened to die.'

'I ain't no killer.'

'You've done some poaching.'

'That ain't killin'.'

'You killed a cow moose the other day.'

His eyes darted sideways at me. 'Mebbe I did. So what?'

'You dressed her out and hung her at the burial ground. You wanted to make it look like Woody did it. You used his crossbow. Then you sent Phil Rolando there. You planned to kill him up there, didn't you?'

'I don't know what you're talkin' about.'

'But I came along,' I said. 'Messed up your plan. So you had to wait till that night. Which turned out pretty well for you. You framed Woody, anyway. And Thurl Harris bought it.'

'You can talk all you want, Mr Coyne. But I ain't gonna.'

'I was hoping we might have a conversation while we drove to town.'

'I got nuthin' to say to you.'

'Okay,' I said. 'Have it your way. Take the whole rap if you want. We'll pretend you did it all by yourself, if you want. I expect Asa Danforth won't give a shit one way or another.'

'What are you talkin' about?'

'The two Rolando men. And Gib, of course. Did you wedge a stick into the engine of Gib's plane, too?'

He didn't answer. He started up the engine and put the truck into gear. 'What makes you think I had somethin' to do with all that?' he said.

'I know what you did,' I lied. I didn't know. But it was a reasonable guess. 'You got Ken Rolando the same way you tried to get me. You dumped his body out here in the woods somewhere. It will be to your advantage at some point to tell the sheriff where the body is. And, of course, it was you who killed Phil Rolando. Plunked him with Woody's crossbow. Then scalped him and dumped him into the lake. I suppose you didn't have time to hide his body, the way you did Ken's. And I know why you did it.' The latter was also a lie. I hadn't the foggiest idea why the murders were committed.

I glanced at him. He was frowning.

'Did you know they were United States marshals?'

His head jerked around. 'They what?'

'This is big-time stuff, Bud. The two Rolando men were U.S. marshals. Heavy business. You want to face it alone?'

'You're just guessin',' he said dubiously.

'Gib knew all about it.'

'Gib knew?'

'What do you think he was going to do today? Why do you think I was going with him? Don't you think he explained it all to me? Come on, Bud. Why else would you try for me if you didn't know that Gib had spilled it to me. Hey. You're in way over your head. You're not the only bad guy here. There's somebody else, and you know damn well he's not going to walk in and confess to get you off the hook.'

He didn't speak for a long time. He drove slowly, glancing occasionally at the shotgun that I had trained on his liver. Finally he said, 'What chance have I got, anyway?'

'I don't know if they still execute people in Maine or not,' I said. 'Seems to me they've got an electric chair. A lot of states are moving over to lethal injections, though. Reasonably painless, they say. Out in Utah they give you your choice. Firing squad, if you want. They hardly ever hang people anymore. I dunno. Maybe they do in Maine.'

'I mean if I tell you all of it,' said Turner.

I lit a cigarette and squinted at him out of the corners of my eyes. 'I'm a lawyer. I can advise you.'

He touched the little scabs on his face with his fingers. Then he nodded. 'Okay, okay, then. I'll tell you. Listen. I was just followin' orders. You've gotta understand that. Just doin' what I was told. The hired man, see?'

'I know, Bud.' I sighed. 'It wasn't your fault.'

Chapter Sixteen

A week later I was back at my desk, gingerly flexing my right leg and wondering if it would hold up for an afternoon of wading a trout river. The abrasion along the length of my shin had scabbed over. Julie, in fact, had insisted on examining it when I limped into the office. Her verdict: 'It has scabbed over rather nicely, hasn't it?'

I had never before thought of scabs as being nice.

The bruise on my knee had undergone a series of transformations. Now it was a dull, sickly yellow, barely tinged pale green along the edges. Julie had proclaimed it ugly.

There was a gentle tap at my door. 'Come on in,' I called.

Julie entered, bearing iced coffee.

'You must be angling for the afternoon off,' I said.

'I am just ministering to the lame and the halt. I like to care for the infirm and the elderly. I think I have a calling.' She placed the glass on my desk beside me. 'Speaking of angling,' she said, 'I bet you're going fishing this afternoon.'

'Thinking of it,' I admitted.

'Then, thanks, I will take the afternoon myself. Before we depart, I want to remind you to return Mr Smith's call. Also that you have a round-trip airplane reservation to Nantucket tomorrow.'

I sipped the iced coffee. I am the only person I know who prefers it black. Julie makes it just right, pouring freshly brewed hot coffee over a glass of ice cubes. 'I remembered both of those things,' I said primly. 'I wrote myself a note.'

'And you've got Mr McDevitt on Friday.'

'Right.'

'And I really think you should see a doctor. That's the same knee you had operated on.'

'Entirely different injury, dear heart,' I said.

'You looked so distinguished on your cane. Don't you need a cane now?'

'I do not need a cane. I'm tough.'

She raised her hands in a gesture of surrender and stood up. 'Well, then. Excuse me for caring. I'm leaving.'

I blew her a kiss, and she grinned at me over her shoulder.

After Julie left, I called Seelye Smith in Portland, Maine. Kirk answered. When I told him who it was, he put me right through.

'Mr Coyne. Thanks for calling back. Had a spot of trouble up at Raven Lake, I hear.'

'Word gets around.'

'Airplanes exploding, United States marshals getting themselves killed. I understand they found the one who was missing.'

'They found his body, yes, what there was of it. Kenneth Sadowski. The scavengers had gotten to it. Crows, coyotes, whatnot. Bud Turner told them where to look. They say he died from massive trauma to the skull.'

'Ay-yuh,' drawled Smith. 'Had his head smashed in. And they're holding the cook, Turner. And he's the one who killed the other marshal . . . '

'Right. Genetti. Philip Genetti.'

'Which particular homocide,' said Smith, 'they had been holding the Indian for.'

'Woody. Yes. And Turner sabotaged Bailey Gibbons's

airplane, too. He knew that Gib was planning to spill his guts to the DA. He thought I was going to be on that plane. His idea was to blow up the both of us. It would have finished the job of cleaning things up. I was lucky that Gib took off without me. So Turner made a try for me with a Stilson wrench out there in the woods. I got lucky. It was Turner, all right. Bud Turner did it all.'

I heard Smith chuckle. 'But Turner's not the real villain here, now is he?'

'No,' I said. 'It doesn't look that way. It'll all come out in due time.'

'Meaning you can't talk about it right now. Fair enough. I only called because I have figured out who tendered the offer to buy the Raven Lake Lodge. It's probably academic now.'

'No, not really. Who was it?'

'Last time we talked, I told you that it was some out-of-state party using the Indian law firm.'

'Boggs and Kell. Same firm that was going to defend Woody. What was the connection?'

'They're the biggest Indian firm in the area. They defended Woody Pauley because he asked them to and because it was the kind of case they liked. That's the only connection.'

'Oh,' I said. 'So do you know who the out-of-state party is?'

'Yes. I know who the out-of-state party is.'

'And?'

'It's interesting.'

'I'll bet,' I said. 'Come on, Mr Smith.'

'Stanley P. Chalmers.'

I hesitated. 'Stanley P. Chalmers,' I repeated. 'No kidding,' I said. I sighed. 'This is a disappointment, Mr Smith.'

'Never heard of Stanley P. Chalmers, eh?'

'No. Never.'

'If I told you he was an assistant regional director for the FBI, would it mean anything to you?'

'FBI, huh?' I said. 'He wasn't interested in his own little vacation retreat or a source of retirement income, I gather.'

'No, indeed. This was official Bureau business. And that, Mr Coyne, is all I know. It cost me a few points to find out that much.'

'I'll buy you dinner next time I'm in Portland,' I said.

'Chalmers's offer, by the way, has been withdrawn.'

'Mmm, figures.'

'I suppose this all makes sense to you, Mr Coyne.'

'It's beginning to. I should know more in a few days.'

Seelye Smith and I exchanged promises to get together again, and I sat back and swiveled around to stare out my office window. Below me, Copley Square teemed with shoppers and sun worshipers on their lunch hours. The street vendors were there – Franz, the guy with the hot-dog cart, Jennifer, the old black lady who sold hot pretzels, Max on the corner with his magazines, the Puerto Rican lady with her bunches of carnations. A couple of college-age boys were peddling silk-screened T-shirts. Secretaries and young executives lay sprawled on the concrete walls and benches with their brown bags containing yogurt and cottage cheese and celery sticks. And around the edges rose the architecture that momentarily marked the passage of Boston's centuries – the Old South Church and, diagonally across, dour old Trinity. The Public Library, part new and part old. The old Copley Plaza and the new Westin Hotels. The mirror-faced Hancock building. Bookshops and drugstores. Restaurants – Chinese, Italian, Greek, and fast. Shoe stores and fur merchants.

I was a helluva long way from Raven Lake. There hadn't been a loon spotted in Copley Square for ages.

Meeting with Vern Wheeler proved to be a bit more complicated than usual. Instead of a leisurely stroll down Boylston Street to the Public Garden, I had to take a taxi over to Logan Airport, board the little commuter plane for a rocky half hour's flight to Nantucket Island, and then catch a cab to Vern's imitation Frank Lloyd Wright summer retreat across the road from Cisco Beach.

I found him sprawled on a chaise longue on the back deck in sunlight that dappled through the lattice roof grown over with flowering vines. He wore red bathing trunks and reflector sunglasses. He held a sheaf of legal-sized documents against his chest.

I cleared my throat, and he groaned, twitched, and pushed his sunglasses to the top of his head. 'Why, Brady? What're you doing here? Nice surprise. I must've dozed off. Did Susan let you in?'

'I just walked around back, Vern. Sorry to barge in on you.'

'You should've called from the airport. I would've sent Susan down for you.'

I waved my hand and sat down on a redwood lawn chair. 'No problem.'

'How was the flight?'

'Bumpy as usual.'

He touched the empty tumbler on the table beside him. 'Something?'

'Gin and tonic would be good.'

'Susan!' he called. 'Damn woman. Watching those damnable television stories again. Susan!'

In a moment Susan appeared. She wore the bottom to a flowered bikini bathing suit and a sloppy white T-shirt.

I guessed her age at twenty. She had molasses-colored hair, cut short, and a mahogany tan all over. 'Sir?' she said. I detected the soft drawl of a mountain girl. West Virginia. Tennessee, maybe.

'This is Mr Coyne, dear,' said Vern. 'He'll be our guest for a few days.'

'Just this afternoon,' I said quickly. 'I'm booked on the five-thirty back to Boston.'

'I'm disappointed,' said Vern.

Susan dipped her head and bent her knees quickly in a tiny curtsy, which barely managed to fall short of a mockery. I thought I saw the crinkle of an ironic grin in her eyes. 'Mr Coyne, sir,' she murmured.

'Hi,' I said.

'Couple gin and tonics, please,' said Vern. 'Make one for yourself, if you like.'

'Very well,' she said. She pivoted and took her time leaving.

I turned to look at Vern. He was grinning at me. 'Wellesley girl,' he said. 'Going for her doctorate in bio-chemistry at MIT next year. Keeping house for me down here in the summer. An attractive piece of furniture, wouldn't you say?'

'I wouldn't say, no. She is a beautiful girl.'

Vern cocked his head and then grinned. 'You have an evil mind, friend. Her father is a business acquaintance of mine. I allow her to have parties here when I'm back in Boston, and she has use of the Audi. In return, I know the place is being looked after. And, of course, I have the pleasure of her company when I'm here.'

'Nice agreement.'

'It works well, yes,' said Vern. He hitched himself into a sitting position. 'I must ask the obvious question,' he said. 'Why are you here?'

'I want to hear about Raven Lake from your lips. I want you to tell me that you knew nothing about what was going on up there.'

He smiled. 'You are a man of honor, after all, aren't you, Brady?'

I shrugged. 'Just tell me the truth, Vern.'

'I should keep no secrets from my attorney. Quite so.'

Susan appeared with a drink in each hand. Vern and I accepted them. 'Mind if I run to town?' she said to him. 'Need to pick up some groceries.'

'You'll be back in time to drive Mr Coyne to the airport?'

'Of course.'

When she left, Vern turned to me. 'I knew,' he said simply.

'Why? I need to understand.'

He shrugged. 'You couldn't understand.' Vern tilted his head back and stared up through the vine-covered latticework. Then he leveled his gaze on me. 'My good friend,' he said, 'you are still my attorney.'

I nodded.

'Then,' he said, 'I will not lie to you. I knew who Bud Turner was. Bailey Gibbons, too. I knew what they did and why. I was forced to hire them. Of that I am guilty.'

I put my drink down. 'I hoped,' I said, 'that you would tell me that you knew nothing of it. That you were as surprised and as shocked as I that the place you loved – the people you loved – were being used this way. Vern, I wanted you to look me in the eye and say, "Brady, as God is my judge, I knew nothing of this."'

Vern shook his head. 'I can't say that.'

I stood up. 'I'm going to take a walk down to the beach. See if the surf casters are catching any. I'll be back in time for Susan to drive me to the airport.'

Vern stood and put his hand on my arm. 'I wish you'd try to understand.'

'I doubt I ever could.' I left him standing there. In his baggy red bathing trunks and his city white skin, he looked very old.

Charlie McDevitt and I took a cab from his office at Government Center to Fish Pier off Northern Avenue, where Jimmy's Harborside restaurant is located. The maître d' greeted Charlie, asked after his wife, and led us across the broad dining room to a small table against a window.

Charlie is a master at what he calls 'power dining'. He knows all the tricks. He cultivates relationships with hostesses, waitresses, owners, and maîtres d'hôtel. It didn't surprise me that they had the best table in the place waiting for us. I knew that somewhere along the line Charlie had slipped the man a ten-spot. I looked for it. But I still didn't see it happen.

I ordered an old-fashioned, and Charlie settled for a bottle of Heineken.

'Okay,' I said, lighting a cigarette. 'I think I've got most of it figured out now. Those guys on the tape – that Uncle Fish and Ceci – they're – what? – do you still call them the Mafia? La Cosa Nostra?'

Charlie grinned. 'Close enough.'

'Whatever. So Ceci was a professional hit man. Killed people on orders from people like Collucci. When things got hot for him, he called Uncle Fish. He wanted salvation, he said. Meaning he wanted a way out of the country. Fifty angels. What, fifty thousand dollars? Anyway, Collucci was in the business of arranging for bad guys to escape. Have I got it?'

'You're doing good. Keep going.'

'Okay. The way out was Raven Lake. Collucci would sneak people like Ceci Malagudi into Raven Lake, and when the coast was clear, it was a short hop in Bailey Gibbons's Cessna over the Canadian border to some other remote lake, where forged papers, passports, whatever, and a bundle of foreign currency would be waiting. From there to Brazil or Sicily or someplace.'

'Right,' said Charlie. 'It was a regular pipeline. Collucci had a nice little business going for him. Sort of an underworld travel agency. Over the past several years, a number of major league fugitives have slipped out through the same route. For a price, of course. Ceci Malagudi was the most recent one.'

'If I've got the timing of it right,' I said, 'I met him. He called himself Frank Schatz. I should've suspected something. The guy didn't know squat about fishing. He was at Raven Lake when I arrived. He got there practically the day after the first marshal, Kenneth Sadowski, disappeared. That was Turner's work. Keeping the coast clear. And Malagudi, or Schatz, or whatever his name was, left the day before the next marshal, Philip Genetti, arrived. I didn't think anything of it at the time.'

'No reason you should,' said Charlie. Our drinks arrived. The waitress told Charlie it was nice to see him again. He asked after her kids and told her we'd wait for a while before ordering.

'And the guy who made the whole thing work,' I continued when she left, 'was Vern Wheeler.'

'He let it work,' said Charlie. 'A silent partner. Collucci was the one who arranged it all.'

'He forced Vern to hire Bud Turner and Bailey Gibbons.'

'Right,' said Charlie. 'Turner was one of his killers. Turner wasn't his real name, of course. Something ending

in a vowel. Happened to have a flair for haute cuisine. S●
Collucci told Vern to hire Turner on as cook, where h●
could keep an eye on things.'

'Kill people if necessary.'

'Sure.'

'And Vern went along.'

'He probably had no choice.'

'And Gib?'

'Bailey Gibbons,' said Charlie, 'was his real name●
Maine boy, matter of fact. He'd done some small-tim●
drug smuggling out of Mexico, flying small planes ove●
the border under radar. Finally landed in a jail dow●
there, which is like a death sentence. Collucci manage●
to get him out, and Vern had to hire him, too.'

'And nobody up there suspected a thing. Vern arrange●
the bookings for people like Frank Schatz – excuse me●
Ceci Malagudi. Tiny went along. Had no idea tha●
anything was out of whack.'

'Well, of course, the FBI suspected,' said Charlie
'Their method of investigation was to pretend to want t●
buy the place. A way to cover their investigation an●
maybe see who might jump in which direction. Lik●
picking up a bag and shaking it vigorously to see wha●
might fall out. Typical Bureau operation. Oblique. Com●
plex. Secretive. Self-serving. The marshals, naturally
knew nothing of what the Bureau was up to. And vic●
versa. Competition, not cooperation. The operative stan●
dard for just about all government agencies. The mar●
shals, typical of them, were more direct. They went righ●
the hell up there. They'd been a couple of steps behind ●
previous fugitive, who was also connected to Uncle Fis●
Collucci, and they figured Ceci Malagudi just might b●
headed for Raven Lake. They were right, of course. The●

didn't expect Collucci to be one jump ahead of them, so they weren't ready for Bud Turner.'

'So Turner murdered both the marshals. On Collucci's orders.'

'So it seems.'

'And he booby-trapped Gib's plane when he thought Gib was going to spill the beans,' I mused aloud. 'For all I know, he thought I was going to be on that plane, too.'

'For all you know,' said Charlie, 'Collucci told Turner to get rid of you. Hell, Brady. For all you know, your client, Vern Wheeler, knew that Turner was gonna try to kill you. If not on the plane, then later, on the way to Greenville in the truck.'

I sipped my old-fashioned. 'I'd prefer to believe that Vern didn't know any of those details,' I said.

Charlie shrugged. 'Believe whatever's comfortable for you.'

After a moment of silence I said, 'What's going to happen to Vern?'

'Dunno. Maybe nothing. Hard to prove the connection. Vern's well placed. Lots of money.'

I nodded and let it go at that.

Charlie lifted his hand about an inch off the table, and our waitress appeared almost instantly at our table.

'You gonna have the lobster, too?' he said to me.

'And pass up the finnan haddie? Not a chance.'

I lit a cigarette after the waitress left. 'There are a couple things I still don't understand. For example, how did Bud Turner know that those marshals, who both called themselves Rolando – how did he know what they were?'

'Uncle Fish,' said Charlie. 'Uncle Fish Collucci told him. How did he know? Listen. There's a girl runs a Xerox machine in a government office in Washington. Nice kid. Husband, two little boys. When she was younger, she made a mistake. She listened to a guy who told her he was gonna make her a movie star. So this girl was in a movie.'

'Stag film,' I said.

Charlie nodded. 'You can probably figure out the rest.'

'Collucci got ahold of the film, let the girl know that he might be able to use some of the junk from the office wastebaskets. Probably even paid her for it. Little carrot, little stick.'

'You got it,' said Charlie. 'Collucci learned a lot that way.'

'The big question,' I said. 'What did Collucci have on Vern Wheeler that he would go along with all this?'

Charlie shrugged. 'I don't know. But you can bet the Bureau will find out. They love that kind of shit. It's what they're best at, figuring out stuff like that. Paperwork. Computers. Backtracking. All that complicated, tedious stuff. Going over old tax records, contracts, deeds, bank records, anything they can lay their hands on, cross-checking here, refiguring sums there. Those guys can do that, day after day, week after week, happy as pigs in mud. They haven't found it yet. But they will. Because you can bet your rosy red fanny that it's there.'

I shook my head. 'I can't believe it. A man like Vern Wheeler.'

Charlie sipped thoughtfully at his beer. 'Go figure it,' he said, gazing out the window at the boats moored alongside. 'Maybe Wheeler needed some quick up-front money one time. Maybe there was a contract he was bidding on. Somebody whispered a sum into his ear, or one of his competitors mysteriously dropped out. Not that Wheeler necessarily asked for help, understand. Guy like Collucci, he does people favors. He's in a position to do that. He's got people close to other people. Legislators, aides, trustees, boards of directors. Uncle Fish comes up with these delicious tidbits of information, he looks around, tries to figure who might enjoy them, profit from them. Then he shares them. Later on – hell, maybe years later – Uncle Fish shows up on the doorstep. "Hey, remember me? I'm your uncle, did you a favor, right? Now it's my turn. Time to pay the piper. You get nothing for nothing in this world. Understand you've got a nice quiet spot up there in the wilds of Maine. Nice state, Maine. Not that far from Canada, your place. Place where a man could lay low for a while, do a little angling if he were of a mind to. I've even got a fella for you who can fly an airplane, and a real good chef." Like that. What could Wheeler say?'

'No,' I said. 'He could say no.'

'Practically impossible.'

I shook my head. 'You've got to say no.'

'You just don't say no to Uncle Fish Collucci,' said Charlie. 'If you do, you find nasty stories about yourself in the *Globe* or the *Washington Post*, all documented, that are guaranteed to get you hauled in front of a grand jury, with all the attending headlines. Or, if Uncle Fish thinks that tactic might not be effective, the next man who shows up on your doorstep is someone like Ceci Malagudi, with a little .22 automatic tucked in his belt with a long thing screwed on to the end of it so that when he shoots holes into your head with it, it sounds like somebody snapping an elastic band.'

I sat back and downed the dregs of my old-fashioned. 'A real disappointment,' I said.

'What, Wheeler? Don't be too harsh on him, Brady. He got sucked in. By little tiny increments. Takes quite a man to see that coming and resist it.'

'I used to think Vern Wheeler was quite a man.'

Charlie shrugged. 'There aren't that many left.'

Epilogue

Seelye Smith and I had lunch at a no-nonsense little restaurant right on the edge of the Portland waterfront. We both had fresh-caught lobsters, which we selected from a big glass tank against the back wall. Smith put up only token resistance when I insisted on paying.

After lunch, I shook his mangled hand and climbed into my BMW. It was a muggy August day, and the road from Portland to Greenville was still and dusty as I drove through the sandy scrub oak and pitch pine countryside.

The new pilot was named William. He wore a starched white short sleeved shirt and pressed chino pants. His hair was cut military short. His plane was spanking new. The cockpit was equipped with all sorts of electronic gadgetry. William called me sir, even after I told him my name was Brady. He offered to point out the sights, but I told him I knew them already. So we cruised through the silent skies without talking. He seemed very competent.

When we taxied up to the dock, Tiny and Marge were standing there waiting. Tiny had his arm slung casually around Marge's shoulder. She rested her hip familiarly against his.

Marge gave me a quick hug. I shook hands with Tiny. We went up to the lodge and arranged ourselves in rockers. It seemed like years, rather than scarcely a month, since I'd been there.

Polly, they told me, had gone to spend some time with a friend and her family in a small town outside of Bar Harbor. They had horses and some chickens. She would be back to Raven Lake for a week at the end of the month before she started classes.

William, the new pilot, was working out well. Very careful, very conscientious. Polite with the guests.

They had found a young married couple to do the cooking. Of course, they weren't as good as Bud Turner.

Woody had returned to Raven Lake. Tiny said that he and Lew Pike played cribbage together every night in the lodge. The sports liked to gather around to listen to them argue. When I saw Woody just before dinner, he strode up to me and shook my hand. Wanted to take me fishing. Said he had a new place he was saving for me. He never mentioned his arrest or the way he had looked at me when Thurl Harris took him away. I didn't mention it, either.

The fishing had slowed down. You could take bass in the evening and early morning off the shoals on the west shore. If you wanted to troll with wire line, you could still pick up a togue or a salmon. But it was slow. Things were due to pick up when the cooler weather arrived.

That night before bed I wandered down to the dock. I had been there a few minutes, savoring the vast silence and waiting for the loons, when Marge arrived. She had drinks for us.

I patted the dock beside where I sat, and she eased herself down. I lit cigarettes for us and handed one to her.

'Thanks,' she said softly. 'Haven't had one of these since you were here.'

'How've you been?'

'Good. Real good, Brady.'

'I'm glad.'

'Tiny and I are doing good now. Thanks to you.'

'No thanks to me.'

In the moonlight I saw her smile. 'Whether you know it or not, yes, thanks to you. It's like – like the place has been purged. And our relationship has been, too.'

'I'm happy for you.'

'Of course, Tiny's real upset about Vern.'

'I am, too.'

Marge sipped her drink and took a long, pensive drag on her cigarette. 'Can you stay long?'

'I'll be heading back tomorrow. I only wanted to pick up my gear. And say hello. Or good-bye, maybe. I never did say good-bye.'

She leaned against me and kissed my cheek softly. 'Hello, Brady Coyne. And good-bye.'

We sat together for a long time, not saying much. After a while we got up and strolled back to the lodge. We didn't hear the loons that evening, but it was all right. I knew they were out there.